ASHER'S FAULT

Visit us at www.boldstrokesbooks.com

ASHER'S FAULT

by

Elizabeth Wheeler

2013

ASHER'S FAULT

ISBN 10: 1-60282-982-9
ISBN 13: 978-1-60282-982-4

This Trade Paperback Original Is Published By
Bold Strokes Books, Inc.
P.O. Box 249
Valley Falls, NY 12185

First Edition: September 2013

Credits
Editors: Lynda Sandoval and Ruth Sternglantz
Production Design: Susan Ramundo
Cover Design By Sheri (graphicartist2020@hotmail.com)

Acknowledgments

With gratitude to my family for my love of story and Florida heritage, my friends for their unceasing support, my colleagues and mentors for their collaboration, the University of Chicago Graham School's novel writing program for developing my authorial identity, Science Screen Report and Allegro Productions for permission to reference their film, the team at BSB for championing my debut novel, and my resilient students for trusting me with stories of their own.

I am nothing without the loving support of my silly, slaphappy husband, Ross, and my two fellow writers—Dewey and Matthew. You are my miracles.

Most of all, thank you God for guiding me through this process, breaking my heart wide open, and blessing this journey.

Dedication

For friends who drift, moms who mourn, dads who leave, brothers who die, and anyone else who feels at fault.

CHAPTER ONE

{Photo of curved pine tree}

I might as well have been blind for the first fourteen years of my life. The evidence was there—all of it—but I didn't see a thing. Back then, I trusted people to give me the answers. Not that I blame them. It's not their fault. The truth is: most people can't help lying.

Photographs don't lie.

Sometimes people doctor them digitally and call it a partial truth, but it's still a lie. And my mom wonders why I won't use a digital camera. After what Dad did, you'd think she'd get it. People use more than Photoshop to justify the crap they do to other people.

Take the day I got my old-school Minolta, for instance. The entire afternoon Dad was plotting to move out, but I didn't have a clue. In all fairness, none of us saw it coming. Sure, Mom got nuts about Dad's perfectionism and work, but it all seemed fine in comparison to the yelling matches Levi's folks had.

I suppose I might have noticed something if the UPS truck hadn't pulled up as Dad and I headed to the grocery store. The driver chatted with Dad like usual, but Dad said *uh-huh* and nodded, glanced at the package, and handed it to me. I was too busy trying to figure out why I'd gotten something in the mail to notice Dad. It wasn't my birthday. It wasn't Christmas. It was the middle of summer, one of those days my best friend, Levi, would call hotter than the hinges of hell.

On the way down the driveway to our spit-shined minivan, a lizard skittered over my foot. I almost dropped the box. Funny the stuff you remember. I set the package on my lap and put on my seat belt as Dad backed out of the driveway.

I waved a hand at my little brother, Travis, who chucked a pinecone at the van. It fell short. I expected Dad to roll down the window and yell at Travis—Dad maintained the Windstar like it was a Lamborghini or something—but he didn't. He kept on driving like he hadn't noticed, but I knew he had. He gripped the steering wheel a little too tightly. I glanced back to see Mom coax Travis back into our ranch house. He'd wanted to go to the store with us, but Dad said no. I didn't feel sorry for Travis; he was eight years younger than I was and got his way most of the time by throwing tantrums. I might have had more sympathy if I'd known Travis would die the next summer because of me.

I picked up the heavy package. The return address was Chicago, so I knew it was from Aunt Sharon, a sure sign it contained something interesting.

"So, are you going to open that thing?" Dad asked. His smile seemed forced.

I took this as lingering irritation with Travis, something I understood. I pulled the tab on the side of the package, and something black and heavy covered in Bubble Wrap slid out. A fancy note card with a thin red border was taped to the outside.

I came across this the other day and thought you might like it. It was a great companion in Europe.
        Love you, Aunt Sharon

I unrolled the Bubble Wrap. A camera. I turned it over in my hands. As I inspected buttons and knobs, Dad's cell phone rang. He held the face of the phone close, glanced at the incoming number and tossed the phone to me. I barely caught it. It was Levi.

"Hey," I said.

"Where the hell are you?"

"Going to the store and out to the rental."

"Man, why didn't you call me?"

I didn't say anything.

"You suck," Levi said. "Did you ask about tonight?"

"Not yet. Hey, I got a camera from Aunt Sharon."

"What kind?"

I read the words stamped on the front right side of the camera. "Minolta Maxxum Panorama Elite."

"How many pixels?"

"It's not digital."

"Sounds like a piece of crap. Ask about tonight and call me."

"Right."

I handed the phone back to Dad.

"What's panorama mean?" I asked.

Dad pulled into the center lane and put on his turn signal, never taking his eyes off the road. "The root's *pan*. Like the Pantheon, right?"

"I guess."

"Well, what do you know about the Pantheon?"

Like I didn't get enough of this at school. "Is it Greek?"

"What's a pandemic?" he said, ignoring my question.

"A disease?"

Dad drove across the road into the Thrifty Foods parking lot. He stopped and let Wild Bill, the crazy guy who hangs out at the post office, cross in front of us. Wild Bill wore the same clothes every day and lived with his mom in a run-down place across the street from the post office. He'd gone to school with Mom and Dad. Bill hadn't been quite right since his senior year when he'd run over the Martins' toddler. Dad rolled down the window.

"How's it going, Bill?"

He stopped and smiled. One of his front teeth was chipped.

"Fair to middlin', Price."

"Glad to hear it." Dad rolled up his window and went right back to my question. "A pandemic is a *worldwide* disease. The Pantheon is a building in Rome built for *all* the gods."

I nodded like that cleared it up. Travis would have reminded Dad that he was an insurance salesman, not a teacher, but I wasn't

Travis. While I waited for Dad to continue, I poked through Aunt Sharon's box and found a manual buried at the bottom. I set the camera in my lap and flipped through the booklet until I found *panorama*. The manual said it was for landscapes—wide views. You just slid a button on the side if you wanted to take panorama shots.

I lifted the camera and found the button.

Dad pulled our minivan into a parking space right in front of the grocery store. Levi would call it rock-star parking even though the parking lot was hardly ever full. I paused with my hand on the door handle, then slung the camera strap around my neck.

"You taking that thing in?" Dad asked.

I nodded.

He ran his hand over his neatly trimmed brown hair, but he smiled.

I stepped out of the car into the shade of the building. Even though we weren't directly in the sun, I could feel the heat of the pavement rising up through the soles of my shoes. Dad grabbed the handle of a stray cart someone had left outside the store and didn't break stride as he swung it around in front of him. The sliding doors opened and cold air rushed out.

I took off the lens cap and slid the button on top from *lock* to *on*. The camera whirred to life. I held the viewfinder to my eye and pulled the zoom back so I could follow Dad through the lens. He didn't go down every row like Mom. He usually shopped like he was racing a timer, darting down aisles, grabbing items off the shelf, and swerving his cart around the other customers. When Mom wasn't with us, he would toss cans for Travis and me to catch and put in the cart. He used to throw jars of spaghetti sauce, but after I missed one, he stuck to cans.

That Saturday, Dad pushed the cart down every row. It should have been another clue that something was up, but I was just glad he was moving slowly enough for me to play with the camera.

"You want to go get some film for that thing?" he asked, motioning toward the photo department.

"Sure."

"I'll meet you in produce."

I turned off the camera and attached the lens cap as I walked up to the counter. A hundred little film boxes in yellows, greens, and blacks lined the shelf. Which one should I get? I was just about to run out to the car for the manual when I heard a deep voice behind me.

"Need help?"

Great. It was Iggy, a skinny high-school sophomore who kept trying to start a rock band. His brown hair hung over his eyes. People said he wore it that way so no one would know he was high. I figured the collared polo was regulation since he usually wore Zeppelin shirts. Rumor was he was bisexual. I checked to make sure the aisle was clear of anyone I knew. It was stupid, I know, but Iggy made me nervous.

"So," he said. I jumped a little. Just a little. I don't think he noticed. "I see you got a camera there so…" He spoke sort of slow. Not Southern slow. Just slow.

"It's new."

He stared at my camera.

"Well, new to me, anyway."

"What kind?" he asked.

"Minolta Maxxum Panorama Elite," I said.

"Let me see it." He stood so close to me that I could smell the greasy deli chicken he must have had for lunch. I felt his hand brush my chest through my T-shirt as he took the camera in his hand. "It's 35 millimeter," he said.

I glanced at the camera to see where he'd found that number, but he was already looking back at the film choices, so I did, too.

"You taking pictures inside or out?"

"We're going to my dad's old place."

"Yeah, that's cool. We've had some good times in the woods out there."

He wasn't talking about me, although Iggy hung out with a pretty varied crowd—mostly goth types, but he managed to navigate some of the jock world with relative ease. Still, I'd heard him called a faggot more than once. I pictured Iggy's cool crowd out in a scrub of palmetto bushes or under the oak canopy where I'd spent my childhood exploring. Years ago, my grandfather had planted all of these exotic tropical bushes and trees around the property. Tourists paid fifteen bucks to see the same thing at the Edison & Ford Winter Estates in Fort Myers. The Edison property was like walking through a tidy garden. Grandpa's place was more like a jungle. My grandfather died the year before I was born and no one kept it up, so the vines and bushes and trees took over. Recently, Dad started complaining about finding empty beer bottles and roach clips out there. I looked more closely at Iggy's face, but he just seemed interested in the film display. He turned and looked at me.

"You're gonna be a freshman next year?"

"Uh, yeah."

"You friends with Josh?"

I shrugged. Josh was a year older than Levi and me. Josh called Levi *Husky!* all through seventh grade and used to shove me against the wall every time he saw me—*Hey, smasher.* When he came to school, he reeked of alcohol and cigarettes but charmed his way out of trouble.

"His brother Evan's having a party tonight."

"Oh."

Iggy flipped his hair out of his eyes. "So you're gonna be outside taking pictures, right?"

"Yeah, outside."

"Okay. You can choose from any of these." He pointed to a section. At the bottom was a single box of film just hanging on its own.

"What's this?"

"Black and white. It's the last one."

"Lots of people use it?"

He snorted. "No. They're discontinuing it."

"Really?"

"Yeah, you got to go to specialty stores like Harmon Photo to get it now. We're not selling it anymore." He shrugged. "Everything's going digital, anyway."

I slid the black-and-white film into my hand and hurried off to find Dad. He wasn't in the produce aisle. I found him in the checkout line. He seemed startled to see me, like he'd forgotten I'd come with him. He tucked his polo into his belted jeans.

"Got some film?" he asked cheerily.

"Yeah. Black and white."

"Didn't they have any color?"

"Yeah, but this is the last black and white. I got the last one."

I put the film on the conveyor belt next to the toilet paper. Our gray-haired cashier, Cathy, chatted with Dad as she scanned the film and put it in a plastic bag. I didn't think to ask Dad why he needed to stock the rental house with everything from mayonnaise to laundry detergent.

❖

I always got nervous when we drove over the wooden bridge that led back to Grandpa's old place, even though Dad claimed there were twenty telephone poles holding it up. I wasn't so much worried about the bridge collapsing as I was about going over the edge and landing in the creek. The side rails had long since rotted away. Dad had told us more than once how he'd thrown a party while his folks were out of town. The next morning, Johnny J, who was now our district attorney, had driven his grandmother's Buick off this same bridge on his way home.

I never met my grandparents on Dad's side. They'd both died before I was born, but Dad says I remind him of his father. Not because I like plants. Maybe it was because he was a nervous guy, too.

I sighed a breath of relief after we crossed the bridge. The minivan rocked from one side to the other as we drove over thick tree roots and potholes in the gravel road. Dad took the driveway fast, avoiding holes by making the tires straddle the worn path on one side or the other. I gripped the door handle and looked out the window, trying to figure out what I could photograph. Twisting, thick oak branches blocked out the sky above us. I wondered if I'd made a mistake getting the film for outside—it was pretty dark under the oaks. I thought about how the Spanish moss hanging from the trees would look on camera. There was the gardenia bush and the hibiscus tree Travis and I picked flowers from for Mom. A quarter mile down the path, the canopy of trees opened up into a wide, sun-filled field. On the left, palmetto bushes and scrub ran thick, with an occasional pine tree shooting up. The middle of the field to the right was clear and open, except for the crooked pine tree.

I watched how the curve of the tree changed as we got closer. In the moment just before we turned into the driveway, the curved part faced me dead-on, and it disappeared behind the trunk itself. It looked just like any other pine tree from that angle. You couldn't tell it was crooked at all.

"Why's that tree like that?" I asked Dad.

He'd just turned off the engine and was reaching for the door handle. He glanced past me to where I had nodded, and he was so close that I noticed he'd trimmed the hair between his eyebrows. Travis called him *unibrow* just to harass him, but there they were now—two separate lines of hair right over his eyes. It wasn't the kind of thing I usually paid attention to, but I noticed it then. I tried to picture him squinting in the mirror with the tweezers like Mom did. I didn't say anything about it, though. I wasn't like Travis. Instead, I pointed to the curved pine tree.

"Was it struck by lightning or something?"

"No, it's always been that way, as far as I can remember."

I got out of the car and started for the trunk to help unload groceries, but Dad said, "Why don't you go try out that camera?"

I thought he was being nice. I really thought he was thinking of me, and I put the film in the camera and walked around the property for a long time, trying to decide what to take pictures of, since I only had twenty-four shots. I considered the vines that hung from the branches, the ones so thick I could swing on them until I shot up three inches and filled out a little last summer, but it seemed like it was too dark under the oaks. I looked at the gardenia and hibiscus bushes for a long time, but I couldn't bring myself to make a camera that had been to Europe take pictures of lame flowers.

In the end, I found myself standing in the open field with the sun hot on my head and neck and arms. I studied how the bark turned black when the sunlight was directly behind it, how the longer I stood there, the longer the shadow grew on the ground. I watched how the clouds changed beyond the tree. Last summer, I had hoisted Travis up to perch on the flat part of the curve. His legs were longer now; he could probably scramble up there on his own. I circled the tree again with the camera against my face.

The sun grew a shade brighter. I could actually see the veins on the bark through the viewfinder. I held the camera steady and adjusted the zoom. An internal light warned red until I pressed the button halfway down. The camera whirred and focused for me, and the twisted trunk of the pine tree came clear in the square of the viewfinder. The red light blinked and turned green. I felt the pinch of a mosquito on my forearm and a trickle of sweat running from my hairline to my jaw, but I didn't brush either away. I took my first picture. That afternoon I used the whole roll on that pine tree.

It wasn't until after the divorce that I framed a picture of the curved tree and centered it on the wall above my bed. In the background of the shot I can make out the blurry image of our minivan parked in the driveway of Grandpa's old house, where dad now lived, the open trunk stuffed with evidence.

CHAPTER TWO

"S he probably couldn't give it away," Levi sneered as we trudged through the dark down the row of orange trees behind his house. He knew the grove better than anyone, except maybe his dad.

"I like it."

"You have to go like an hour away just to get the film developed. That sucks, Asher."

"I think I can order the film online."

"The camera's a dinosaur. It's practically extinct."

I ignored him. After Dad and I got home from Grandpa's old place, I'd spent the rest of the afternoon reading the manual and searching online for information. When Levi called just before dinner, I remembered I was supposed to ask if I could sleep at his house. I really wanted to learn more about the camera, but Levi called me a douche bag, so I knew I'd hurt his feelings. When I asked, Mom hesitated, but Dad said with school starting soon I should hang out more with my friends. He seemed eager to get me out of the house. I'm pretty sure Dad wasn't eager for me to prowl around in the orange grove at midnight muddying my sneakers.

"So, I've been thinking we need to stake our territory the first day," Levi said.

"Our territory?"

"Claim our space. You know, get a table in the courtyard at the high school. The guys on the team tell me that you got to have one right off, or everyone thinks you're a freshman."

"We *are* freshmen."

"Yeah, but we don't want to act like we are." Levi punched my shoulder. "We don't want to be on the sidelines, see? We don't want to be stuck waiting for seniors to graduate to get a spot."

I rubbed my shoulder. The view from the sidelines seemed okay to me.

"Shit," Levi said. I watched him flail his arms around in the moonlight.

"Spiderweb?"

"Yeah."

I inspected the space in front of me for the web remnants, but Levi had managed to snare the whole thing. I patted down his back to make sure a spider didn't cling to him. He brushed off his face and arms.

"Damn, I hate those things," he said.

He started walking again. I didn't. I heard something skitter. He got two tree lengths ahead of me before he turned around.

"What?" he said.

"Did you hear that?"

Silence.

"Maybe we should go back," I said.

"You're such an ass."

I kept imagining Levi's parents peeking in to check on the bodies we'd made out of blankets and pillows in his room. I didn't think Levi's mom, a police officer, was that stupid.

"Jesus, Asher. Come on."

The last time Levi and I snuck out of his house, stray dogs chased us. I'd sworn I'd never do it again.

"It's *Evan Llowell*," Levi said, like he was talking about a rock star.

"I know."

"Iggy practically invited you."

"He mentioned it. Not the same thing."

"Why would he have mentioned it if he wasn't inviting you?"

I shifted my feet. It'd been a mistake to tell Levi about it. We'd been through it a dozen times after my mom dropped me off at his house.

"You weren't there, Levi. He didn't mean it like that."

"When else are we ever going to go to one of Evan Llowell's parties?" He started back down the row. I followed him.

Evan, the town's star athlete who almost single-handedly ended our losing streak in football, had bought a place a year ago, right after he'd graduated from high school. It wasn't like he'd earned it. He'd taken the money his folks had put aside for college and bought it, right after the housing market bottomed out. Josh, Evan's little brother who was a year ahead of Levi and me, bragged that his brother had been scouted by UCF, but Evan wasn't interested in playing for anyone other than Florida State. No one from FSU came for Evan, though, and his grades couldn't get him in anywhere else but the community college. So instead of college, Evan bought a $250,000 house for under $100,000 and played pool, drank beer, and watched games on his big-screen television. Mom complained about how Evan, a kid just out of school, had more house than we did and paid less. A couple of other guys rented rooms from him, and all the respectable adults we knew started to complain about Evan Llowell's place. Which made it all the more cool. And it was just on the other side of the orange grove behind Levi's house.

The grove butted up against a paved road. Residential homes lined the other side of the street, and seven houses down from where we exited the grove stood Evan Llowell's place. Cars lined the street for a quarter mile back. I only recognized a few of them, and I didn't see Iggy's black CRX. Levi tapped each vehicle with a long twig he'd yanked off an orange tree. As we neared the house, a truck pulled into Evan's driveway. Two guys I recognized from last year's football team slid out of the cab. The stockier of the two grabbed several cases of beer from the truck bed.

"I'm sure as hell gonna miss just running for the border. You figure every town's got a liquor store that turns a blind eye?" said the stocky guy.

"I got one of them fake IDs, just in case."

"You serious? Let me see."

He dug in his pocket with one hand and flipped open his wallet. The stocky guy angled the wallet to face the streetlight. He squinted and let out a low whistle.

"Bet that cost a pretty penny."

"My uncle can hook you up with a guy."

They loaded their arms with beer, and Levi and I followed them up to the door where they paused. The taller of the two, the one with the fake ID, turned to us. I wasn't sure until then that they'd even noticed us.

"Hey, you mind?"

Levi stood closest to the door. It took him a fraction of a second to figure out the guy wanted him to turn the knob.

"Right. Sure."

He held the door open wide for them, and a cheer rose up as they entered with the beer. Levi grinned wildly at me as we followed them inside.

The muggy place bulged with bodies, but the lights were surprisingly bright. Music thudded from one of those Bose speakers, but no one was dancing. It looked like Evan spent all his money on toys and technology because the couch had a tear in the side but the pool table, in what should have been a dining room, looked brand-new. All the guys measured a solid foot taller and wider than Levi or me. A bunch of people slammed coins on the living-room table and hollered at one another. A second group crowded around the big-screen television. Although most of the people looked vaguely familiar, I'd be hard pressed to name them. This wasn't a high-school party; some people looked around the same age as our parents. I didn't see Iggy anywhere.

"Holy shit," Levi said. "Look at that." Some of the people in front of the TV shifted. There on the screen were two naked girls going to town on each other. He grinned. "The only way this could get any better is if I had a beer."

I inched closer to the wall, but Levi trotted in the wake of the beer guys.

"Uh, Levi," I called, but he either didn't hear or ignored me.

I considered following him, but I spotted the guy Dad hired to fix our AC. He was sitting on a stool in the kitchen, so I redirected to the living room. The last thing I needed was for someone to report this back to my parents. Jennifer, a popular girl from my class, was perched on an armrest, her gaze averted from the movie. Levi sort of lusted for her, so I knew he'd be thrilled to know she was here. She took a swig from the beer she was holding and grimaced before she noticed me. Immediately her expression changed to a smile. Jennifer saluted me with the beer and waved me over. She tended to be severely intense, but in my yearbook she'd written I was *the nicest, kindest guy ever*. I maneuvered my way through the crowd to her.

"Thank God. Someone I know," she said to me under her breath.

"What are you doing here?" I asked.

She gestured toward the sofa across the room where Kayla, her best friend, leaned against Josh Llowell's chest. She had her arms wrapped around him. It was like watching someone dive headfirst into the shallow end of the pool.

"Is she drunk?" I asked.

"Nope, just stupid."

Josh's hand rested possessively on Kayla's hip.

"I can't believe I let her talk me into this. I mean, is this what high school is supposed to be like?" Jennifer asked.

I glanced around the room.

"I don't think these people are in high school," I said. "Except Josh, and he's only here because it's his brother's party. And us."

Jennifer sipped the beer again, and her face soured like she'd sucked on a lemon. "I don't know how people can drink this." She pushed it toward me.

"Uh…"

"Just take it, Asher."

I placed it on the far edge of the coffee table.

"And that's gross," Jennifer continued.

"What?"

She gestured toward the television screen.

I heard someone shout "Husky!" from the other side of the room. It was Josh. He held Levi in a bear hug.

"And why does he call Levi that?" Jennifer asked.

"Husky? He thinks Levi's fat. That's the name of those jeans they make for fat kids," I said.

"No, I know that. It's just Josh is such a jerk. What is Kayla thinking?"

Kayla sat on the sofa looking up adoringly at Josh as he continued to berate Levi. I would have felt sorry for her if it weren't so nauseating.

"Who let this kid in here?" Josh called.

A flash of panic spread across Levi's face, but then Evan walked past and shoved Josh hard.

"Shut up! You're lucky to be here yourself, little bro."

Evan held a joint in his hand as he waltzed in front of the television set like he was royalty. The group around the TV grumbled in protest.

"Oh, shut the hell up! It's my party," he said as he stepped out of the way and leaned against the wall close to where Jennifer and I stood. He took a hit from the joint and offered it to us. I shook my head.

"You?" he asked Jennifer.

"Uh, no thanks."

His puffy eyes appraised her.

"Could you do that?" he asked, pointing toward the girls on the screen.

"What, me? No," she stammered, then stood up straighter and flipped her hair over her shoulder. "Could you, with a guy?"

"That's not the same thing. I'm no fag." Evan laughed. "You got a name?"

"Jennifer. I came with Kayla. Josh invited us." She pressed her lips together and scanned the room. "Where are they, anyway?"

"You're friends with my brother?"

"I wouldn't say that."

Evan laughed. "Good girl. So, you're in high school?"

"Not yet."

Jennifer didn't notice Evan's stoned eyes, blinking drowsily at her.

"I don't remember the freshman girls looking so good. What's your name?"

"I just told you. Jennifer."

She tucked her hair behind her ear and gazed down at the floor. He grinned and then seemed to notice me standing there like some sort of unpleasant growth.

"And who are you?" The charm left his voice. He eyed me confusedly.

"Asher." I dug my hands into my jean pockets.

"Sorry, what?"

"Asher."

He busted out laughing.

"What kind of name is Asher?"

If looks could kill, Jennifer's would have annihilated Evan. "It's in the Bible," she hissed. "One of Jacob's sons. You know, the story of Joseph?"

"I'm sorry, what, angel? You say something?" Evan asked.

Just then, a red light flashed through the large front window of the house.

"Po-po," someone yelled. "Turn the music off!"

It took Evan several seconds to switch gears. It's like the whole room had delayed reactions. Several faces turned fearful.

"Turn it off!"

It got quiet.

"Hold this," Evan mumbled. He handed me the joint, then walked across the living room to the front door. He peered through the peek hole, then turned back to the crowd of people and winked. He pointed toward Jennifer. "You stay right there. I'm not done."

Jennifer's wide, panicked eyes mirrored mine.

"What am I supposed to do with this?" I whispered. My heart thudded. I could feel beads of sweat breaking out on my upper lip.

A flood of people headed toward the back of the house, and I tried to spot Levi among them. He had reason to run. The law enforcement in our town consisted of four police officers. Even though Levi's mom wasn't working tonight, she'd definitely get a phone call if someone saw us here.

"Do you see Kayla?" Jennifer searched the crowd. "Lovely. That's just great. Look, there's no way I'm getting arrested. If you see her, tell her I left."

She ran for the back door. I held the joint awkwardly in my fingers. I'd never seen drugs before. Years of incarceration flashed before my eyes, and for some reason I thought of Iggy. It would be just my luck that the one person who didn't drink or do drugs would get busted. I felt like I was going to be sick.

A toilet. That's what I needed. I could get rid of the evidence and vomit. I hurried down the lighted hallway and turned the knob of the first door on the left. Locked. Panic welled up in me. I pounded on the door.

A muffled voice hissed, "Go away."

I recognized Josh's voice.

"Is there a bathroom in there?" I asked, my voice too high.

"Second door on the right."

I hesitated. "Is Kayla in there?" No answer. "Jennifer was looking for her. She had to go."

I heard a police radio crackle from the front room, so I raced down the hall. I turned the knob of the second door on the right. Locked. I could hear someone retching inside. I knocked on the door hard. "Hey, open up."

Another retch. I pounded.

"Come on, open the door!" I said, frantic.

"I'm sick," a voice moaned.

"Open. The. Door," I demanded.

The door opened a crack. A girl I didn't recognize sat on the floor wiping her mouth with a grayish towel that had probably once been white. I quickly slid into the room and dropped the joint in the toilet where it sizzled to its death among the pink chunks, tossed a handful of toilet paper on top, and flushed just as a voice called from the hallway.

"All clear. Carl says we got to keep the noise down." It was Evan.

I opened the bathroom door and slinked back to the living room. Only a few guys remained; everyone else had vacated the house. While they talked about dodging the police, I started for the back door, but then Evan saw me.

"Hey. I said to stay right there," he called to me. Ten minutes ago he could barely stand up, but now he was clearheaded. Perfect.

"Uh, she had to go."

"Who?"

"Jennifer. You told her to wait, but she had to go."

He stared at me like I was an idiot. "No, my smoke. Where is it?"

"I..."

He stepped toward me. I stuffed my hands in my pockets, glanced at him, and sort of smiled nervously.

"You think it's funny?" Evan asked.

My attempt at a friendly smile vanished. "No! No, not at all. Clearly. Because you told me to wait." We glanced back and forth at each other. I gestured to the back door. "Only, I thought you meant Jennifer. Not me."

Evan sighed, and I stopped making noise. My mouth still opened and closed like a guppy, no sound, just a couple of O-shaped attempts at securing my safe return home. The guys on the sofa grinned at me. Every drug cartel movie I'd ever seen played through my head.

"What'd you do with it?" Evan asked.

"I—I didn't want anyone to get arrested or anything." I eased toward the kitchen, planning my escape. "I thought they might search the place, so I flushed it."

Evan stared at me. Something to my left moved and I jumped reflexively, but it was just my own reflection mirrored in a Budweiser sign that hung on the dining-room wall next to the pool table.

"I'm really sorry. Really." I licked my lips and pointed to the back door. "Anyway, I think I'm just going to go now," I said, but I didn't move. "Okay?" I think I was hoping someone would give me permission, a nod, something. No one moved. "O-kay." My feet started toward the door.

"You look like you're about to crap your pants," Evan observed. Was that concern on his face? I took a deep, audible breath and nodded vigorously.

"Yeah, pretty much."

Evan grinned. His teeth were even and white.

"It's Asher, right?"

"Yeah."

"Let me tell you how it is." He came over and wrapped an arm around my shoulder. Now I really thought I was going to throw up. He smelled like eternal groundings. "Folks call and complain about the noise, so the cops come out and tell us to settle down. They know better than to mess with a Llowell. Am I right?"

The stocky guy who brought the beer in from the truck nodded. "That's how they roll." He belched.

Evan patted my head. "You need to relax, my friend."

"Yeah," I said. "Actually, I'd feel a lot better if I could just go now."

I ran the entire way back to Levi's house, which is quite a feat for me, considering I generally only run when something terrifying is chasing me, like those dogs the last time Levi convinced me to sneak out. Jerk.

When I tapped on Levi's bedroom window, I could see him sitting at the computer, the blue screen the only light in the room. He bobbed his head from side to side to the beat of some song on his iPod while he scrolled down Facebook. I swatted at a mosquito buzzing around my ear, and glanced at a pair of headlights turning into Levi's street. I ducked into the bushes to wait for the car to pass, but instead it slowed enough for me to recognize it as our minivan. It pulled into Levi's driveway.

They couldn't see me on the side of the house, so I jumped up and banged on Levi's window. He turned in his chair and stared dumbly at his bedroom door. Idiot. I banged again as the engine of the minivan shut off. He noticed me at the window, pulled his earbuds out, and sauntered across the room.

"Where the hell were you?" he said as he cranked open the awning window.

I swung my leg up through the open window the same time the doorbell rang.

"My parents," I frantically hissed as I maneuvered my leg through the narrow window and scrambled into his room.

"Shit."

I kicked my shoes off as Levi shut the window behind me. The doorbell rang again insistently.

"What happened?" he asked, all curious for details.

"I almost got arrested," I whispered. "Shut up."

Footsteps and voices carried from deeper in the house. Levi dived into his bed. I grabbed a pillow and dropped to the floor before I noticed the image open on Levi's screen.

"Computer," I whispered.

"Damn."

Levi leapt up and turned off the monitor. The room was dark. I could barely make out the muffled voices in the hall.

"Did he indicate where he was going?" Levi's mom was saying. She sounded like she was working, like she was interrogating a suspect. They were just outside Levi's bedroom.

"No." It was Mom. Her voice rose and cracked as she added, "He just packed his bag and said he was leaving."

Dad.

They must have had an argument.

A bad one.

I held my breath and pressed my eyelids closed as the door squeaked opened.

"See? He's sleeping. Why don't you come back for him in the morning?" Levi's mom whispered.

"I don't know," Mom said.

"Look, most of these types of things resolve themselves."

"I'm sorry. I thought he might come here. I just needed to make sure…"

"Shh. He'll likely be back tomorrow. You guys can work it out," Levi's mom's said. "Right? No point worrying Ash."

"I'm sorry. You're right. Okay." The door closed. My eyes shot open as I listened to her voice trail off down the hallway. "I just can't believe he's done this to us." Her voice cracked.

It wasn't until the next morning that I learned that Dad had moved out. At the time, Levi and I were just relieved we hadn't gotten caught. It never occurred to me that Dad wouldn't come back.

CHAPTER THREE

{Photo of man burying cat}

I think it would have been easier if he'd died. Instead, he disappeared from our lives. Well, he didn't totally disappear. He still lived in our town, just not in our house. We still saw him around, but we pretended not to. It was as if Dad died, but he had an evil twin who moved into town the same day we lost him. Mom blamed Helen from church, and that seemed sort of reasonable since Dad was seen all over town with her within a week of leaving. And while Mom was losing it, she had to search for a job. As for me, I kept taking pictures.

One of my favorites happened about three months after Dad left when I was home from school.

My stomach had started cramping in the early morning. By the time Mom was up getting ready for work, I felt better, but I didn't tell her that. The last thing I wanted was to be stuck at school with diarrhea. I ran to the bathroom every ten or fifteen minutes to build my case, but when I was stretched on the sofa between runs, I heard Mom on the phone with work.

"But he's sick." I turned down the volume on the television a little. She walked into the living room. "Oh. When does that kick in?" She sat down in the chair across from me, picked up the pencil on the coffee table, and tapped it nervously against the surface. "Well, what am I supposed to do? He's sick." I tried to figure out if her irritation was at me for being sick or at work. Abruptly she stood up and walked out of the room.

She'd just started this job as a telemarketer. I wasn't *that* sick. And anyway, give me a break—I was a freshman; it wasn't like I needed my mom to take care of me. She hung up the phone and sank wearily onto the sofa beside me. She was sitting on my leg. I wanted to move it, but she was crying.

"This is all his fault," she muttered.

"You don't have to stay home."

"I can't stay home. They won't pay me." She smoothed the hair on the top of my head like I was little. It took a concentrated effort to let her.

"I'll be fine."

I wanted her to leave. I mean, who wants company when you might start crapping water at any moment?

Travis rounded the corner dressed for school, but with disheveled hair. He held his stuffed dog, Og, in his hands.

Mom glanced at him. "Put it back."

"Why does he get to stay home?" Travis whined, pointing to me.

"Because he's sick. Put it back in your room."

"I want to stay home."

"You want to be sick?" I asked.

"You're not sick," Travis said. "It's picture day."

Mom spun on me. "It is?"

I didn't say anything. I avoided eye contact. The fact that I had managed to keep myself out of the yearbook all through middle school had not escaped my mom's notice.

"Asher."

"Mom. I'm sick."

Mom sighed and turned back to Travis. "You're not taking Og to school."

"Why not?"

"Kindergarteners do not bring stuffed animals to school. Put it back."

"No." His chin jutted out defiantly as he clutched Og tighter.

Mom clenched her fist and hit the coffee table. "We're going to be late! They'll dock my pay. Put it back in your room now!"

"Why can't I stay home?"

"You're not sick."

"Neither is he." Travis poked his chin out. My stomach rolled. I felt like I was going to puke.

"Asher doesn't lie," Mom said.

She was right. I probably would if I could, but I'm no good at it so I just don't say anything. Travis lied so well that I would know the truth about something and listen to him and think I'd dreamed up what really happened.

"Faker," Travis growled.

I hurried off to the bathroom. I was still in there when Mom knocked on the door and said, "I'll stay home if you want me to."

I could hear her keys jingle in her hand.

"Seriously, I'll be okay."

"Keep the phone nearby. I'll call you."

"Mom. *Go.*"

I watched the hands of the clock on the wall in the bathroom move while I waited. Another ten minutes of Travis whining and Mom muttering passed before they finally left the house. When I was sure they were gone, I flushed the toilet and ran my hands under the faucet. I splashed some water up on my face, dried it off, and headed back to the sofa.

We used to have cable, but Mom had to cancel it after Dad left. And she wondered why Levi never came over to hang out at our house anymore. I flipped through the five channels we had—two were in Spanish. Levi hated that. On the Jeep his dad bought him for when he turned sixteen next year, there was a bumper sticker that read, *Why should I have to press 1 for English?* There are enough Hispanic migrant workers around that I thought for sure the Jeep would get keyed the first week they parked it in their driveway, but so far no one had touched it.

I settled on one of the Spanish channels. This mother and her older daughter were begging this guy for something. They were overacting. The guy looked like he could be in high school—his skin was so smooth. He wasn't saying much. He looked worried and sad, and when he did talk it was just a whisper. It made me wish I knew more Spanish than one through twenty and "Hello, my name is Asher." My belly rolled and churned.

I stood up and started back to the bathroom when I noticed Mr. Williams, my neighbor, through our sliding glass door in the kitchen. He peered at something in the red- and yellow-leaved crotons that lined the side of their house. I went on to the bathroom because, frankly, even if Mr. Williams had discovered an alien growing in his hibiscus, it wasn't worth crapping my pants over. But when I finished, he was still by the side of the house, only now he had a shovel. I could barely make out the small gray heap next to him on the ground. Sam.

Sam had been the Williams's toothless, old gray tomcat who couldn't hear anymore. He couldn't lick himself clean and stunk like things do when they're overripe. He had been a good cat. More dog than cat, really. Sam would actually come when you called until he lost his hearing. One time when Travis and I were playing in the yard, Sam killed a rattlesnake. We saw him wrestling with something, darting and batting at it, and then he brought the still-twitching dead thing right up to our front door. Mom almost had a heart attack when she found it. I read in a book that cats kill things and leave them for people they like because they can see what bad hunters humans are. I explained that to Mom, but she still didn't like it. Now Sam was dead. I guessed Mr. Williams was burying him before Kristen and Michelle got home from school.

The way Mr. Williams's shoulder slumped as he pressed the shovel into the earth caught my eye, the way his body turned to dump dirt. The crotons framed him on either side, and the morning sun cast a long shadow of his figure against the house. I wanted to preserve it—this light, this moment—because one day everything's normal, and the next day it's all changed. I hurried to my room, grabbed my camera, and slid out the front door. The ground was wet from dew, but I didn't care that I wasn't wearing shoes. I avoided the fire-ant hills that had cropped up in Dad's absence and ducked behind the palmetto bush that separated our house from Mr. Williams's. My heart was beating fast, but Mr. Williams was so busy burying Sam he didn't hear the whir of my camera.

Through the viewfinder I studied the sharp points of his bent elbow and the edges of the shovel. His foot forced the blade into the earth. On film, the dark brown dirt, his shadow, and the shovel would look black against that bright stucco wall of the house. Mr. Williams wore a white shirt, made whiter still by the direct sunlight. I centered him in the viewfinder. I could have taken the picture just like that. Mr. Williams wasn't facing me, and it wasn't like he would be grinning like some sort of idiot even if he were looking toward me. Still, it didn't feel right.

I moved the camera down and over, taking his head out of the image, focusing on the shadow instead of the objects. Better. The shadow of the shovel against the wall, of Mr. Williams's body, of the croton leaves. Sam rested in the lower corner of the photograph—you'd have to look for him, but he was in it. I took the picture. I was just thinking that it was kind of like listening to an adult talk to a little kid about Santa and wishing I was still young enough to believe when I felt a tap on my shoulder.

"What are you doing there?" a scratchy voice demanded.

It was Pearl from next door. She wore a faded mint-colored, zip-up bathrobe and dingy slippers that weren't made for going outside. She was a talker who was hard to stop. And despite the fact that she could sneak up on a ninja, she was a loud talker. I glanced toward Mr. Williams.

"Are you skipping school?" she asked, pointing a bony finger at me.

"No." I started to move away from the palmetto bush, positioning myself to keep the branches between Mr. Williams and me. I lowered my voice. "No, I'm sick."

She leaned in toward me. "What?"

It took every ounce of willpower not to roll my eyes. I took a deep breath and said, louder this time, "I'm sick."

I inched in the direction of my house, but she was still standing beside the palmetto bush. Why wasn't she following me to the front?

"Sick? Like hell you are." Pearl folded her arms across her chest.

"It's my stomach."

"Where are your shoes?"

I glanced down at my feet.

"You lying to me? Don't you lie to me." She wagged her finger, and the sun glistened off a diamond tennis bracelet. She put her hands on her hips and stood to block my way, her gray slippers planted like dead cats in the ground.

My stomach cramped. I grabbed my belly and turned to walk away. "Look, I'm sorry, but I need to get inside," I called over my shoulder. She followed me with slow old-person steps.

"What have you got there?" she asked.

I glanced back to see what she was talking about. She pointed her twiggy finger at my camera.

"My camera?"

"You spying on neighbors?" she asked.

"No. No, not like, you know, spying."

I thought for sure I was going to crap my pants.

"Hmm. Taking pictures." She eyed the camera. "It's a nice camera. You're a lucky boy." She looked more closely at it. "You know anything about cameras?"

"A little." She handled it. She was standing close. She smelled like mothballs. "I'm still learning," I said.

"What kind of photography do you do?"

Photography. I liked the sound of that. "Black and white."

"Black and white? Why?"

I didn't say anything.

"Color is easier," she said.

"Not really," I said.

"Humph. It's the lighting. If it's too dark or too light. All those different shades of gray. Why black and white?"

"It's what I like."

She backed away a bit and tucked her hands into the pockets of her bathrobe.

"Okay, but what kind of photography?" When I didn't answer, she continued, clearly irritated with me. "Landscape, people, animals, portraits?"

"Not people," I said and thought about the picture I'd just taken of Mr. Williams. But that didn't really count since I'd chopped his head off in the shots. My stomach gurgled loudly.

"Good."

I was glad I'd answered right. Maybe she'd let me go now.

"Good," she said again. "Taking pictures of people is hard. You like landscape?"

"Yeah, but I really need to—"

"You know, when you take a picture of a mountain, it never comes back to complain about what it looks like. People hate pictures because photographs don't lie. You know that, though, don't you?" She chuckled and then glanced at her watch. "Look at that. You almost made me miss my show."

I was thinking that Pearl probably had cable as I watched her move slowly down her driveway past her black mailbox. I noticed that the number *4* had completely peeled off it. The others would be gone soon. I had helped Dad attach the numbers to Pearl's mailbox a few summers ago. I remembered carefully peeling the sticky black numbers off the sheet and handing them to him. He showed me how to space them out and press them down carefully. Dad had let me do the *4* myself.

I ignored my grumbling stomach as Pearl wobbled back to her front door. After I was sure she had gone inside, I looked at her mailbox through the viewfinder. I adjusted the zoom and took a picture of the peeling numbers.

A few days later, ten-year-old Kristen came over to tell me that Sam had run away. She asked me to let her know if I saw him and gave me a flyer. I promised her I would keep an eye out for him. It was easier for Mr. Williams to lie than to tell the truth, and honestly, Kristen might prefer the lie. People lie all the time, but I wasn't lying. I would keep my eye out for Sam…in my developed photo.

CHAPTER FOUR

{Photo of Budweiser mirror}

"So Josh kept stopping and crying about how hot it was and how he thought he was gonna die, and coach got up in his face, yelling and screaming like this close." Levi held his finger and thumb two inches apart. "Josh threw up right on coach's shoes. Man, was he pissed." Levi tossed one of Travis's marbles into the air and caught it. "You should have heard him, all 'Jesus H. Christ' and 'What the hell's wrong with you, boy?'"

I loaded a roll of film into my camera. "Do a lot of guys throw up at practice?"

"The stupid ones do. That's why I don't eat right before."

I closed the camera back and turned it on to advance the film. It clicked and whirred. I checked to make sure the number *1* appeared in the box on the top and then switched it off.

"You should have tried out, Ash."

I shrugged and slung the camera strap around my neck. "I'm not interested in cracking my skull."

"That's why they've got helmets, idiot." Levi tossed the marble into the plastic trash can beside my computer desk. "Seriously, Josh and Manny are all right."

I didn't reply. Manny had been pretty cool in Spanish class, but every time he hung around Josh he turned into a jerk. I raised my eyebrows at Levi.

"Okay, they're mostly assholes, but Manny is hilarious," Levi admitted. "You should come tonight."

"I need money," I said.

"You won't be mowing after dark," Levi said. "Come on. Mom will let you."

"I'll think about it."

He stood up, walked over to my dresser, and stared at the black-and-white picture hanging above it. "Who the hell is that?"

"Mr. Williams."

"What's he doing?"

"Digging."

"No shit. What's he digging *for*?"

"Sam."

Levi squinted at the picture. I grinned as I sat down on my bed and pulled on my blue Converse sneakers.

"That nasty old cat?" Levi shook his head. "Man, your room creeps me out."

"It's better than sports posters."

"Hey, my room is cool. You wait 'til I get my girls up."

"Right."

"And I got my *Keep Out* sign," he said.

I snorted. "Yeah, but you've got to go inside your room to see it. What's the point?"

"Uh, it's cool."

"And that denim bedspread."

"So?"

I laughed. "Your name is *Levi*."

"Shut up. And anyway, when did you become an authority on interior decorating? I mean, black curtains and a black-and-white bedspread. And not a color picture anywhere. I don't know, Ash. Seems to me there might be some vampire in you."

I adjusted my camera. "Are you ready?"

"I vant to drrrink your blood," he mocked, arching his hands like imaginary talons.

What an idiot. We walked into the kitchen where Mom was folding an endless pile of clothes. A stack of mail sat on the dining-room table next to her. I picked up the one on top marked *Past Due*.

She glanced at me.

"What's this?" I asked.

"Put it down," she said.

I stared at her.

"I've got it. We're fine. Put it down."

Levi helped himself to a handful of chips from the pantry.

"Is it okay if I take Asher for a while?" he asked.

"Asher needs to cut the grass," Mom said and looked pointedly at me.

"He'll do it first thing tomorrow, won't you, Ash?" Levi said.

I noticed Mom's clothes hanging on her. She'd lost a lot of weight, maybe fifteen pounds.

"We can hang out tomorrow, Levi," I said. "I've got stuff to do around here."

Mom folded a pair of Travis's jeans, her lips tight as she considered.

"Oh, come on," Levi said, his voice crunchy with chips. "Let Asher come out and play for a while."

She never could say no to Levi.

"Where?" she asked.

"We thought we'd hit that Mexican liquor store outside of town," Levi said, "followed by a strip joint."

Mom glared at him, and Levi smiled, his teeth all full of chips. She rolled her eyes and sighed. "Stay out of the woods. And be back before dark."

Travis rounded the corner. "I want to go."

"Hell, no," Levi said.

"Levi!" Mom threw a sock at him. He caught it.

"Hell, no, *thanks*."

Travis grinned. Levi tossed the sock back into Mom's laundry hamper.

"Okay, that's enough," she warned him, but she was smiling.

"We'll play with you later," he said to Travis. "Got some seriously boring camera action this afternoon."

Travis kicked the wall and stormed off down the hall. Levi whistled.

"Man, that kid needs a therapist," he said.

"Are you kidding me? He acts just like you," I said.

"Are you two going or not?" Mom asked.

Levi sauntered up to my mom. "Maybe you need a therapist, too." Mom swatted at him.

Outside, the air buzzed with heat and insects. Levi and I walked east toward the woods where we'd built a fort a few years back.

"So, how'd it go with the shrink, anyway?" Levi said.

"John's not a shrink. He's my youth director."

"Have you been directed?"

I regretted telling Levi that Mom had arranged for me to talk to John. She'd suggested it last month after she found me sleeping in the driveway the morning after Dad showed up at church at the same time we were there.

"We shot some hoops," I said.

"You?"

It was no secret that I lacked coordination despite being almost six foot.

"We just hung out. No big deal," I said.

"So are you mental?"

"My parents are mental. Not me."

"Who's the one taking pictures of dead animals?" Levi teased.

"Shut up."

The sun angled from behind us, making my shadow taller and lankier. I looked like a stick figure. Levi's shadow was taller and thicker but not nearly as bulky as it had been at the start of the school year. I hadn't really noticed until then how much he'd slimmed down between football practice and weight training. The chubby goof I'd hung out with since preschool was disappearing.

Levi stopped. I took a few more steps forward, but when he didn't start walking again, I stopped, too. I took a deep breath and started to turn around, but he wasn't paying any attention to me. He was staring at something past my shoulder. The way he tore off across the street, I thought he must have seen a robbery in progress. I caught up to him, but not as quickly as I normally did. He'd gotten fast, too. Levi knelt down next to a heap of trash, inspecting a red, white, and silver mirrored Budweiser sign.

"Have you ever seen anything this cool?" Levi demanded, touching the mirror surface with a gentle hand.

"Your mom won't let you keep that," I said.

"Shut up, Asher. Who would ditch this?"

"Evan Llowell."

The garbage can stood in front of Evan's beige and brown ranch home. His blue Chevy truck sat in the driveway next to an immaculate yellow Volkswagen Bug. The picture window was covered with a thick white curtain. A sign in the middle of the yard advertised Shaw Realty. Attached to the sign was a plastic tube with the words *take one* printed on the side. I'd heard Evan had met some girl from Miami and was moving to the city to start a repo business.

"Man, can you believe it? I never thought I'd see Evan Llowell give it all up for some chick," Levi said. He touched the edges of the Budweiser sign, searching for any nicks. Satisfied, he wrapped his arms around it and said, "C'mon, let's go."

"Hold on." I lifted my camera.

He glanced up at the house. "We don't have time for this."

"Levi, I don't think Evan cares if you take the sign. It's sitting on the curb." I flipped the camera on. "Move."

He hesitated.

"Get out of the picture," I told him.

He reluctantly stepped aside. Through the viewfinder I could see him standing with his arms crossed in front of his chest, glancing around nervously like he thought someone else was going to come along and steal his treasure. I zoomed in to the Budweiser sign and moved to the side so the Volkswagen and Chevy were visible just behind it. I snapped the shot. I started to take another one, but Levi rushed forward, stuck the sign under his arm, and started walking toward the orange grove.

"You coming?"

"Where?" I asked.

"My house. I've got to get this thing home."

I shook my head. "I should get back. Mom said—"

"Yeah, I was there. Go do the Catholic boy thing, and be at my house at nine," he called over his shoulder.

"How many times do I have to tell you we're Methodist, not—"

"Whatever," he hollered as he turned down a row of trees.

❖

I stopped in the grass between our house and Pearl's. Both yards needed mowing, but Pearl would pay me to do hers, and I needed money to develop my film. Mom would understand. I walked across the lawn and rang Pearl's doorbell. As I waited, I stared at a big brown spider connecting its web to a basket of faded plastic ivy hanging from the ceiling of her front porch. It took a long time for her to answer the door.

"Oh, it's you." She had on a different flowered robe. I wondered if she bothered to get dressed anymore. Maybe that happened to old people.

"You need your grass cut?" I asked.

She eyed the lawn over my shoulder.

"Still charging fifteen dollars?"

I nodded.

"You can do it for ten."

Pearl's yard stretched twice the length of ours. I pursed my lips and shifted my weight in my blue Converse. I needed more than ten. Ten barely covered the gas.

I swallowed hard, then said, "Michael charges twenty."

Pearl folded her arms across her chest. "His mower catches the grass. Ten."

I stared at her wrinkly, pinched face. I needed cash to pick up my film from Harmon. I'd dropped it off over two months ago, and they'd already left three messages that it was ready.

"Okay. Ten."

❖

"You need to mow *our* grass," Mom said that night at dinner.

I picked at my green beans. "I know."

"Tomorrow morning. First thing. I've got another two loads of laundry, and we need to go get groceries, too."

"It's Saturday," Travis said.

"I know," she said.

"Bobby's going to Sea World."

Bobby was in the same kindergarten class with Travis, and they had spent the year terrorizing the teacher. Mom made sure they would be in different first-grade classes, but I figured they'd still manage to get in trouble together.

"He said he's gonna see dolphins and stingrays and sharks."

"Good for Bobby," Mom said stiffly.

"Why don't we get to do stuff like that?" he asked.

"Let's focus on what we *do* get to do, okay?" Mom's fork and knife scraped against the plate. She stuffed a forkful of chicken in her mouth.

Travis made his bulldog face. "We don't get to do anything."

Mom clanked her fork down onto her plate. "Yep. That's right. We don't get to do anything." Then with deliberate control she wiped the corners of her mouth with her napkin, grabbed her half-full plate, and marched into the kitchen. Dishes crashed; a cabinet door slammed.

"Way to go," I said.

"Shut up."

Travis tried to kick me under the table, but his legs were too short. He slid down in his seat and kicked his foot at me again. When I grabbed his heel, he squirmed and landed with a thud on the floor just as Mom rounded the corner. I dropped his foot.

"He kicked me," I said.

She ran her hands through her mousy brown hair. "You know, I'd like to do things, too, but I've got to work two jobs and take care of this place."

"So?" Travis said, sitting cross-legged on the floor and pulling on a loose string in the carpet.

I gently nudged his shoulder with my foot.

"We don't have to make things harder," I told him.

Travis jumped to his feet and shoved me hard.

"You knocked me out of my chair!" His face turned blotchy red.

I gave Mom my wide-eyed look and pointed at Travis.

"Enough!" Mom shouted. "I've had it with you two! I just…" She struggled to find words, but instead she ran out of the room. I heard her bedroom door slam.

I glared at Travis and stood to clear the dishes. I reached for his plate, and he knocked my hand away.

"I'm not done," he said, taking a big bite of chicken.

"Then sit down."

I headed for the kitchen. I rinsed the dishes, put them in the dishwasher, and dried my hands off on the towel before heading into the dining room. Travis still picked at his food. I sat down next to him at the table.

"I'm sorry," I said.

He looked at me, then continued to move his food around the plate.

"Are you finished?"

"No."

"Okay." I stood up and headed back to Mom's room. "Mom?" I asked and knocked gently on the door.

"Come in," she said.

I opened the door. Mom sat cross-legged in the middle of her king-size bed, a box of tissues and a pile of crumpled ones next to her.

"Sorry," I told her.

"No, I'm sorry. I'm just tired. Sometimes I get so mad at *him*." She meant Dad.

"I know it's not fair. I hate that Travis doesn't get to go to Sea World, but what am I supposed to do?" she asked. We were quiet for a minute.

"Manny's parents are divorced," I offered. "His mom gets child support for—"

"No." Since the start, Mom refused to accept any financial help from Dad. She insisted he made a choice, and it wasn't us. I didn't understand it, but Mom refused to discuss it.

"Don't you have film at Harmon?" Mom asked, changing the subject.

I hesitated. "Yeah."

I lingered in the doorway for another minute and then headed back to the dining room. Travis had smoothed his mashed potatoes flat and was drawing designs in them with his fork. Mom followed me into the room.

"We'll go to Harmon tomorrow if you mow the grass," she said.

Travis stopped building. "That's not fair. Why does he get to do what he wants?"

"They've already left two messages," Mom said, gathering the stack of mail.

"Three," I said.

"If you used color film, you wouldn't have to wait for a ride to Harmon," she suggested. "You could ride your bike right downtown."

"I don't like color."

"Why don't you just try it?"

I started out of the room. Why did she have to do that? She knew I didn't like color.

"I'm just saying you might like it," Mom called after me.

I rounded the corner to the hallway just as I heard Travis say, "Bobby's got a digital camera."

Bobby was an only child, like Levi. He'd probably get a new car when he turned sixteen, too. I went to my bedroom and took my photography notebook off the shelf above my computer. I flipped it to the last entry. If I had seven rolls of film waiting for me at Harmon at $17.60 each, then I needed around $120.00. I checked the math again: $17.60 a roll times seven equaled $123.20. I got my wallet and counted my money: $87.00. I was short $36.00. Plus, I needed to buy film.

Great.

I opened my wallet and counted again, but I wasn't surprised when nothing extra turned up. Just to be thorough, I went through my keepsake drawer and opened every birthday and Christmas card

I'd ever received. Aunt Sharon always sent cash for birthdays, but I usually lined up what I was going to get with it way in advance. Nothing in the cards. But I did know someone who had extra cash. I walked down the hall and pushed the door open to Travis's room.

"Hey," I said.

The Transformer in Travis's hand leapt off the edge of his bed onto a Matchbox car. The car flipped and he made a noise sort of like an explosion.

"Wanna play?" he asked like nothing had happened earlier. That was the cool thing about Travis. He didn't harbor hurt feelings about stuff.

I sat down on the floor beside him. He handed me a green car, one of his older ones. He grabbed the black one with flames painted on the side. I put my car beside his on the edge of his unmade bed. I rested my arm on top of the covers and felt a mound underneath. Digging under it, I discovered Travis's smelly stuffed dog. I dropped it and rubbed my hands against my shirt. When Travis was smaller, he'd slept with Og between his legs, and he wet the bed. No amount of washing ever got the stink out of it.

"Give me that," he demanded.

He snatched Og off the floor and tossed him to the top of the bed.

"Leave Og alone," he said absently, then made a revving noise. "You think you can take me, sucka?" he yelled. He looked at me. "You ready?" I nodded. "Ready, set, go!"

We launched the cars across the room. Travis's landed in a pile of dirty clothes. My green one sat in the middle of the room a good two feet shy of the clothes, but at least it wasn't upside down.

"I win," Travis said. He scrambled to gather our cars and handed the green one back to me. "Again. Ready, set, go."

This time I threw mine, too, but not as hard as I knew Travis would. Both cars landed in the heap. Travis ran to investigate.

"Me again." He held the cars high in the air. "Hey, I know. Let's make ramps."

He started pulling books off his shelves, mostly old ones of mine about space, airplanes, and dinosaurs. I helped him stack them, making ramps up and down, a series of steps. Then I remembered why I had come into Travis's room in the first place.

"You got any money?" I asked.

"No."

He kept building and wouldn't look at me, a pretty good indication he was lying. Aunt Sharon had given him money for his birthday two months ago, and he never spent any. It wasn't like he was saving it for something special; he just liked having it. He kept it stashed somewhere top secret in his room.

He leaned the makeshift ramp against his bed and put the flaming car up high on the edge of the book. It raced down the ramp and flipped. I let the green car go and it landed on its wheels, but then Travis decided to level the ramp with his Transformer. The book flipped, and the pointed edge of it landed on my hand. I yelped.

"Would you be careful?" I asked, rubbing my hand.

"Sorry," he said.

I started to inspect my hand, but then I noticed something scamper across the carpet. I jumped to my feet and stepped back. Travis lunged forward. He cupped his hands against the floor and carefully scooped. He smiled as he held the lizard between his thumb and fingers.

"Look. He lost his tail and it's growing back." Travis held the lizard out to me. A tiny stump stuck out of its back end. I nodded and fought back a shudder. "Wanna hold him?"

"That's okay."

"Wuss. I'll take him out." He stopped in the doorway and waved one of the lizard's legs at me. "Bye-bye, Asher."

Sometimes Travis hunted for lizards and attached them to his ears. It freaked me out the way they dangled like green and brown earrings, their bodies all stiff and arched. A moment after he disappeared into the hall, I heard Mom shriek.

I smiled and started stacking the books like a house of cards, balancing a flat one on top of two others on end. When Travis came back in the room, he flopped onto his bed. He grabbed Og and tossed him into the air a few times, then he turned on his side. I could feel him watching me.

"Get out," he said.

"Why?" I was holding two books up with my legs while I tried to balance the third on top.

"I have to do something. Just go."

The books toppled as I stood up and brushed past him. In my room, I sat down at my computer and went to a couple of photography sites. If I got up early, I could mow Mr. Williams's yard, and then I'd only be a little short. Maybe Mom would lend me the rest.

There was a knock on my bedroom door.

"What?" I asked.

Travis poked his head in. "Hey."

I swiveled my chair toward him. "You can come in."

He walked into my bedroom and put a ten-dollar bill on my dresser. "It's all I've got," he said. "And I need it back next week."

I picked the bill up and smiled at Travis. "Thanks."

He didn't say anything. He walked back out. I glanced at the clock in the lower corner of my computer screen. It was nine thirty, a half hour past the time Levi told me to meet him. I'd never really planned on going, anyway.

❖

That night I stayed up until well past midnight checking out photography links on the Internet. I guess it was no surprise that I slept in late the next morning. As soon as I got out of bed, I threw some clothes on and hurried out the back sliding glass door toward Mr. Williams's house. Mom would be ticked if she saw me mowing his grass before ours, but I needed the money now. I stopped. Neat, diagonal lawn-mower rows lined his yard. Blades of grass littered the sidewalk and driveway. I hadn't even heard the roar of the mower. He must've done it before I'd crawled out of bed. Twenty dollars would have given me enough money to pay for the film. If Mr. Williams hadn't mowed his grass that morning, I would only be short five dollars or so. Mom would have given me that much, but I knew she wouldn't give me twenty. I sighed with resignation and cranked up the push mower and started along the front edge of our lawn. Across the width of our yard, pivot, back, repeat.

❖

Thump, thump, thump.
"Stop it, Travis," I said, swatting behind me at his foot.
Thump.
I spun around to glare at him. He looked me dead in the eye and smiled before kicking the back of my seat again.

"Knock it off," Mom said, gripping the steering wheel even tighter. Highway driving made her nervous enough.

I felt a gentle nudge against the back of my seat. I leaned forward to grab the plastic grocery bag on the floor in front of me. I counted the rolls I had to drop off. Five rolls of film at $17.60 would cost $88.00. If I mowed seven lawns at $15.00 a lawn, then I should make enough to cover the gas to run the mower and pay for the developing. I pulled out my photography notebook and wrote the date in the far left column. Then I wrote the number five in the next column. In the far right corner I wrote $88.00—the amount I'd need for next time. That wasn't so bad.

But I was still short twenty dollars for today.

I thought about telling Mom, but I knew she'd just rant about the three hours she was giving up on a Saturday to drive me to Harmon and the money she spent on gas to get me there. She'd tell me I should have mowed more lawns instead of watching television or getting on the computer. I closed my notebook. Everyone was so edgy lately.

The store had two doors—one on the left for the photography studio and one on the right that I went through. Camera bags, frames, and tripods lined the walls and display cases. I tried not to look—there was always something I wanted—as I made my way to the back of the store. Alice was on the phone behind the counter in the back. She smiled and waved at me.

While I waited for her to hang up, I studied the restored black-and-white photographs of old Florida scenes displayed on the back wall. Boxy black cars were parked on the beach in one photo. Another showed Lee County airport trucks with an OK Used Car dealership in the background. Two of the photos were of gas stations. I liked how the branches of a tree framed the top of the picture. The last photo was an aerial view of planes. They weren't in regular frames—the pictures stood alone in a glass case without any border at all. I'd love to do that with mine, but it looked expensive.

Alice hung up the phone and said, "Asher. We were starting to think you weren't coming back for these."

Mom and Travis walked in as Alice flipped through the files of photo envelopes. She pulled several out and stacked them next to her.

"How many?" she called.

"Seven."

She took three more out of the file. Then she counted them and brought them over to the cash register to ring them up. Travis drifted into the studio and Mom followed him. There was a statue of an old butler in there. Travis liked to stick his finger in the statue's nose.

"Excuse me," I said.

Alice's hand paused over the register. Her eyes met mine.

"I…I only have enough money for five."

She stared at the register and tucked her brown hair behind her ear.

"I know you aren't supposed to hold them for this long. I'm really sorry."

She took two of the envelopes off of the stack and put them to the side.

"I'll just ring up five. Don't worry, we'll hold them for you," she said.

I was relieved, but I wished I could go through the pictures. I wanted to see how the photos had turned out. It was my own fault.

"That will be $88 exactly," she said.

I counted my money again. With Travis's ten, I had $97. "I have enough extra for one roll of film."

Alice smiled and crossed to the black-and-white film, where she took down a roll of T-MAX 400 without asking. "Should we wait to develop the rolls you're dropping off today?"

Instead of seven lawns, I'd have to mow ten.

"Can you go ahead and develop them? I'll make sure I have enough next time."

Alice nodded. "Your total is $95.51."

I handed her $96.00. She gave me the five white envelopes, the film, and forty-nine cents. I put the change in my pocket and opened my notebook. I felt her eyes on me as I adjusted the numbers in the columns. When I finished, she smiled, waved at me, and went back to making phone calls. I opened the top envelope and took out the first batch of shots.

It wasn't until I heard the drawer of the cash register open again that I noticed Mom standing next to me. Alice handed her a receipt and added two envelopes to my stack on the counter.

"Maybe we'll get Travis to Sea World sometime this summer," Mom said. "What are they going to do, take the house?"

She tucked her wallet back into her purse and ruffled my hair.

Take the house?

"Mom."

"Travis?" she said. "Come on, it's time to go."

CHAPTER FIVE

{Photo of cross in front of clouds}

On the way to church, I flipped through the stations and settled on Fall Out Boy. I could see Mom's neck stretch forward as we pulled into the parking lot.

"Do you see it?" she asked as we drove down the first row.

"No," I said.

She snapped off the radio.

"I was listening to that."

"I'm trying to look."

She didn't use her ears to see, but I didn't want to argue. She was in a bad mood every Sunday. Dad and Helen attended the eleven o'clock contemporary service, so to avoid them we had to go to the nine o'clock traditional service. The one time they came to the early service, we ran into them in the entryway. Since then, Mom scanned the parking lot for their shiny maroon Land Rover every Sunday, driving up and down the rows just to be sure they weren't there.

"I don't know how he can show his face here," she said.

I'd asked my youth director, John, about that. He said if the church doors were only open to people who did everything right, then the pews would be empty. But the times I'd seen Dad at church, he didn't act like someone who thought he'd done something wrong. That morning, Mom rushed us out of the sanctuary, his smile disappeared, but he didn't look guilty. More like…sad, I thought.

I looked at the clock on our dash. "We're going to be late again."

"Do you want to see him?" she asked. "Do you want to see *her*?"

"I do," Travis said.

I slid down in my seat. That kid had a knack for sending Mom into a tailspin.

"Why?" Her eyes narrowed as she looked at Travis in the rearview mirror.

"Just want to. I forget what she looks like."

"She looks like a home wrecker."

I wasn't sure if that was true, either. John said there were always two sides to every story. Not that I could say that to Mom. No way. If I blamed anyone for Dad taking off, it would probably be Travis—I'd had time to think about it, and it seemed like everything changed when he was born—but that was something I couldn't say, either.

Turned out, we weren't late after all. We made it to our seats before the acolytes lit the candles. I was glad we didn't have to slide into the last row again, meeting the kind looks of people around us who had come in late, too. That morning, we sat toward the middle, like we were normal.

We were saying the Lord's Prayer when I noticed Travis making these exaggerated facial expressions and gestures. He flipped the pages of the pew Bible and swung his legs. I bumped him with my elbow. He elbowed back, hard. Mom touched Travis's arm.

"What?" Travis asked just as Pastor Cole requested a moment of silence. I gripped my hands together.

Mom mouthed, "Stop."

"Tell him to keep his hands off me," Travis said loudly, shouldering me.

It wasn't enough to make me lose my balance, but I pressed my lips together and shook my head. Travis went back to flipping the pages of the Bible. Mom unzipped Travis's rolling blue-and-yellow book bag. He kicked at it. Mom looked at me.

"Og?" she asked.

I took the bag from her and rummaged through it. Nope.

Travis started smacking the Bible open and closed. Mom tried to take it from him.

"No," he said.

"You're just messing around with it. Put it down," she whispered.

"No."

Miss Gabby, who led the Cherub Choir, spun around from the pew in front of us. "Travis," she hissed, her mouth a perfect upside-down U.

"Yes, Miss Gabby?" Travis said politely, still wrestling with Mom.

Miss Gabby took a big gulp of air, and her mouth opened like she was going to say something, but instead she clamped her pink lips together. She shifted her bug eyes to my mom, who half shrugged, but never loosened her grip. I fought the urge to smile. As embarrassing as Travis was, I was glad he wasn't intimidated by Miss Gabby like all the other kids.

"I'm going to have to take him out of here," Mom said to me.

I looked on the seat behind Travis and Mom for Og.

"Come on, honey, let's put it away," Mom said, trying to pry Travis's fingers loose. He held fast and a Bible page ripped. The sound shot through the church. Everyone pretended not to hear. Everyone except one guy who looked about my age, two rows in front of me on the left. His body still poised in prayer, he cocked his head to the right and tossed me a sideways grin. I'd never seen him before.

My cheeks turned red at the scene we must have made, my hellion brother and my saintly mother. I suppose everyone fears being judged, but God knew she wanted to smack Travis's hand and snap, "Damn it, knock it off!" Instead, she appeared to have the patience of Mary from the chest up while she pried the ripped page from Travis and shoved it back into the book.

"No," Travis yelled.

I spotted Og's stubby brown leg underneath the pew. I scooped him off the floor and tossed him into her lap.

"Thank God," she said, handing the dog to Travis.

At first he made a face and shoved Og away. Mom said, "Fine," and passed him back to me.

Travis lunged for him and held Og close. Mom sighed, sat up straighter in the pew, and gave her full attention to Pastor Cole.

A few moments later, the congregation got up and greeted each other. This was Mom's favorite part of church. She hugged Travis and me first and then turned toward the other people around us. Travis held out his hand to me and then squeezed as hard as he could. I even shook Og's paw.

John, who was sitting at the end of our pew, grabbed my hand. "Peace to you, Asher."

"You, too."

I nodded at a woman standing at the other end of the row, but I was watching the new guy wearing a brown T-shirt that read *Jesus is My Homeboy* moving closer until he stood in front of me.

"Hey," he said. "Garrett."

"Asher."

"So, do they have anything to do other than hang out in here? You know, for people under sixty?"

He flicked his head to the right to get his hair out of his eyes.

"Yeah. After Children's Time we go to this other thing."

"Excellent. We'll follow you out."

People started returning to their seats. Garrett went back to his and leaned over to say something to his dad, mom, and some girl with them, and then they all turned toward me. He had this easy confidence—it was crazy. I didn't know where to look, so I settled on my feet. When I glanced back up, Garrett smiled and waved at me. I waved back.

Josh had told Levi that the guy who bought Evan's place had two kids who were in high school—a very hot senior girl and her brother. This had to be that family.

I leaned over toward John to glance at his wristwatch. Nine twenty-something. He caught me looking and held his arm out so I could read the time more easily. Nine twenty-seven. He smiled, and I grinned back and nodded my thanks.

At Children's Time, Travis ran up to the front with the other kids. I waited by the double glass doors until Pastor Cole had finished. I waved at Garrett and the girl to follow us out the door and along the sidewalk.

"I'm Emily, Garrett's sister." She was tall and lean like him, with long hair the same color as his, too. Neither one of them would have any trouble fitting in at our school.

"Where are all the people our age?" Garrett asked.

"They'll be in Bible study. That was the traditional service. Most of the younger people go to the contemporary one. They've got a band and stuff. It's cool."

"Why don't you go to that one?" he asked.

Before I could figure out how to answer his question, Travis said, "Helen the home wrecker." Then he tried to stomp on a lizard.

"Careful," Garrett said. "You don't want to hurt it."

Travis watched the lizard skitter off into the grass and squinted over at Garrett, who smiled. Levi would've encouraged the stomping.

"Our parents divorced last year," I said. "He goes to the contemporary service."

I could tell by Garrett's expression that he wanted to ask more questions, but fortunately we arrived at the kids' room to drop off Travis. We went through the gate of the chain-link fence to the other side of the building. The door leading into the study was open. Short, stocky Vince Llowell unfolded metal chairs around the long table. He didn't look—or act—like a Llowell. Maybe it was because his brothers, Josh and Evan, had harassed him his whole life. When I walked in, his face lit up.

"Hey, Ash, I got a chair for you," he said. He motioned to the seat next to his stuff.

"This is Garrett and Emily," I told him. "They're new."

Vince smiled and said, "Hey. You moved into my brother's place."

"On Washington?" Emily asked.

"Yep. I'm Vince Llowell. The coolest of the Llowell kids." Vince extended a hand to them. Garrett shook heartily, but when Emily went to shake, Vince bowed down like a knight or something and said, "My lady."

I loved this kid. "Yep, you are definitely the coolest of the Llowells," I said.

"I'm in high school," Vince announced.

"Not yet," I corrected as I pulled three soft-covered Bibles off the shelf and handed one to Emily and another to Garrett.

"I'm *almost* in high school," Vince said. "Seriously, I should be in high school. I've always hung out with older kids, right Ash?"

Garrett and Emily sat across the table from us. Garrett traced the picture of the tree on the cover with his index finger while Emily started talking to a junior, Shawna. Over the next few minutes, another half-dozen people arrived. Finally, our youth pastor and my personal shrink, John, came in carrying a red bin. He distributed our folders. Emily and Garrett shared one that belonged to a kid who was absent.

"Glad you could join us," John said to them. "Where are you from?"

"Orlando," Emily said.

"Oh, the city. This must be pretty different for you, huh?"

Emily and Garrett exchanged a look confirming what he said. John smiled.

"Yeah, you can say that," Garrett said.

"James 2?" Shawna asked John.

"Yep. And today's work sheet," he said as he passed around another paper. Then he pulled a plastic bag filled with pens out of the bin and gave one to each of us. I flipped my Bible open to James and looked over the work sheet. It was too bad John hadn't planned something cooler for today, like a play or something.

"How was skating?" Vince asked some of the other kids.

"It was fun!" John answered enthusiastically.

"I almost broke my arm," Shawna said.

"You were fine," John said. "Asher, why don't you get us started?"

"Okay." I folded my hands together. "God, thanks for bringing us all here today to learn the things you want us to know. And thanks for the chance to get to know new people. Amen."

After that, we each took a turn reading from James 2. Emily volunteered to go first. There was no way I'd volunteer to go first in a room full of people I didn't know, but she didn't stumble over anything. I thought it was cool that the passage was all about how to be with strangers, being nice whether they were rich or poor or whatever.

Garrett was next. He cleared his throat and then started, "Listen, my dear brothers." He read the passage as though he'd practiced it before he got here, but not like he was showing off or anything. He squinted and leaned in close, and I wondered if he needed glasses. I realized I was staring, so I looked down and followed along in my Bible.

Usually reading was easy, but today, with the new kids listening, my palms started sweating. Two more people went before I did. I looked down two entries to my passage. I was both relieved and a little disappointed that it was only three lines. I skimmed it, making sure I could pronounce all the words.

Then it was my turn. *"So speak, and so do, as those who are to be judged by a law of freedom. For judgment is without mercy to those who have shown no mercy. Mercy triumphs over judgment."* When I looked up, everyone but Garrett was still looking at the words on the pages in front of them. He did this ridiculously exaggerated wink at me. I fought the urge to laugh.

Once we'd finished the passage, John asked, "So what did you get out of that?"

Garrett said, "I could be wrong, but to me it's like James is saying to take care of people when they need it. Sometimes we judge and think, yeah, they deserve that, but isn't that when they need help the most?"

"Who are the needy?" John asked.

"Everyone is," a girl said.

"When people need food or somewhere to live and stuff, like that mission work we did," I said. I liked getting that in, so Garrett knew we did cool things, not just work sheets.

"Right, who else?" John asked.

"If someone had a hatchet, I wouldn't take them in," Vince said. "Even if they needed it."

Emily's eyes narrowed. "Wouldn't it depend on the reason for the hatchet?"

"Well, Vince, I don't know exactly where you're going with that, but I think Emily brings up an interesting point. How much should we risk as Christians?"

Vince leaned over to me and whispered, "Have you ever seen *Fright Forest*?" I shook my head. His brown eyes grew huge. "Don't."

"How much did Jesus risk?" John asked.

Garrett laughed. "Absolutely everything."

There was a knock at the door. Miss Gabby poked her head in and said, "John, I need to talk to you outside for a moment." She mouthed, "Meredith."

That was John's wife. She was in a wheelchair and looked old enough to be his mother. She always gave me the creeps with her skin like paper around her skull. Sometimes he brought her to church with him, but not today.

"Excuse me. Why don't you guys go ahead and get started on the work sheet? I'll be right back."

As soon as he was out of the room, I heard someone whisper, "What should we write?"

"The answers are in the passage," I said.

Vince leaned across the table to the work sheet John had left out on the table.

"Are you going to copy off the teacher?" Emily asked.

Vince's eyes widened. "What? No. I'm just checking my answers."

John stepped back into the room. Vince scrambled into his seat and started to hum. John's smile was gone. He was a little pale. He didn't look at any of us as he made his way back to the table. Miss Gabby followed him inside, and when Vince saw John's face, he stopped humming. I waited for someone to say something, but when no one did, I cleared my throat and asked, "Everything okay?"

John's eyes were glossy, like he was about to cry. "It's going to be," he said. "Thanks for asking."

He explained to Miss Gabby what we had been doing as she sat down at the table in his place. Then he left.

"What happened?" Vince asked as soon as the door closed.

Miss Gabby opened the Bible.

"I believe you were working on James," she said, ignoring the question.

Vince glanced at me. I raised my eyebrows and looked back at the work sheet without really seeing it. Instead, I prayed in my head for what John said to be true—*it's going to be okay*—but I had a bad feeling about it. Looking around, I could tell I wasn't the only one who thought so. Everyone pretended to work, but people kept exchanging concerned looks. The room was quiet. The only sounds were the low buzz of the air conditioner, the flip of pages, and the click of pens.

❖

"I'll bet she died," Vince said.

"Who?" Garrett said.

"Meredith. That's his wife. She's been sick for years, right?"

"Vince," I warned.

"Sorry, Ash. Just being honest. I gotta go. Josh gets ticked if I'm not waiting out front."

Vince hurried across the grass to the front of the building while Garrett, Emily, and I headed into the church.

"Cool kid," Garrett said.

"Yeah. You know, he's the only one in his family who goes to church," I said.

I found Mom and Travis standing in line to talk to Pastor Cole after the service. Emily headed toward their family, but Garrett followed me. As we joined them, Mom nudged Travis forward and said, "Go ahead. Tell Pastor Cole what you did."

Travis anchored himself to the floor. Mom knelt down beside him. "Tell him."

Travis's head sunk into his shoulder and I would have felt bad for him if Garrett hadn't whispered to me, "I didn't know Methodists confessed."

I couldn't resist a smile. While Mom started to explain the ripping of the pew Bible to Pastor Cole, I stepped aside with Garrett.

"Hey, we might go to the public pool later," he said. "Why don't you see about coming, too?"

"Okay. I'll check."

"Excellent."

Garrett's brown eyes matched his shirt. Mine were murky, an indistinguishable grayish color that changed shades depending on what I wore. "Mood eyes," Mom joked, like the rings that changed color depending on how the person was feeling.

"So I'll see you later," he said and disappeared into the crowded hallway leading to the exit.

Mom thrust Travis's hand into mine and sifted through her purse for the car keys. He attempted to get loose from me.

"I don't need you to hold my hand," he muttered.

I knelt down beside him. "Look, Travis. Travis." Sometimes you had to be loud with him in order for him to pay attention.

"What?"

"I'll let you go, but you have to promise you'll stand right here beside me. Mom's going to have a coronary if you take off. Understand?"

His eyes shifted away from mine and he muttered something under his breath.

"I know it was tough apologizing—" I started.

"Will you *not* talk to him about that, please?" Mom said, pulling the keys from the depths of her purse. "Let's just go."

We squeezed through groups of people and hurried to the parking lot. Mom glanced around for Dad's car. She unlocked the back and reached through to pull the latch up on the passenger door. Travis refused to climb into the car. I'd miss Garrett at the pool if he kept this up.

"Get in," Mom ordered.

"No."

"One," Mom warned. Travis stared her down. "Two!"

"What are you going to do on three?" he asked.

"What do you think will happen?"

They glared at each other. Travis kicked at the asphalt a few times and reluctantly climbed into the backseat. Mom brushed past me and was already in the driver's seat clutching the steering wheel by the time I sat in the passenger seat. Travis pushed the back of my seat with his feet, but he stayed silent. For a moment I thought we would enjoy a short, quiet drive home, but as soon as Mom turned out of the parking lot, Travis said, "Can I have a hermit crab?"

"You know how I feel about pets."

"Bobby has one. Did you know if a hermit crab loses a leg, it grows another one?"

"That's lovely." She fixed her eyes on the road.

"I wonder if you poke its eye out if it'll grow a new one," he said.

"That's enough, Travis."

"I'm just—"

"Enough."

I thought we'd spend the rest of the drive in silence, but I heard Travis rummage through his stuff. He piped up again.

"Where's Og?" he asked.

"Did you check your book bag?" Mom said.

"He's not there. I left him at church."

"We'll look in the car when we get home."

"He's on the bench. Someone could take him. They've got those people from that other service. Someone might take him."

"No one is going to take that thing," I said.

"Shut up. We have to go back for him," Travis insisted.

She softened, whispered, "I can't go back in there right now."

I thought about Dad and Helen sitting in the contemporary service watching Mom step inside and walk down the aisle. Would Dad recognize Og? Would he even remember?

"You would if it was something of yours," he said. "Not fair. *Not fair.*"

"Oh, please, Travis," Mom said. "Who said life was fair?"

But we'd only scratched the surface of what wasn't fair. We had no idea how unfair life could get.

CHAPTER SIX

{Photo of the footprint on fire-ant hill}

"You need to take care of the fire ants," Mom said as we pulled into the driveway after church.

Our yard grew weeds and fire-ant hills and was downright hostile toward anything resembling the lawns of the houses around us. Granted, most of them had sprinkler systems, but that wasn't a decent excuse. When Dad lived here, the yard looked great.

"It's too hot," I said.

"Wuss," Travis said. He swung the back door open, hopped out, and slammed it closed.

"You wait until you're old enough," I said as I stepped out of the car.

"It is hot," Mom said. "And you need to eat. Why don't you do it later this evening when it's a little cooler?"

"I was thinking about maybe going to the pool. That new kid at church invited me."

Mom glanced at Travis crushing anthills. She unlocked the door and said, "That's really thoughtful, Asher. You and Travis can go while I get some things done around here."

"Uh," I said, "well, actually, I was hoping I could go on my own."

"You can still see your friends," Mom said.

Then it occurred to me that Travis might not want to go. I decided to try it from that angle.

"I don't know. It is pretty hot out. Do you even want to go to the pool?" I asked as I held the door open for Travis.

He shrugged. "Maybe."

"Because I need you to watch my camera when I'm swimming."

Travis glared at me and raised his voice. "I'm not gonna just sit there with your stupid camera."

"You won't have to sit there the whole time—just most of the time."

"Why do you want to bring your camera?"

"You can stay here if you want," I suggested.

"Asher," Mom warned. "Just take him to the pool. Look, if he doesn't go, you don't go. Got it?"

How was that even remotely fair? I opened my mouth to say something, but she looked so pale I couldn't bring myself to do it.

"Never mind. We'll just stay here." I was halfway down the hall toward my bedroom when I heard Travis holler, "Fine. I'll watch your stupid camera."

The public pool was just far enough away from our house to warrant a ride from Mom, but she told me we'd have to walk there since she had a list a mile long of things to do. At least she gave us some cash to get something to eat at the concession stand. We changed quickly, and I stuffed the money in a Velcro pocket of my black-and-red swim trunks.

The sun burned down on us as we walked. It wasn't long before my upper lip was beaded with sweat. I could feel the heat on my scalp. Travis poked along beside me.

"Do you have to go so slow?" I asked.

"It's hot."

"It'll be cooler at the pool."

"Take my picture."

He knew better than to ask.

"You took that one of Mr. Williams," he said.

I shook my head. "Doesn't count. His face isn't in it."

"What's wrong with faces?"

I didn't answer him.

"Is that why you hate picture day?" he asked.

"I don't hate picture day."

"You could take a picture of a part of me," Travis said. He wiggled his bottom at me.

"No. Will you stop that? Come on."

"Why not?"

I walked faster. He ran to catch up.

❖

It cost three dollars each to swim at the community pool, a total rip off since the place was so dilapidated. I tucked the change back into my trunks as we stepped out from under the moldy awning. I spotted Levi and Josh sitting at the pool's edge. I scanned the pool for Garrett. At first I thought I'd missed him, but then I spotted him gliding under the surface of the water down at the deep end.

Travis yanked at my arm.

"I want to swim."

"We're going to see Garrett first."

"No."

"Do you want me to take you home?"

Travis bolted. I was about to chase after him when I heard, "Hey, Asher." Garrett stood near Levi and Josh who turned to look at him when he called my name. He motioned me over with a swoop of his arm. I caught sight of Travis at the far end of the pool, dodging people. My eyes stayed on him as I circled in the opposite direction. I figured I'd meet up with him on the other side.

"Glad you made it," Garrett said.

"Hey," I said.

Levi strolled up beside me. "Who's your friend?" he asked.

"This is Garrett. I ran into him at church."

"I'm Levi. Hey, Josh, this the guy who moved into Evan's place?"

Josh walked over and nodded. "You guys got a good deal."

"It's a buyer's market," Garrett said. "At least, that's what my dad says. You guys going to be sophomores, too?"

"I am. Josh is a junior. We're on the football team." Levi appraised Garrett. "You play?"

Garrett shook his head. "I'm into dirt bikes. And I draw."

"You should go out for the team. It's a good way to get to know people."

Garrett turned to me. "You play, too?"

"No."

Garrett nodded and glanced from me to Levi and back again. Levi flicked the bulky Minolta hanging in the middle of my chest.

"He plays with his little friend instead," Levi said.

"You take pictures?" Garrett said.

"Yeah, he takes pictures," Levi said, "black-and-white ones of dead cats and pinecones and messed-up trees."

"That is so cool. Take my picture." Garrett threw an arm around Levi, stuck his tongue out, and crossed his eyes. Levi pushed him away.

"He doesn't take pictures of people. Do you, Ash?" Levi said.

I opened my mouth to say something but couldn't think of anything. I couldn't figure out why Levi was being such a jerk.

"Why not?" Garrett asked.

"Yeah, Ash, why not?" Levi said.

"Shut up, Levi." I angled toward Garrett. "I like…I just prefer landscapes. The film isn't cheap, and people are sort of…I don't know."

I felt the strap eating into the skin around my neck.

"Unpredictable." Garrett finished my sentence.

I nodded. "Yeah," I said. "Unpredictable."

Which made me remember Travis. I scanned the pool for him. He sat beside the ladder, his knees curled up under his chin while his fingers drew circles in the water. I almost felt sorry for him, but then he caught me looking at him and gave me the finger.

"Nice," Garrett said.

Awesome. Garrett noticed. "My mom made me bring him along. You know how it is."

"Not really. I'm the youngest."

Travis dug at his nose.

"That kid's a mess." Garrett laughed.

"We've got to go by church later. He left his stuffed dog."

"Check it out," Levi said. "Jennifer's here." She was standing in line at the concessions with some of her friends. "I suddenly have this craving for ice cream. You guys coming?"

"I want to swim. You?" Garrett asked me.

"You go ahead, Levi. I'm going to swim, too."

"Suit yourself," Levi said.

Garrett was quiet until Levi and Josh were out of earshot. "What's up with that guy?" he asked.

"What?"

"You didn't catch that?"

"Oh, that's just how Levi is. You'll see."

Garrett jumped up and said, "I think he's an ass. It's hot. Come on." His eyes dared me, and I felt myself holding my breath. He dove into the water barely making a wave. I wanted to follow him.

"Travis," I called.

My brother looked up at me. I held my camera up and motioned for him to come over. Even though he gave me a disgusted look, he got up and walked toward me. I handed him my camera. "Don't mess with it."

"Whatever."

I hesitated, but then Garrett called me. He hung on to the edge of the pool. Drops of water ran down his face.

"Are you coming or what?"

I walked over as Garrett sunk under the water. I slid into the pool with one quick motion. The trick to getting in was to do it fast. The water felt icy against my hot skin. I bobbed up and down a few times to warm my body.

"Come on." Garrett darted toward me and thunked me on the head. "You're it." He shot away before I could react.

Tag. Breathless, stupid tag.

Garrett swam and rolled in the water like an otter. Just when I thought I had caught him, he would slide beyond my fingertips. I kept calling time so I could check on Travis. It ticked me off Mom made me bring him. It would have been easy enough to wrap my camera in a towel or something. She just wanted him out of her hair.

He wasn't sitting where I had left him. He was over by the metal picnic bench, holding the camera up to his face. I swam to the pool's edge.

"Gotcha." Garrett whacked me good-naturedly on the head.

"Travis," I called.

He was standing in front of Levi. Just then, the camera flashed. Travis had taken Levi's picture.

"Travis!" I yelled. Damn it.

Levi was trying to get the camera from him. Travis poked him in the stomach. Levi poked him back, hard. I scrambled out of the pool and Garrett followed me. I didn't like the way my camera was swinging around Travis's neck.

"Travis!" I yelled as I got closer.

But then Levi shoved Travis.

I grabbed Levi's shoulder. "Hey!"

While I distracted Levi, Travis gave him a swift kick in the leg.

"Damn, keep this leech away from me or I'm going punch him," Levi said. He held Travis at arm's length.

I spun Travis to look at me. "I told you not to mess with it." I pulled the camera from around Travis's neck and grabbed him by the arm.

"Shut up," Travis said. He lurched to kick Levi again.

Garrett helped me pull Travis away from the crowd to two empty lounge chairs down at the far end of the pool. He squirmed, but Garrett and I each had an arm.

"Let me go," Travis growled between clenched teeth.

"I told you to sit with my camera," I hissed. "Is it that hard to just sit there for a few minutes? Is it?"

Travis refused to look at me.

I took a deep breath. I needed to calm down. Garret next to me made me hyperaware of everything I said. "Why are you messing with Levi, anyway?" I asked.

He wouldn't answer me. The three of us sat there, the only sound between us the huffing Travis made when he was angry. His cheeks puffed in and out like a blowfish. We'd have to go home if he didn't settle down. I thought about threatening him with leaving, but that didn't always have the right effect. Half the time he would scream, "Fine, let's go." I'd have to leave because the people around me would have heard it.

"We're probably going to have to go," I told Garrett.

"Don't," Garrett said. He turned to Travis. "Hey, you haven't even gotten in the pool yet."

"He can't swim," I said.

"Can too."

"What about ice cream? You want some ice cream?" Garrett asked.

If I had asked, Travis would have told me off, but instead his expression softened a little. There was something about Garrett that made you feel agreeable.

"Hold on a sec. I'll be right back."

I watched Garrett run over to the chain-link fence, where he'd left his towel and shoes. He dug into his shoe and ran back. He gave Travis a five.

"Thanks," Travis said. He pulled his arm away from me and flashed me a smile. "Ice cream." He held up the bill and took off.

"Yeah, that'll teach him," I said.

"At least you're still here."

"I've got money. I'll pay you back."

"Don't worry about it."

I watched Travis cut in front of some people in the food line who weren't paying attention.

"Is he always like that?" Garrett asked.

"Pretty much."

"Why?"

I couldn't remember a time when Travis wasn't a walking time bomb, but it had gotten worse since Dad left. I almost told Garrett that, but it felt like too much. I settled on shrugging.

The splashing of the people around us almost drowned out Garrett's next words. "Can I tell you a secret?"

I nodded. "I'm pretty good at keeping stuff to myself."

Garrett slid the lounge chair a little closer. "When I was little, I had this blanket. I took it everywhere. Couldn't sleep without it."

I had trouble hearing him with his skin so close. I could see the freckles dotting his nose. Blanket. He was talking about being little, like Travis. He didn't want me to be mad at my brother. I never really caught the full story.

He sat back in the lounge chair. "You know, I wasn't sure you were going to show up."

"I wasn't sure I was going to make it here, either."

"I'm glad you did."

I turned to look at him. It wasn't the kind of thing I was used to hearing.

"Hey," he said leaning in even closer.

I could feel my pulse pumping.

"What?"

He smacked my arm and raised an eyebrow. "You're it."

Garrett leapt off the lounge chair and raced through the crowd of people at the pool. I watched him for a brief second—this crazy, free guy with the wild brown eyes. I'd never met anyone like him, so even though I wasn't the running type, I chased him. He glanced over his shoulder at me as he maneuvered. As we passed the food line, Travis saw me.

"Where are you going?" he said.

"I'll be right back," I shouted. "It's okay!"

Travis glared at me. I ignored him and followed Garrett into the shade of the building. I caught a glimpse of him before he disappeared around the corner into the men's room. A group of girls blocked my path. I tried to scramble around them, but they formed a tight group. I nudged through with a quick *excuse me* and sped around the corner. I almost ran right into a dad with his little kid coming out of the bathroom.

"Whoa!" the man said. "Slow down."

I moved to the side to let them pass.

"Sorry," I said as they walked past.

The dad whispered, "You looking for your friend?"

"Yeah."

"The stall," he whispered.

I grinned at him. "Thanks."

I stopped in the center of the bathroom to gather myself. I was still breathing fast. The scent of mold and urine mixed with bleach. Three stalls, two urinals, three showers. Somewhere, water was running.

"Gar-rett?" I called in a singsong voice. "Oh, Gar-rett! Where could he possibly be?"

I looked under the stalls—no feet.

"Is he behind door number one?"

I swung the first door open.

"Hmm. How about door number two?"

I pulled open the second.

"Which leaves us with…" When I got to the last stall, I heard Garrett laugh from inside. I had my hand ready when he shoved it open and pushed past me. "I got you," I said.

"I thought for sure you'd head back to the showers," he said.

Yellow *Caution: Under Construction* tape crossed the shower area.

"I would have," I admitted. "That guy ratted you out. So I guess this means you're it."

Garrett lightly tagged my upper arm. "Not anymore."

I laughed and went to tag him back, but he caught my wrist. I broke his grip and grabbed his forearm. Usually I hated this sort of thing. Levi's competitive nature meant someone—me—usually ended up face-first on the floor. Garrett wrestled me easy, trying to one up each other until we were nose-to-nose, grinning. It felt weirdly normal to stand so close to someone I'd just met.

Then Garrett stepped away, raised an eyebrow—he was really good at that—and ducked under the construction tape. He headed down the hall to the broken shower stalls. I hesitated for a second. I couldn't think straight. I chewed on my lip and listened to the dripping water in the sink, the thumping inside of me, before I followed him.

I'd made it around the corner before my foot slipped on the humidity-slick tile and I fell flat on the damp floor. I froze to take inventory of all my parts to make sure I hadn't broken anything.

"Asher?" Garrett peeked out at me from one of the showers. "Hey, you okay?"

"Yeah. I just…"

"Did you break something?"

I decided to move to show him I really was fine, even though I wasn't entirely sure. I'd never broken a bone. Levi insisted you knew when you broke something, so I figured I was okay.

Garrett hurried over and held out a hand to help me up. I reached up and pulled, but Garrett slipped too and tumbled down on top of me. His elbow caught me in the chin.

"Man, I'm so sorry!" he said, tangled up with me. "Are you okay?"

I started laughing even though it really hurt, and then Garrett was laughing too, our limbs all twisted up together. He was openmouthed, laughing over me, and a string of saliva dripped onto my chest. I could barely talk through my laughing.

"Did you…just spit…on me?" I gasped.

The question made him laugh harder. My face hurt from smiling. Then Garrett rubbed against my hip. That's when I felt how hard he was. I froze. The instinct to shove him off me flickered just under my skin, but I didn't. Garrett's wide grin dimmed as he studied my reaction. I listened to the water drip.

"Are you okay?" he asked.

Did he mean the fall or something else? Both? His eyes searched my face. I must have nodded because he let out a heavy breath and rested his head on my chest for a moment. He smelled like coconut oil.

"Your heart is pounding," he said.

"I know."

Because we were running.

Because I fell.

Tell him.

He hoisted himself up and looked at me.

"I can't believe I was so worried about moving here," he said. Indecision flickered across his face. Then Garrett smiled tentatively at me. "So I should probably tell you I'm gay."

"Gay," I said, like it was new to my vocabulary.

"Yeah." He searched my face.

"I'm not," I said. "I'm not…gay."

"Okay," Garrett said, and a shadow passed across his face.

"I'm not."

He started to move off me, to back away, and I felt myself holding on to him. A panic rose up in me. I blinked back tears. "I'm not."

Garrett's eyes blinked understandingly. He nodded. "Okay," he assured me. "It's okay."

It's okay not to be gay. Then why wouldn't my arms let him go?

I don't know who made the next move. I'd like to say he did, but I'm not sure. All I know is his mouth was as gentle as his eyes, and as much as I hate to admit it, I liked the taste of him and the feel of him against me.

We heard a voice. I scrambled up and ran into a shower stall, which made no sense since the showers didn't work. Garrett was up too, and he gestured toward the other set of stalls past the shower. I ran in there and slammed the door closed, but it sprung open and my fingers fumbled with the latch but the sliding mechanism wouldn't line up. I held the door closed and rested my forehead against it. I chewed on my bottom lip as quick footsteps entered the bathroom.

"Asher," a voice called loudly, like I was lost in the woods. The noise reverberated in the tiled room. It was Levi. "Garrett, you seen Asher?"

I heard the sink water turn on at the same time a faint siren sounded.

"He's taking a crap, I think," Garrett said. "Ash."

He lied really well. I quietly cleared my throat. What did my voice sound like? "What is it, Levi?"

"It's Travis."

Garrett turned the faucet off, and the siren I had assumed was the sound of the pipes continued to wail. I pushed the stall door open, walked past the showers, and stepped under the caution tape. Garrett's face was reflected in the mirror, his eyes wide. He had little square imprints on the skin of his arm from the tile floor.

"What the hell are you doing back there?" Levi asked. "Come on."

"Well, the other stalls were occupied at the—" Garrett said for me. Maybe he wasn't good at lying.

"You got to come," Levi interrupted. "Travis hit his head or something on the diving board and they found him floating and it's bad, Asher, he…" His voice cracked.

A chill crawled across my skin as his words sunk in. Levi shifted his weight from foot to foot and wiped his hand across his mouth.

"It's bad." He shook his head from side to side.

If it had been anyone but Levi—anyone—I would have needed to see for myself. My breath came fast, and I clenched my jaw. I stole a glance at Garrett. He took a tentative step toward me, but I held my hand up and brushed past Garrett and Levi, out of the moldy, musty bathroom and into the sunlight. The pool was empty. Parents quietly ushered kids through the gates to the parking lot.

A little girl, younger than Travis, toddled past me, Floaties on her pudgy arms. "But why can't we swim?"

"A boy got hurt."

"Is he okay?" she asked, but the mom didn't answer. She scooped up the little girl and hurried out to the parking lot.

A crowd of people stood at the far end of the pool near the deep end. I read the expressions of the people watching my brother. They crowded around. I couldn't see him. Jennifer sat on a lounge chair nearby, crying. A couple girls stood around her, their hair stringy wet. One nudged Jennifer and pointed to me. She cried harder. One by one, faces turned from Travis toward me. A paramedic rushed away from the crowd toward the ambulance. His lips were a straight, concentrated line.

I gulped for air.

I thought Travis was getting ice cream.

I blinked hard, squinting at the sun while Levi and Garrett ran up beside me. Levi rested a hand on my shoulder. I twisted away from him.

"Ash," he said. "I called your mom. She's on her way."

Mom. I paced back and forth. I felt them all looking at me. Jennifer got up from the lounge, and her group of friends shuffled toward me. I started to feel caged.

"Did you see anything?" I asked Levi, my breath coming fast. "How bad is it?"

Levi rubbed his face. "Jesus, Asher."

"How bad?" I demanded.

He wouldn't look at me. So instead of walking through the crowd to stand closer to my brother and see for myself, I ran. I ran barefoot across the concrete, through the chain-link gate, and across the parking lot. Someone called after me, but I didn't look back. I put as much distance as I could between my brother and me. My legs sprinted and ached. I didn't think I had a destination in mind until I saw our church in the distance.

The black asphalt of the parking lot burned my bare feet. A few cars were there even though the church services were long over. The cool air hit me as I opened the door. Two men in long pants and short-sleeved shirts without ties stood in the entryway. They paused briefly in their conversation as I ran past them in my black-and-red swim trunks into the sanctuary and down the aisle. My eyes scanned the row to my left. Close to the center of the sanctuary, I caught sight of two faded stuffed paws visible from under the pew. The pounding in my chest faded slightly. I slid onto the bench, inching toward Og. My bare, clammy skin stuck to the polished surface as I moved along. Pews weren't made for contact with flesh. I paused over Og, leaning my head against the pew in front of me. A prayer mumbled from my mouth, but nothing I said made sense. He was directly below me between my bare feet. Travis would want Og. I should grab him and hurry back to the pool or home. Mom was going to be worried, but she'd be glad I thought to get Og.

She'd be glad.

My skin crept, and I shuddered. Yeah, Travis would feel better with Og by his side. I reached down and picked him off the floor. I cradled the smelly dog in my hands, rocked him gently. "Shh. It's okay, Og. It's okay. It's fine." But as I sat there, I could see those faces from the pool in my head. I could hear Levi's kind voice. I could feel Garrett's lips. I closed my eyes tightly.

"Asher?" a voice asked.

I didn't look up.

"Asher?" asked the voice again. "What are you doing?"

I didn't look up. I rocked Og. I kept rocking Og and telling him it was going to be okay.

❖

Later they told me Pastor Cole took me home and sat with me until my mom came home and Aunt Sharon had gotten in from Chicago. I wouldn't let go of Og. They told me that Travis hit his head on the diving board and then drowned.

Here one minute, gone the next.

It was a busy day at the pool. They told me it wasn't my fault. They told me Garrett called four times that night to see if I was okay, but I didn't take his calls. I just held on to Og. I kept rocking him. But Og wasn't Travis, and Travis was dead. Nothing would ever change the fact that my brother died because of me.

Chapter Seven

When someone dies, people bring casseroles and hams. Sympathy food was still arriving the morning of Travis's funeral. Aunt Sharon answered the door while Mom and I got ready. I finished first and took over for her in my new gray suit while she showered and Mom did her makeup. So when the bell rang and I opened the door, I expected another lady from church with a covered dish, but instead I found Garrett standing on my front step.

I didn't even know he knew where I lived.

"Hey," he said. "I tried calling."

"Right, sorry. I got the messages. I was going to call you, but it's been—"

"No, it's okay. Don't worry about it."

We stared at each other for a moment.

"Nice suit," he said.

"Thanks. The funeral."

"It's today?"

"Yeah." My yard looked weird with Garrett standing in it. Had he noticed the cracks in the driveway? "You want to come in?"

"No, I've got a ride waiting. I didn't want to bother you." I noticed Emily in the driver's seat of a blue Civic, the engine still running.

I wanted to tell him he wasn't a bother, but I waited a few seconds too long to respond.

He said, "I just wanted to drop this off."

I hadn't noticed he was holding anything until then. He handed me a bag, the nice department store kind with a handle. I wanted to look inside, but I wasn't sure if that would be rude.

"It's your camera," Garrett said.

My camera.

"You left it at the pool."

"Thanks." I had completely forgotten about it.

"Well, I've got to go. My sister has this thing. I didn't know the funeral was today."

"Don't worry about it."

"I'd like to go. Not *like* to go, but you know, be there."

"It's okay. Really."

"School starts soon," he said.

"Yeah."

"Maybe we can hang out or something before then."

"Cool."

Garrett stuffed his hands into the pockets of his jeans and turned away. I closed the front door.

The only other funeral service I had ever been to was my grandfather's in Chicago. My parents were still married then, and we had flown up so Mom could be with Grandma and Aunt Sharon. My parents argued about whether or not I should be allowed to go to the service. Mom said it was important, that death was a part of life, and that at nine, I was old enough to handle it. Dad didn't say much, so he probably disagreed with her. In the end, Mom won, and we went shopping for this black suit that cost almost a hundred dollars. I only wore it once. At Grandpa's service, I sat next to my mom as she hugged all these people she knew from when she was younger and dabbed at her eyes. She introduced me to a ton of people and I shook hands. I didn't know how to be. Do you smile at people at funerals? Was I supposed to cry like Mom? I had met Grandpa maybe four times, and it's hard to make yourself cry.

Travis was only two then. Dad stayed back at Grandma's with him since the people we knew who would have been able to watch him were all going to the service. Travis had tantrums then, particularly when the pressure was on to be good.

When Grandma died less than a year later, Mom went back to Chicago for a few days to help Aunt Sharon, but that time the rest of us stayed home because Travis was sick.

Travis had never been to a funeral, but the suit Mom chose for him to wear to his own had. She said it would make him feel better if he wore something that had belonged to me. I thought it made her feel better, not Travis, since he hated hand-me-down stuff, and he was dead. To me, it made sense that a part of me was being buried with him.

Mom didn't have a lot of experience with planning a funeral, since Aunt Sharon had done all the work when Grandpa and Grandma died. But between Aunt Sharon and Pastor Cole, everything was taken care of. All the discussions and arrangements had been made at the church. Aunt Sharon asked me if I wanted to say something at the service, but I didn't. Mom asked me about what I thought Travis would have wanted, but I didn't know. I didn't even want to go, but Mom said I had to. "He was your brother," she said. Like that made it easier.

Mom waited until the moment we stepped inside the funeral home to whisper, "*He* is going to be here. Just so you know."

Dad. Great. She said Dad had shown up at the hospital. I don't know who called him. I guess he had a right to know, being our dad and all, but Mom said he had given up his rights to anything when he walked out on us.

For the funeral service, Mom had brought a ton of pictures of Travis, from baby photos to the most recent ones of him in his T-ball uniform. A lot of them were in my photo frames. I had spent a good part of the morning taking my shots out of the frames so Mom could use them for his service. I had stacked my black-and-white photos on top of my dresser as Mom sat on my bed and filled my frames with colorful, smiling portraits of Travis. I watched as she arranged some of the recent ones on a polished table near the entryway of the funeral home.

"I told you to leave that in the car," she said as she glanced at the camera hanging around my neck.

I shrugged.

"Please don't. Not today."

She took my silence as agreement.

I watched her arrange the photos. Travis in his red T-ball shirt and cap, a bat resting on his shoulder, his eyes tiny slits from looking into the sun. Travis's school picture, his black hair cut too short, his cheeks a little flushed as if he'd just come from PE, pink lips with the edges of his mouth turned down like he'd had to hold his smile too long. Travis's preschool class photo, ABCs bright and cheerful, behavior chart next to the dry-erase board. Travis was having a yellow day, he and Bobby side-by-side holding hands, grimacing, trying to see who could squeeze the hardest. I liked that one.

"Where are you going to put the other ones?" I asked. There were still a half-dozen more pictures of my brother in the box.

"In there," she said. "Can you carry this?"

She handed me the heavy box and motioned for me to follow her into the room where the casket was. Another table was set up next to it. I put the box down.

"Is he in there?" I asked.

There were two unspoken *he*s in our life now. She nodded as if she didn't trust her voice enough to answer aloud and started pulling frames out, the larger ones in front, the smaller ones hidden, so I put my hand on her shoulder.

"It's all wrong, isn't it?" she said.

She was in one of the photos. A younger woman with light brown hair and an easy smile angled the baby in her arms toward the camera. It was only six years ago, but she didn't look much like the woman kneeling on the floor next to me. The color of the photo had aged to something in between color and black and white.

"Why don't we just put this one up front," I said, "in between these two…and move this one over a little. Tell me if that's better."

She lifted herself off the floor and backed up a bit.

"Yeah. That's better. Except—the one to your left. Move it back a little more."

Aunt Sharon walked up and stood next to Mom, looking at the pictures.

"The pastor is here," she said. "He has a couple of questions. I wasn't sure what to tell him."

Mom nodded.

"The pictures look good," Aunt Sharon said. "I'm glad you thought to bring them. It's a nice touch."

Mom made the gasping noise and started turning red like she does when she's about to lose it. Aunt Sharon rubbed her arm.

"I know. Okay, sweet girl, you got to hold it together." Mom's hands shook at her side and she clasped them together in front of her. She couldn't talk. Aunt Sharon wrapped an arm around her. "You need a few minutes?" Mom nodded.

"Are you okay here?" Aunt Sharon asked me.

"Yeah. I'm okay."

She pointed to a door to the left. "We'll be in there if you need anything."

I glanced around the room. No one else was around; I was alone. I didn't think I'd have a chance to do what I wanted. I quickly opened my camera case, took the Minolta out, and slung the strap around my neck. I took a deep breath to steady myself.

The casket lid was surprisingly easy to open. I only glanced at his face once, and I was glad I did. It made it easier that he didn't really look like Travis. I'd already decided I wouldn't take a picture of his face, just in case Mom ever came across it. Instead I took one of his hands resting on his chest. Only I would know who it was, when it was.

I closed the lid and backed away. I hated lying to Mom, but Travis had always wanted me to take his picture.

Now, I had.

I wondered where they kept the dead people before they brought them out. Did Travis's body have to lie next to other dead people's? Maybe Meredith—John's wife—was in the back somewhere. I'd heard she'd died the same day as Travis, and that they were going to have a service for her tomorrow. I wondered if Travis had spent the night next to her in the funeral home.

Last year at Halloween, he had talked Mom into letting him watch *Night of the Living Dead*. He acted all cool while it was on, but he snuck into my room that night. When I asked him what he was doing, he said, "Nothing." I asked him if he was scared, and he said, "No." I told him he couldn't sleep with me, and he said, "How about the floor?" He camped out in my room every night for a week.

I guess when you're dead you probably don't worry about things like that. Even so, I hoped Travis hadn't been right next to her. I hoped he'd had his own space that was dark and cool. He would have freaked out if he'd known he spent the night next to a dead person.

I looked at the photos on the table again. Of the eleven pictures, I was in only two with him. One was at the beach, Travis sitting in the sand with me standing behind him. The other was posed. We look like we're in the woods, but we aren't. Travis is holding Og. I'm holding Travis.

I heard voices and turned to look. Dad walked in with a guy who worked at the funeral home. Dad's hair gleamed, wet with gel. I didn't recognize his gray suit.

When he saw me through the doorway, he shook hands with the guy and headed in my direction. I busied myself with putting my camera back in the case. I kneeled in front of the cardboard box, even though it was empty. I hoped Mom didn't walk in. Not here. Not now. He stood tall beside me for a moment and then said, "Asher?"

I glanced up like I hadn't noticed him before. "Oh, hi."

"Are you okay?"

I nodded and stood up. He looked older than I remembered. The last time I had been this close to him, he'd been standing outside our front door. He had come to pick Travis and me up for a visit. We hadn't seen him since he had left, but in the divorce papers we were supposed to go to his house every Sunday and one evening during the week. Mom had a rough time agreeing to that, and when she saw Helen waiting in the car parked in our driveway she started howling like an injured animal. When I answered the door, she was screaming from the other room. I told him, "We can't, Dad." He didn't understand, so I had said, "We're not going with *her*."

Meaning Helen.

He said something about her being his wife and us giving her a chance, but it was hard to hear with Mom all hysterical. Travis didn't seem to care one way or another. He sat in the chair playing his DS, ignoring Mom and Dad. I was sure Travis didn't care now, either.

"Where's your mother?" he asked.

"Talking to Aunt Sharon. In there." I pointed toward the door.

"Are you okay?"

As if he didn't hear me before? "Yeah. Yeah. I'm okay."

But his eyes were searching my face a little too hard, and it made me want to cry so I tried to look somewhere else. The only thing to look at was the casket or the pictures. I settled on the pictures. Instead of seeing Travis, I imagined my black-and-white photos in the frames.

"The pictures of Travis out there in the hall," Dad said. "I heard he was playing T-ball, but I hadn't seen that picture of him in his uniform."

I felt little. I couldn't remember the last time I felt so little.

"These I recognize," he said. "I was around for all of these." But Dad wasn't in a single picture.

He rubbed his hands over his face. "I'm not okay," he said. "I'm so sorry." His voice was all jagged and raw in my ear. Then he put his arm on my shoulder and forced me to look at him. "I can't talk to you here. Not now. But I'm going to fix that."

He said it like I knew what he was talking about. Was he sorry for leaving us? For marrying Helen? Or was he just sorry that Travis was dead? I couldn't figure out how he could fix any of it.

"Mom is going to come out soon," I warned him.

"Right. Okay. I'll go find Helen. We'll be keeping our distance because Pastor Cole said that would make it easier for her." He meant Mom. I wondered if they called her *her* like we did him. And now, Travis. "But we are here. And if you need anything…" He put his hand on my shoulder.

If I need anything…

"Mom's fine." I pulled my shoulder away from him.

He blinked at me, shook his head a little like he knew better, and for a moment I was so angry, I forgot all about Travis being dead.

"I've got to go," I said.

I picked up the box and rushed out the door to our car, like it was really important for me to put it in the trunk. He didn't follow me. The car was locked. Mom had the keys. I took my camera case out and put the strap around my neck. I yanked the box flaps up, folded it flat, and jammed it as best I could under the tire so it wouldn't blow away.

My eyes burned. I blinked hard and looked skyward, trying to get the tears to dry. Then I noticed the church steeple across the street, tall and black against the cottony clouds. It was the Catholic church, and it looked cool. There was something about the clouds that made me think of the fair.

Wispy clouds of cotton candy.

Grainy, melt-in-your-mouth clouds.

I pulled my camera out of its case and slid the button on. I removed the lens cap, peered through the viewfinder, and adjusted the zoom lens. It whirred as I pushed the button halfway down. The inside light was red, then the camera's autofocus took over. The lens spun, tweaked, and the green dot appeared. A perfect picture. Click, horizontal. Click, vertical. What about making the clouds the focus instead of the cross? I tried to get the camera to focus on the whiteness beyond the cross. What would it look like if the sharp lines of the cross were blurred? The lens shifted and adjusted. The red light stayed on. I tried to press the button to take the picture, but it refused to focus on the clouds. I fought it, moving the cross out of the line of vision and then returning the cross to the picture, but the camera wouldn't let me take it.

I recognized the F-150 that pulled into the parking space across from where I was standing. Levi's dad adjusted his tie as he stepped out of the truck. He waved awkwardly at me. Even from across the parking lot I could see the lines in his face. Anyone who thinks a tan makes you look better hasn't seen skin that works in the sun. He walked across the parking lot to the front doors. I wasn't sure I'd ever seen him wearing anything but jeans and boots. Levi wasn't with him.

I left the box under the car and followed Levi's dad into the building where my mom, my dad, and my dead brother waited for me.

CHAPTER EIGHT

"What's gotten into you?" Mom yelled over the roar of the vacuum cleaner.

I finished a last run between the coffee table and the couch before turning it off. Dust I'd kicked up floated in the light pouring in through the front windows.

"Nothing," I said. "Trying to help out is all."

She leaned on the armrest of the couch watching me. I yanked the cord out of the outlet and started to wrap it around the two plastic hooks on the back of the sweeper.

"Don't pull on the cord like that. You'll break it." She moved a stack of magazines from the coffee table to the rack beside the couch. I could see the rectangular outline of the magazines in the dust on the table. I wiped it with my sleeve.

"Why don't you get a dust rag for that?" Mom asked. "If you're so eager to clean, you might as well do it right."

It wasn't like I had cleaned the whole house—just my bedroom and the living room. I'd put the stack of mail Mom hadn't sorted through on her bed. I'd stashed the dishes in the dishwasher. What was the big deal? I hadn't swept and mopped. And I hadn't cleaned the windows, even though they needed it.

I stored the vacuum cleaner in the hall closet and went to the bathroom. A glob of toothpaste stuck to the counter. I took a couple of pieces of toilet paper off the roll, wet them under the faucet, and rubbed off the toothpaste. The toilet wasn't too gross, but I went ahead and wiped the rim with another handful of toilet paper just in case and flushed it.

He probably wouldn't even come in here.

Then I noticed marks on the mirror. I looked at the clock on the bathroom wall. I didn't want the bathroom to reek of Windex, like I'd slaved away making the house nice.

I ran my hands under the water and dampened my hair at the top of my head. Stupid cowlick. Gray T-shirt. Jeans. I sniffed my armpit.

"Asher," Mom called from farther down the hall. She was back in Travis's room.

"What?"

"Come here."

She stood in front of his open closet door with a rumpled shirt in her hands.

"Smell this."

I didn't move. Mom brought the T-shirt up to her face and breathed in deeply. I recognized the Spider-Man logo.

"Come here."

"I don't want to smell his clothes," I said, but I moved toward her.

"It doesn't smell bad. It just smells like him."

I didn't ask her why she was going through the dirty clothes Travis had tossed in the bottom of his closet. She went into his room every day for an hour or two. Sometimes she called me in to show me something. Sometimes it made sense. Most of the time it didn't.

Yesterday I'd found her car keys in the freezer. I took a picture of them sitting there with a package of frozen peas in the background before I put the keys back in her purse.

"Garrett's coming over," I said.

"I know."

"Are you going to be okay?" It was as close as I could get to asking her not to cry in front of him.

She nodded. Her face puckered up. Her chin dimpled.

"I'm going to my room," I said.

"Okay," she said. "I'm fine." She wasn't. She wanted me to stay with her while she cried and snorted the fumes of Travis's sweaty

Spider-Man T-shirt. After Dad had left, my youth director, John, told me it wasn't my job to stop her from crying. I wasn't sure if the rules had changed now that Travis was dead.

Back in my room, I stretched out on my bed and looked around. What would Garrett think of my photos? I tried to picture him standing in the doorway, taking it all in.

"Asher, come here," Mom called from Travis's bedroom.

"I'm busy!" I hollered back. Sort of busy.

A long pause.

"No, seriously. Come here."

I climbed off the bed and smoothed the wrinkles out of the comforter before returning to Travis's room.

She wasn't sniffing his clothes anymore. Now she sat in the center of the room, leaning against the twin bed. In her lap was Travis's book bag, with the zipper open wide. Her hand was hidden inside it. She looked amused. When she was certain she had my full attention, she said, "Guess what I just found."

I shook my head and shrugged. Garrett was going to be here any minute.

She withdrew her hand from the book bag and revealed a Bible from church. I scanned her face for a clue as to how I should react.

She started laughing. I joined in.

"Can you believe this? He stole it! I made him apologize, and the whole time he was saying sorry he had it stuffed in his book bag." She laughed. I watched for her tears but they didn't come. I sat down beside her on the floor.

"So we'll take it back Sunday?" I asked.

"No. Of all the things he could have taken, it's just as well." She put the book in my lap. "You keep it."

A stolen Bible. "Uh…Mom."

"I'll put some extra money in the collection plate."

She moved on to the other stuff in the book bag. She pulled out a long piece of rope, three rocks, and a plastic dinosaur. I stared numbly at the objects. She stopped and rested her head on my shoulder. She rubbed the Tyrannosaurus rex's bumpy green skin. "Asher, what am I doing?"

My mind searched for what she wanted to hear. The obvious—sorting through Travis's things—didn't seem like the response she was looking for. Small, random stacks surrounded us. The toys weren't organized by type, color, or anything. Legos stuck out from three different piles.

"You're missing him, Mom."

The doorbell rang. I took the Bible in my hand, moved my shoulder out from under her head, and stood up. "Garrett."

"I know."

I hesitated at the bedroom door a moment, tempted to look back at her. Instead, I hurried down the hall and through the living room to the front door. I reached for the handle, but I was still holding the Bible. I laid it on the coffee table, rubbed my hands on my jeans, and opened the door.

Garrett wasn't facing me. He was looking out across our yard.

"Hey," I said.

"There's a snake over there."

About halfway across my yard I saw the grass ripple. I saw a flash of black.

"It's an indigo," I said. "They aren't poisonous. They keep the bad ones away."

"Really? I never heard that."

"I'm not saying I want to keep it for a pet, but as far as snakes go…" I shrugged. "Didn't you have snakes in Orlando?"

"Not that I know of. We lived downtown."

I thought about telling him about the time Travis had caught a little black snake and set it loose in the house, but I didn't want to talk about Travis. The indigo slithered into the palmetto bush at the edge of our house.

"Come on." I held the door open.

"Is my bike okay?"

I glanced at the blue Mongoose in the driveway.

"You rode your bike here?"

He nodded. I noticed his hair was matted to his temples and forehead.

"It should be okay. You thirsty?"

He grinned. "Yeah."

We headed for the kitchen. I pulled a Gatorade out of the fridge. "Blue okay?" I handed it to him.

"Ah, my favorite."

"Mine, too."

He popped the top off and tilted his head back, taking long gulps. I pulled a bag of chips out of the pantry and put them on the counter. Garrett helped himself to a big handful, but he wasn't as blatantly messy as Levi.

"Come on," I said. I grabbed the bag of chips and started down the hall.

"Can I bring this?" He held up his drink.

I nodded.

"You're lucky," he said. "My mom freaks out if I take food into my room."

We passed Travis's closed bedroom door. I stepped inside my room and tossed the chips onto my computer desk. I wasn't quite sure what to do with myself, so I just sort of stood there and tried not to stare at him or anything.

Garrett walked up to my dresser and looked at the framed photos. "Did you take all of these?"

"Yeah."

I reached into the bag and took a handful of chips. I sat down on my computer chair and swiveled toward the screen. I felt jittery, nervous. I clicked the mouse, but I wasn't really paying attention to the computer. I watched Garrett put his drink down on my dresser and move along the wall. I heard the familiar squeak of Travis's bedroom door opening through the crunching of the chips in my mouth.

"Is that a footprint?" Garrett asked.

He was looking at the photo of the fire-ant hill Travis had stomped on with his bare feet. The ants had scurried out in a swarm.

"Yeah. It is," I said, impressed.

The footprint wasn't easy to see—you had to really look for it.

Mom walked in and handed me the stolen Bible I'd left on the coffee table. Her eyes were swollen, but she wasn't crying now.

"Hi, Garrett. I met you at church, right?"

"Yeah. Hi."

"It's good to see you again."

He didn't take his eyes off the photo of Mr. Williams. He leaned forward and squinted.

"Is that guy in the picture your dad?" he asked.

"No. Our neighbor, Mr. Williams," I said.

Mom cleared her throat. "We're divorced."

I turned in my chair. Mom's hands fidgeted in front of her. She stood with one leg slightly bent, her weight on the other. Her eyes focused on the corner of the room where no one was standing. I gripped the Bible.

Garrett said, "My mom was married to some guy before she met my dad. He was a musician. She said getting divorced was really hard."

He treaded in dangerous territory talking to my mom about the divorce. I tried not to move, in that way small animals do when a predator wanders into the clearing.

"It's easier if it's something you want." Mom shrugged. "I don't know. Seems to me there are worse things than divorce."

She smiled weakly at me. I waited for her to crack like the nut she sometimes was. God, just get her out of my room.

"Thanks for coming by. We haven't had a lot of visitors since…" Her voice drifted off. I fought the urge to get up and shove her out into the hall. "You boys have fun."

Finally. I heard Travis's bedroom door squeak closed.

"Is she okay?" Garrett asked.

"I don't know."

"I can't even imagine. I think about my sister, you know?"

Garrett returned to looking at the photographs on my wall. I stared at the stolen Bible. I'd gotten a Bible for confirmation. It was white. This one was red. I opened it. I turned a few of the thin pages and closed the Bible. I slid my fingers along the edges. Something snagged my finger.

"So, how are you doing?" Garrett asked.

I'd been so fired up about him coming over, like hanging out with Garrett would magically make things better, but I felt sort of emptier. Not his fault.

"I'm okay," I said.

"Do you ever think about that day?"

I suddenly felt the urge to shove him out of my room, too.

"Not really," I said. I tried really hard not to think about that day.

A page was poking out of the book. I felt along the side and dug my nail in where the paper was. I opened the Bible and flipped to the section. The page had been clumsily shoved into the book. I took it out and smoothed it. The top was torn. From the middle of the crumpled page I read the words:

O God; my sins are not hidden from you.

My breath started to come faster. Garrett removed his drink from my dresser and sat down on my bed.

"I think about it a lot," he said. "It was such a great day, and then…"

I stopped listening to him. I couldn't take my eyes off the page. I smoothed the paper in my hands and looked at the top of the passage.

Save me, God,
for the waters have come up to my neck.

I felt panic rise up in me and glanced at Garrett, but he was just taking a gulp from his drink. "He was getting ice cream," he was saying. "And we were only gone a couple of minutes, right?"

I'd managed to bury it, but the truth was I should have been watching Travis. Mom told me to keep an eye on him. I knew better than to leave him like that—he never listened. Why hadn't she ever asked me where I had been when it happened?

"Are you okay?" Garrett asked.

I handed the ripped page to him. He skimmed the front and flipped it over.

"Where'd you get this?"

"My mom found it in Travis's book bag."

"Huh."

He handed it back to me.

"Waters have come up to my neck," I read.

"What is that?"

"It's a psalm. Travis ripped this page out of the Bible the morning before he died."

Garrett silently read it over again. I waited, my palms sweating. He shook his head from side to side. "It doesn't mean anything," he said.

"Waters have come up to my neck," I pointed at the words on the page. "Right there, Garrett. It's right there."

"He hit his head though, right?"

"My sins are not hidden from you."

"You think we did something wrong," Garrett said. "I thought about that, too. But it's not like we meant for something to happen to him. We weren't even there. It was an accident. Accidents happen sometimes, Asher. I'm pretty sure God wouldn't want—"

"What do you know about what God wants?"

I didn't mean for it to come out so cold. I closed the Bible in my lap and swiveled my computer chair away from him.

"What, because I'm gay?" he asked.

An apology stuck in my throat. Not because he's gay, I wanted to say, but because how would he know what God would want? And there it was in black and white on the page. My head pounded like all of this was too important, too big for me. I could feel Garrett's eyes on my back, but I remembered God's eyes were on me, too. I heard Garrett shift on the bed. I stared at my dark computer screen. I could see him in its reflection, looking uneasily around my room.

"Your pictures are really cool."

I sat still.

"I like the one of the tree. The one that's curved."

I closed my eyes. It was my favorite. How could he know that? I took a deep breath.

"What made it like that?" he asked.

I wanted to tell him. I wanted to tell him my dad said it had always been that way. I wanted to tell him it was my first photograph, point out the minivan in the background, Dad's plan to leave, but I just kept my eyes closed. It was quiet a long time. My bed creaked. He was standing up.

"Asher?"

"What?" I whispered.

The Bible felt heavy against my thighs.

"Are you okay?" he asked.

I didn't answer him.

"Asher? It's just a piece of paper."

I kept my eyes closed.

"Are you just going to ignore me?" I heard him laugh uncomfortably. "Okay. That's mature." He was walking around my room. I could hear him moving. "You want me to go?"

Absolutely. Yes. And no. I stayed silent.

"Aren't you going to say anything? Look, I'm really sorry about what happened to your brother. Really sorry," he said. "But I'm not going to apologize for what happened with us."

Didn't he get it? Couldn't he read? Instead I waited for him to just leave. I was good at waiting.

Eventually, I heard his footsteps move down the hall. I heard him make the appropriate small talk with my mom before the front door opened and closed. I opened my eyes and looked back down at the Bible. I took the ripped page from it and stood. I walked over to my dresser and pulled open the drawer. A blank picture frame sat on top. I undid the swivels and removed the backing.

The page didn't fit right in the frame, but I put it in there anyway. I took a long, hard look at the passage before I buried in under my socks and shoved it back, deep in my drawer. I'd commit it to memory eventually, but not that day. I had time.

I made my way down the hall past Travis's room to the bathroom. I locked the door and turned on the shower. I pulled my T-shirt over my head and stepped out of my jeans and underwear. A few moments later, I was naked under the hot stream of water. My skin turned pink. The water filled my ears. I sat cross-legged in the bathtub holding my head in my hands long after the hot water had turned cold.

CHAPTER NINE

I tucked my schedule in the back pocket of my jeans and adjusted my book bag. I glanced back to see if Mom had pulled away, but the car still idled at the curb. She was watching me walk up to the school. I motioned for her to go on, but she took it for a wave. Why didn't she just go? She'd gotten weirdly protective, but I suppose that was natural. I turned and started walking up the sidewalk.

I passed Manny from my freshman year Spanish class. He nodded at me. His last name was something Spanish—Hernandez, I think. The first day of class, Mrs. Morales had started talking to him in Spanish. Turned out, Manny knew less Spanish than I did. His first name was Manuel, but everyone had been given a new Spanish rendition of their name. My Spanish name was Arsenio, which sounded like a guy who set things on fire. My first choice had been Alejandro, but I hadn't raised my hand fast enough. I nodded back at Manny. He was talking to his girlfriend and didn't see me. I headed for the main entrance.

The school opened up into the round concrete courtyard with planter palm trees. In the far right corner I spotted Levi, sitting at our table with a bunch of guys from the football team, including thick-neck Josh, and a couple of girls. I realized I didn't score high with a single person at the table other than Levi, and the last time I'd seen him was at the pool. He hadn't come to the funeral. His dad was there, but Levi wasn't.

We had claimed the round metal picnic table the first day of school our freshman year, just like Levi said we should. Most freshman were stuck standing around waiting for seniors to graduate to find a place, but Levi's plan to mark our territory from the first day of high school worked. His mom had dropped us off while there were still stars in the sky. Levi had wanted to take the center picnic table, but I told him that was asking for trouble. Better to go to a less-conspicuous table. We had settled on the table farthest away from the entrance. When a couple of upperclassmen approached us, I was ready to bolt, but Levi pretended he didn't see them hovering around. He stood up and adjusted his pants as he continued talking to me about his trip to the Everglades with his dad, his voice getting deeper and louder.

"Did I tell you we got a pet? Yeah—water moccasin. Keep it in a tank and all. I got it from my uncle. You know, the one who has reptiles and snakes and shit. You know how gators get into houses and pools and stuff? My uncle's who they call to get 'em. Police don't do it. They call my uncle."

I'd met Levi's uncle. He was an accountant.

I decided instead to wait outside my first-period class for the bell to ring. I dug my schedule out of my pocket. Room 48—English 2. I'd had English with Mrs. Flor last year in the same classroom. She had taught my dad when he was in high school. She was ancient and strict, but I'd pulled an A.

I walked past the doors to the auditorium and the gym and headed down the long hallway. A couple of people nudged each other as I walked by and stopped talking. Russ said, "Hey, Ash," as I moved past him. We weren't good friends or anything. I couldn't remember him ever really saying hi to me before.

I reached the room and waited along the wall with the other people in my class. A couple of them stood in groups talking—girls, mostly. The rest of us were quiet, like we weren't quite awake yet. I recognized everyone. Josh, Manny, Jennifer, Ian, Shawna…

Garrett rounded the corner. He held his schedule in his hand. He looked at the tops of the doors where the numbers were affixed as he made his way down the hall. A huddle of girls watched him as he walked by, checking out the new kid. He didn't seem to notice.

"Hey, how *are* you?"

Hannah, captain of the cheerleading squad, touched my shoulder. I stood up a little straighter. She looked all concerned.

"I'm fine."

She leaned forward and whispered, "I was at the pool." Her eyes got all misty, like it was *her* brother or something.

I nodded slowly.

She squeezed my shoulder. "I just wanted you to know that... well...you know."

Garrett stopped in front of room 48. He put his schedule inside the folder he was carrying. He looked up and saw me, then turned away. Hannah was still standing there, waiting for me to say something, or break down, or whatever it is people expect you to do when your brother dies.

"Yeah, thanks, Hannah. That's nice," I said.

She moved along the hallway. I watched two other cheerleaders join her farther down the corridor. They huddled in as she walked up to them. They glanced back at me as Hannah talked. I leaned against the wall.

The click of high-heeled shoes against the floor got my attention. A woman who didn't look much older than we were hurried toward us. She had short brown hair and wore a vest with purple beads all over it and a floaty black skirt. She smiled at me as she rushed toward room 48. Keys jingling in her hand, she unlocked the door, reached inside, and turned on the lights. The bell rang.

"Just in time. Come on in."

I hung back a minute, letting most of the other students get inside first.

"Good morning," she said. She talked fast with a northern accent. "Welcome back."

Josh yawned.

"Come on, let's move," she said.

Garrett moved into the classroom. I was standing right beside the door. He didn't even glance at me. Jennifer was behind him. She stopped and motioned for me to go ahead. I followed Garrett into the class.

"Sit where you'd like, for now," the teacher said.

The back rows had already been taken. Garrett sat toward the front and center. I sat in a desk two rows behind him and to the far right. The teacher picked up a piece of chalk and wrote *Ms. Hughes* on the board.

"I'm Ms. Hughes and this is English Two. Please take your schedules out and put them on your desks. I need to check to make sure you're in the right place."

A couple of kids exchanged looks. Jennifer raised her hand.

"Yes?"

"What happened to Mrs. Flor?"

"She isn't working here anymore."

"Is she okay?"

"I assume so."

"She broke her hip," Kevin said. "She's okay. She moved to be closer to her daughter." Ms. Hughes blinked at him. "My mom works in Dr. Taylor's office."

The announcements came on and we stood for the Pledge of Allegiance. The principal talked while Ms. Hughes circulated the room and checked each of our schedules. She was still at it after the announcements ended. Shelly leaned toward Garrett's desk.

"Hey, I'm Shelly."

"Garrett."

"I know. Where you from?"

"Orlando." He paused. "You know?"

"You've got a sister, right? A senior. Emily."

"Yeah. *How* do you know?"

"My brother works at the Taco Bell. She came in to fill out an application. So, what brings you here?"

"My dad got a transfer."

"What does he do?"

"He's an engineer."

Shelly lifted an eyebrow. "Your mom?"

"She's a…wait. What's with the inquisition?"

I leaned forward. "Back off, Shelly. It's his first day."

She opened her mouth to say something to me but closed it again. She scooted away from Garrett's desk a little, but then leaned forward again.

"You don't mind, do you?" she asked.

Garrett shrugged.

She turned to me. "See? He doesn't mind." Shelly tapped Garrett. "Didn't you guys move into Evan Llowell's place?"

"Yeah."

"He used to have orgies."

Garrett just looked at her.

"Shelly," I said. "Come on."

"I'm just being friendly." She glanced back at Jennifer and giggled. "Can't a girl be friendly?" Jennifer smiled without showing her teeth.

Garrett didn't turn around in his seat. He didn't say thanks. He looked down at the schedule on his desk.

I watched Shelly mouth, "Oh my God, he's so hot," to Jennifer. I clenched my jaw and fought the urge to tell her to back the hell off.

❖

The whole day was weird. In history class, a guy I'd gone to school with since kindergarten said, "I heard you were dead."

When I explained that my brother had died, he said, "Oh, well, that's good."

That's good.

Like I said, weird.

I caught a lot of the people I would have called friends staring at me. Manny nodded at me in the morning but pretended to be busy reading the Spanish textbook when I sat down next to him in Spanish 2. He had never cracked the book before unless the teacher told us to. And during class, he kept glancing at me. When I looked back, he looked away. On my way to my next class, I saw him talking to his girlfriend. His back was to me, but when she saw me, she whispered something to him. He turned around and looked right at me but didn't nod. He didn't say a thing. What was wrong with people? My brother died. It happens.

After Spanish, Jennifer stopped me in the hall.

"Hey. I've been trying to find a time to talk to you. I just wanted to tell you I'm really sorry about Travis." She chewed her lower lip. The button she wore on her shirt read *I'VE GOT SPIRIT HOW 'BOUT YOU?* "My grandmother died last year."

She handed me a note. It was folded into a rectangle with a little triangle on the front. On the triangle, she had written the words *pull here.*

"Call me," she said.

She touched my shoulder. As she turned to walk away, her left boob brushed my arm. I don't think she meant to do it. Girls probably accidentally brush their boobs against things all the time, right? Still, a blush spread across my face. Jennifer's heeled sandals clicked on the floor as she headed down the hall.

I pulled the *pull here* tab and unfolded the page. Inside the note Jennifer had written *I know how you feel* and her cell-phone number. She mingled with a group of her friends at the end of the hall. I watched her from the distance, her white capri pants bright against her tanned calves. She caught me looking, flipped her hair, and shot me a sweet smile. What the heck? I nodded awkwardly at her, folded the paper in halves, and stuffed it in my pocket.

Biology. Mr. Stevens handed each of us a course outline as we walked into class. A stack of textbooks sat on the front table. I watched the door to see who I would have to work with in labs. I hardly recognized Jennifer's best friend Kayla walking in the room. Her hair was dyed a purplish red. Her lips were black. She wore a trench coat even though it was eighty degrees outside. Come to think of it, she hadn't been with Jennifer and the usual group in the hall.

"New look?" Derrick asked.

"Screw you," she said, not even giving him the benefit of a glance.

Kayla dropped her folder on the desk beside me.

"Hey," she said. "What a jerk."

"Uh, hey."

I tried not to stare at her black fingernail polish and drummed my own fingers on the desk. The bell rang, and Mr. Stevens got people to hand out textbooks while he called roll.

"Adams, Garrett." Mr. Stevens called. He took his glasses off and scanned the class. "Garrett?"

"That's the new kid, right?" someone said from the back.

"He got in a fight," Kayla said.

My head spun toward her.

"That wasn't a fight," Derrick said.

Kayla pinched her face at Derrick.

"Okay, enough. He obviously isn't here," Mr. Stevens said. He pushed his glasses back onto his face and made a disapproving clucking noise. "The first day of school."

When he called my name, he lowered his glasses and nodded at me. He hadn't done that with anyone else. I looked away. Kayla passed the textbook sign-up sheet to me.

Mr. Stevens opened his laptop. "Would you dim the lights, please, Derrick?"

He started his slideshow presentation, but my brain checked out. Garrett in a fight? It didn't sound right. But then, I barely knew the guy. Maybe he'd told someone else he was gay. You couldn't just tell people around here something like that.

I stored my textbook in my book bag and stared at Kayla's profile. She'd seen the fight. I tapped my eraser on my desk, considering my options. Just ask, like a curious bystander. I turned my course outline over and wrote *What happened with the new kid?* on the back in the upper-right corner. Nice touch, the new kid part. Like I didn't even know his name. I slid the paper over to Kayla. She glanced down at the note. She looked back up at the screen. I slid my pencil over to her, but she scooted her chair away from me and folded her arms in front of her. Since when did she get so interested in Mr. Stevens's slideshow? Something wasn't right.

I glanced at my other option, Derrick. He was whispering in the ear of the guy sitting next to him, but pointing directly toward me. He saw me and pretended that his hand had been in mid-motion to scratch his head, but there was no missing that he had been talking about me. He picked at a zit on his chin while the guy next to him inspected the lead of his pencil.

I felt my face go hot. Something *definitely* wasn't right.

The lights came up. Mr. Stevens placed a paper on my desk. A pretest. To see what we knew. I read the first question, but even though I read the words they didn't seem to make any sense together. Mr. Stevens circled the room like a vulture, sticking his beak-like nose over shoulders to make sure people kept their eyes on their own paper. I read the first question again. I needed to get started. I spied Mr. Stevens looking at me and panicked until he smiled encouragingly.

It wasn't one of those pity smiles. I'd had plenty of those today. I could have been wrong, but it seemed like he was letting me know he knew my brother was dead, and he was cool with my mind being mangled. Not like he was going to fix it or wanted to talk to me about it. Take your time, his smile said. We all get mangled. I took a deep breath and read the first question again. It finally registered.

After class, I walked in the opposite direction of my next class just so I could catch up to Kayla.

"Okay. Stop dodging me. So, what happened with the new kid?" I asked. I tried to sound mildly concerned.

"He was in a fight."

"Yeah, I know. What happened?"

"He got blindsided." The way she said it, so quick and disgusted, I knew that part was true.

"That sucks. Is he okay?" I asked. Not too concerned.

"It was bad. His nose was all, you know." She wrinkled her own nose.

I swallowed hard. I didn't want to ask, but I had to. "What was the fight about?"

"You."

"What?" My heart started pounding. "Why?"

"Something about you taking a crap. Look, Asher. I've got to go." Kayla turned into the girls' bathroom.

Me. About me. Taking a *crap*? Then I thought to ask, "What happened to the other guy?"

"Levi?" her voice echoed. "They took him out in handcuffs."

CHAPTER TEN

The front door slammed.

"You're not going to believe this," Mom said.

I was flipping through my first copy of *Photography Today*. I had finally found an article on something other than digital cameras. I closed the magazine and put it on my lap, but my index finger marked my place just in case this wasn't a big deal. I'd been through enough at school.

Mom twirled her keys, set her purse down, and then picked it up again. "I went to the attorney today."

She had been debating about going to see one about Travis's death. Several of the people she worked with had insisted she had a case against the public pool. The whole thing made me sick.

"I went to Charles." She said it like I knew him. "You know Charles. The tall guy who goes to our church."

"Oh, yeah." I had no idea who she was talking about.

"Well, he won't take the case. Won't even talk to me about it. And guess why?" She didn't wait for me to answer. "He said he's in the middle of filing some paperwork that involves *me*. He wouldn't give me any details. 'Client confidentiality,' he said. I'll bet it's your father." She slammed down her purse again on the table. "Do you know anything about this?" She narrowed her eyes at me as I put the magazine down. "Asher?"

I was thinking. "Not exactly."

She tilted her head slightly. I took a deep breath.

"It's just that at the funeral Dad said something to me about trying to make things better or something. I didn't know what he was talking about."

"I didn't see him talking to you."

"When you were in with Pastor Cole or something," I said.

"And you didn't tell me this because…?"

"I didn't know what he was talking about. I still don't know what he was talking about."

"What else did he say?"

I sighed. "I don't know, Mom. What difference does it make?"

Her voice got all high and cracked. "What difference does it make? Asher, he's hired an attorney. Don't you get it? He's going to do something to us."

"What could he do?"

"Oh, Asher, sometimes you're so…" She half laughed and didn't finish.

"So what?"

"So innocent. Naïve."

"I am not," I said.

"I bet it's the child support. Now that Travis is…I can't even say it. I can't believe it. I'm driving down the road thinking I need to pick him up for T-ball, and then I remember and it hurts all over again. And you know, if *he* hadn't left us, this never would have happened."

"You," I whispered.

"Excuse me?"

"He left *you*."

She shook her head. Her arms folded in front of her and she drummed her index finger against her elbow. "Oh no. We're not playing this game, Asher. No."

"I'm just saying, you always say he left *us*."

"That's because he did. He didn't just walk out on me. He left everything. He left me, you, Travis. He left every photo. Don't you think he'd want a picture of you? What kind of father just walks out?" She started marching through the house, hollering from the hall. "He left his books, his diploma, that office chair that was so damn important to him." The closet door in the bedroom crashed open, and she hurried back to the living room where I sat with my finger still holding the page of my magazine. She threw two pairs of dress pants onto the coffee table. "He left his clothes. His clothes, Asher. What kind of man does that?" She was breathing hard from yelling and scurrying about.

I was breathing hard, too. "Dad left *you*. *I* left Travis. And then *Travis* left us." The magazine got mangled in my grip. "What I can't figure out is how everyone else got lucky enough to get out and *I'm still here*."

She looked at me like I had pulled out a pistol and aimed it at her.

And that's when I felt the tears coming. It was true—I hated being stuck here with her. Stupid tears stung the rims of my eyes, and I jumped up off the sofa and hurried past her to my room. I locked my door and tried to shove the tears back in with my fists as I paced the floor. I hated that Dad got to take off when he decided he didn't like it here anymore, that even Travis had gotten out. I coughed up a sob from somewhere deep, grabbed my iPod off my dresser, and blasted music. I buried my head in my pillow and gripped it until my arms ached. I cried with the world all black underneath my clenched eyelids for a long time. It wasn't until I settled into hiccups that I sat up and wiped my nose on my shirt. My body ached. I pulled my earbuds out and listened for sounds of Mom between my own wheezing, snotty sniffles. Nothing. I sat up and considered apologizing to her, but the truth was I'd meant what I said. Even so, I grimaced when I thought about my saying everyone else got out.

"Mom?"

I hauled myself up off the bed. She wasn't in the kitchen. I thought she'd be in Travis's room, but the dark wooden door was closed. The letter *t* was etched in the door at waist-high level from when Travis had tried to write his name on it. Mom had taken the ballpoint pen away from him before he could get to the next letter. He hadn't capitalized it. The doorknob turned easily. I reached in and flicked the light switch on.

"Mom?"

She wasn't there.

I headed toward her bedroom. Not there, either.

I went back down the hall. The bathroom light was off, but I wouldn't put her past sitting in the tub with the shower curtain closed. I turned the light on.

"Mom?"

I pushed the bathroom door farther open. I stepped inside and opened the shower curtain. Just the washcloth, stiff and dry, hanging from the showerhead.

I saw my swollen, blotchy face in the mirror. My eyes were little slits. I turned the light off and went back to Travis's bedroom to look in his closet. Sometimes he used to hide in there when he was mad. I thought maybe Mom was doing the same, but the closet was empty.

It wasn't until I went back to the living room and noticed Mom's purse was missing that I thought to check the driveway. The car was gone, too. While I was crying, Mom had taken her keys and left.

She'd gone all nutty before, but she'd never left. In all the times I'd sat and watched her cry, I'd never just walked out on her. Anger started to rise up again, but when I played over what I had said to her, I realized I'd gone too far. I slumped down on the couch and heard a crunch underneath me. My mangled photo magazine was wedged between the sofa cushions. From the house phone, I tried to call her cell. It went straight to voice mail. I hung up. I wasn't ready to apologize, and I didn't know what to say.

I settled back on the sofa and flipped through the magazine pages, pretending to try to find my place, but I kept hearing cars driving past and peered out the window to see if it was her pulling up in the driveway. I picked up the TV remote and killed some time flipping through our meager stations. I kept glancing at the wall clock. When the sky turned black, I started worrying that she wouldn't come back.

I called her cell phone four more times, and each time it went straight to voice mail. What the hell? For a second I thought about calling Dad. I could find his number easily enough, but when Mom did come home, she'd kill me. I pictured Mom hysterical, driving recklessly, our minivan crunched against a telephone pole, her cell phone buried under metal.

It would be my fault.

Should I call the hospital?

Levi's mom was a police officer. I dialed the number from memory. Maybe his mom would pick up.

"What?" Levi said.

I almost hung up.

"Asher, I know it's you."

"Let me talk to your mom," I said.

"Why?"

"Just put her on."

Silence.

"Come on, Levi."

"I've had a shitty day," he said.

"So I've heard."

More silence.

"Please? It's about my mom," I said.

"Hold on." I could hear Levi moving. When I heard music get louder, I knew he wasn't trying to find his mom. He was in his bedroom. "Is she okay?"

"Your *mom*, Levi. It's important."

"Tell me first," he said.

I didn't say anything.

"I'm not getting her until you tell me," he said.

"My mom and I got into it and I think she might have taken off."

"*Might* have taken off?"

"Well, the car isn't in the driveway…"

"Doesn't she have her cell?"

"Yeah, I think so, but she isn't picking up."

"So what?"

"She's never done this before. Not ever," I said, my voice catching a little.

Levi's voice lowered. "You think she's going to off herself or something?"

I paused. "I don't know. She's probably just driving around to clear her head."

"How long ago did she leave?"

"It's been about three hours. Seriously, I just want to talk to your mom. Put her on."

"Wait, so you got the house to yourself?" he asked.

"Of course I've got the house to myself. Mom's gone. What, you think my dad is here? I'm just wondering, since your mom's a cop and all…Maybe she went to Cheryl's from work." I should have thought of Cheryl earlier. "I'm going to try Cheryl. It's fine."

"Bullshit. I'm coming over."

"No." But Levi had already hung up.

It actually took longer to drive from Levi's house than to walk because you could cut through the yards and empty lots faster on foot. It wasn't three minutes before his voice called, "Hey," from the back sliding glass door.

I took the pin out of the top and shoved the pane of glass along the track. It ran off the track and got stuck, but Levi managed to squeeze inside the small gap I'd made. He easily closed it behind him.

"Heard anything?" he asked.

"No." I noticed his right hand was wrapped in gauze. "Are you grounded?" I asked. Levi's mom didn't tolerate altercations.

"Yeah."

"But she let you out?"

"I'm not even allowed to pick up the phone. Unless it's you. Because of Travis. You're the only way I'm ever getting out of the house. You look like shit. What happened?"

"Nothing. It was stupid. I shouldn't have called you. Why'd you come over, anyway?"

"What happened to make her take off?"

"I lost it." When I said it aloud, I got scared I was going to lose it again, so I didn't say any more.

Levi nodded. "Yeah. Things have been pretty shitty. You have good reason to lose it."

I swallowed hard. "I think I made Mom lose it."

"I'm not sure she ever had it. You still keep the alcohol above the stove?"

He was wearing me out. "Come on, Levi."

"You don't think this calls for a drink?" He grabbed two glasses out of the cabinet and set them on the counter.

"Not for me, Levi."

"You let me decide what you need." He started to unscrew the cap. "Don't worry. I'm grounded 'til hell freezes over. What's the difference?"

"Put it away." My hands started shaking.

"Why are you always such a pussy?"

"What, you think drinking's going to make this better? You've got all the answers, right? Like beating Garrett up. That was a great idea."

Levi stiffened. "What do you know about it?"

"Nothing. Why don't you tell me?"

"Look, that faggot is not your friend," Levi said.

I could feel the heat rise to my face again. "Like you are," I said. I didn't recognize the sarcasm in my voice.

He shoved my shoulder hard. His eyes got all buggy. For a second I thought he was going to cry. Instead he shoved me again, only this time I bumped against the table. I launched back at him, but he easily blocked me. Levi clenched his wrapped fist and pulled it back, cocked and ready. I flinched. We stood staring at each other, each breathing hard. Finally he shook his head and lowered his arm. "Go to hell," he muttered.

Levi flung open the sliding door and left, leaving a three-foot-wide gap behind him. Well, that was helpful. I stood for a full minute trying to gather my thoughts, but it proved a useless effort. The gnats started coming in, so I stepped up to close the door, but no matter how much I grunted, shoved, and contorted myself, I couldn't slide it shut.

My stomach rolled. I went back into the kitchen to store the rum back in the cabinet. I started to put it away, but then I unscrewed the cap and poured an inch of the liquid into one of the glasses. I held it up to my face and sniffed. The rum smelled like medicine. I took a swallow. It burned my throat. I poured three more and then chugged a glass of cool water. It didn't get the taste out of my mouth.

For a second, I thought I was going to be sick, but then I remembered I hadn't eaten anything for dinner. I opened a can of mini raviolis, spooned them into a bowl, and nuked it for a minute in the microwave. I put the rum away. I rinsed the glass and put it in the dishwasher. The counter seemed as good a place to eat as anywhere else. I stood in the kitchen and gulped down my dinner. The centers of the raviolis weren't even warm.

I don't know how long I stood at the sink rinsing the bowl, but by the time I stopped, the skin on my hands looked like Pearl's. I put the bowl in the dishwasher and tried the sliding glass door again. I thought a little food might give me the edge I needed, but it still wouldn't budge. I stepped onto the concrete slab outside the opening to get a better angle. The air was cool against my skin.

At least I wouldn't have to worry about Mom being angry because of the wasted AC. If I'd known it was going to be this cool, I would have turned the air off and opened a few windows. I stepped toward our yard and set off the motion-activated light. Insects swarmed the brightness. Our sliding screen door leaned against the side of the house. Travis had knocked it out months ago. Mom had asked me to fix it, but I hadn't gotten around to it yet.

Most of the ranch houses had screened-in porches along the back. We didn't. Years ago, Mom had pestered Dad about screening the slab in, but he said he wanted to wait until we could put in a pool. We never did put in a pool. Travis could have learned how to swim. But Travis didn't drown because he couldn't swim. He drowned because of me. I stepped barefoot onto the prickly grass and peered up at the sky. Clouds blocked out all the stars and the moon.

A stream of water hit my leg. I heard a cackling laugh.

"Gotcha!"

Through the dark I made out Pearl standing in her side yard. She held the nozzle of the hose in her hand like a gun.

"Thought maybe you could use some watering, too," she said.

"Thanks." Levi would say she was nuttier than squirrel shit.

She sprayed the water right up to the edge of her lawn. "Can't do this during the day with the water ban, but I'll be damned if my grass is going to turn brown."

Two bands of light crossed over Pearl in the side yard. I could see she was wearing another flowered robe and plastic slip-on shoes. She held her hand up to cover her eyes and peered toward the front yard.

"Looks like your mother's home. Late night for her, huh?"

I went inside the house and met Mom as she came in the front door.

"Where were you?" I said accusingly.

"Thinking." She handed me a Taco Bell bag.

I set the food on the kitchen counter. "I tried to call."

"I was talking to Sharon." She put her purse on the dining table.

"I was upset."

"So was I." She noticed the sliding glass door was open and tried to push it closed.

"You just left. I didn't even know you'd gone."

"I needed to think."

"You left."

"Isn't that what you wanted?" She stopped working on the door and stared at me.

"No."

"Look, I just needed to drive around for a while."

"What if I'd taken off?"

She blinked at me. "That would kill me," she said. Mom inspected the sliding glass door, gripped the edge, and lifted it. "Are you going to eat your dinner?" she asked.

If it had been McDonald's, I would have said no, just to make sure she knew I was really mad. But I liked Taco Bell.

"The cell phone bill is going to be high," I said. I dug a burrito out of the bag.

"I didn't talk to Sharon the whole time. I went to Cheryl's, too." She peered at the door tracks and stepped back into the house. "And then I got hold of Pastor Cole." Her steady hand eased the door shut. It glided along the track. "I made an appointment for you to talk to him tomorrow."

CHAPTER ELEVEN

A gray cat moved in my open window. A screen divided us, but I could feel the chill in the air. The cat's tail twitched. Padded feet made figure eights on the windowsill, brushed against the screen, and circled back again. And my hand felt the fur through the holes in the screen. The cat pushed back, leaned into my palm. Such soft fur. His motor ran, he purred. Sam blinked, blinked, blinked. Lights flashed like red-eye reduction, but it was thunderless, rainless lightning.

Sam low-growled, darted into darkness, and a figure chased him—smaller than me, taller than Sam. A shadow of a boy I know—Travis.

My window was a door, a sliding door. My hand reached to glide it open, a foggy screen that disappeared, evaporated, and was gone. Travis skipped after Sam. My bare feet on the crackly ground, stepping on fire ants I didn't feel. I ran after Travis in a yard that was a field. He sat in the crook of a twisted tree, blinking, blinking up at Sam who clung vertical on the tree. I reached for Travis, who reached for Sam, who crawled up the pine tree, which creaked and cracked and bark splintered and the trunk slithered skyward, straightening. Cat ears folded, claws dug, tail swatted. Sam molded to the tree. I grabbed for Travis, who grabbed for Sam, who grabbed the tree that stretched up.

Flesh at my fingertips.

I am Jack.

The tree is giant.

Sam hisses.

Thick sticky sap seeps and blood oozes from picked, scabby bark. Travis waves from up high. He wants me to look. He is yelling my name, perched on the wooden board, about to jump, but I cannot hear his low growl. Sam shakes a gooey paw, and they both propel off the tree and fall, and the ground is water and they are sinking in waves of rich, black dirt, deeper and faster than I can dig, and I yell—Travis, Travis, Travis—as his pale hands disappear into the ripples of earth.

And then the bathroom light blinded, and the water in the sink browned, and Mom scrubbed at my hands with soap and said, "It's okay, Asher," but she wasn't listening because I was telling her that Sam was alive and I couldn't figure out why she was crying. Then I was on the floor leaning over the toilet watching lettuce float and swirl while the rest sank in lumps to the bottom. Then my pillow was cool, and Garrett was whispering in my ear or on my eyelids, but I couldn't hear what he was saying, I could only feel his breath, and when I opened my eyes, Mom was sitting on my bed, and I asked her why she had made him go home.

❖

I blinked several times at the light coming through my blinds. The black curtains were pulled back. The windows were closed, but the blinds were open. I strained to see the clock across the room, but my head felt heavy. I tried to lift it. I shivered, pulled the covers up. Mom was there, a cool washcloth on my forehead and a thermometer in my mouth. I heard her voice drifting in and out from the other room: "Won't be in school today…Need to cancel appointment… Staying home to make sure he's okay…Things have been so hard."

The room tilted. I threw up on my pillow.

By noon, I felt good enough to sit up in bed. Mom placed a glass of ginger ale and a straw on my nightstand. She sat down on my bed and felt my forehead. I propped myself up. I'd done it again—sleepwalking. I picked at the dirt under my fingernails. Mom took my hand.

"Where was I?" I asked, averting my eyes.

"In the neighbor's yard," she whispered.

The neighbor's yard.

I'd gone outside.

"Which one?" I asked, like it mattered.

"Williams." She stroked my hand gently, like I was really little. I let her.

"Did they call you?"

"No. I heard you."

I winced. "What? Was I yelling?"

"It's okay. No one thinks a thing about it."

So, yes, I yelled and woke everyone up. "Mom, I haven't done that since I was like ten."

"Except for that one time, when we saw your Dad at church."

She said Dad. Not *him.*

"Ginger ale?" she offered.

I nodded, and she put the straw in the glass and handed it to me. I took a small sip and gave it back to her. I looked down at my hands.

"What's with the dirt under my nails?"

"You were digging in their planter."

❖

I sipped more ginger ale and nibbled saltines on the living-room couch. A trash can sat beside me on the floor. I held the TV remote in my hand. Mom brought me the cordless telephone.

"Seriously, Mom, I'm good."

"Call me if you get sick again." She tucked the blanket under my feet. "I'll call in a little while to check in, okay?"

I nodded. She checked her watch and tucked her purse under her arm. She opened the front door. "I love you," she said.

"I know."

❖

The doorbell rang while I was watching this old movie about this Amish kid who saw someone get murdered and thinking of how cool it would be to be Amish. Mom had only been gone an hour. I peeked out the window before opening the door. I didn't recognize the car in the driveway. Some lady sat in the driver's seat. The person at the door was so short, I couldn't see who it was. Then I recognized the lady and the car. They belonged to Bobby, Travis's friend from school. I opened the door and shaggy-haired Bobby held a large plastic cage out to me. He glanced at his mom in the car, and she pointed at me.

"My *mom* says I've got to give this to you."

The cage didn't appear to contain anything but some sand, water, and some shells.

"What is it?"

He rolled his eyes in disgust. "A hermit crab."

"Why are you giving me a hermit crab?"

"It's not for you. It's for Travis."

"Travis is dead."

Bobby shook his head. "Yeah, I know." He sighed. "Look, do you want the crab or not?"

"Why would I want it?"

"Bobby," his mom called from the car. He ignored her and stared me in the eye. I was used to staring wars with kids. Travis had been the master. "Bobby!" she yelled.

"What?" he called to her, not breaking eye contact.

She was hanging out the window. "Give. Him. The. Crab."

He thrust the cage into my hands. "I didn't want the stupid thing anyway."

He bolted down the driveway, flung open the back door, and climbed inside. He stared out the other side of the car, toward Pearl's house. His mom turned around in her seat. The car window was open and I couldn't hear what they were saying, so I knew she wasn't yelling at him. Finally, she got out of the car and walked up to the front door, smiling apologetically at me.

"Hi, Asher," she said. "I'm Irene. I was at the funeral. I'm sorry about this, but I had to follow through with Bobby. You understand."

"Sure." I had no idea what she was talking about.

"How's your mom doing?" People were always asking that.

"She's okay."

Irene turned back to the car to glance at Bobby. "I can't even imagine what it must be like for her." Her voice quivered a little. "They were such good friends. Bobby's having a tough time, but this was the right thing to do."

"Right."

"Well, enjoy Hector." She turned and hurried back to the car.

Hector the hermit crab. Great.

I closed the door, went inside, and put the cage on the kitchen counter. I grabbed some Doritos out of the cabinet and munched on those while I watched the tank. A few minutes later, Hector started moving around a little. At first, I thought there might be several crabs inside since there were three shells in the cage, but it looked like the other two were empty.

I was in my bedroom on the computer doing research on hermit crabs when Mom came home from her shift.

"Asher, what is this thing?" she hollered from the kitchen.

"Hector the hermit crab."

She was quiet until she stood in my doorway. "Why is it in our house?"

"Bobby came by with it, earlier today."

"Why?"

I shrugged. "I don't know. Hey, remember when Travis was talking about hermit crabs growing new parts? A hermit crab really *can* grow a new eye if it loses one." I scrolled down the computer screen.

"I'm calling Irene."

Mom returned ten minutes later. Her eyes were all red from crying.

"So what's the deal?" I asked.

"Travis won the crab in a bet with Bobby. Bobby was going to bring the crab by on Monday, but then Travis died Sunday."

"So why didn't he keep it?"

"When his mom told him about Travis, he was *happy* because he thought it meant he could keep the crab. She was so upset about it, she made him give us the crab anyway." She sat down on my bed. "Bobby's just a kid. It's a natural reaction. It doesn't mean anything."

I smiled. "Travis would have done the same thing."

"I told her that. I just wish she would've asked me about it first. She said she'd be happy to take it back to the pet store for us if we don't want it."

"I really think Bobby should have it."

"His mom won't let him. 'It's the principle.' What will we do with a hermit crab?"

"I've got room on my dresser. This site says we can feed him regular food. He doesn't need anything special. And I'll clean the tank."

"I don't know, Asher. I'm not big on pets."

"It's Travis's pet," I said.

We both knew if Travis were alive, she never would have let him keep it.

"You feeling better?" she asked.

"Yeah."

She sighed, then stood up and ruffled my hair while she looked over my shoulder at the computer screen.

"Your hair's getting long," she said.

I'd found a website for people who raced hermit crabs.

"Hector, huh?" she asked.

"Yep."

"If he smells, we're getting rid of him."

CHAPTER TWELVE

I stepped off the bus and walked through the main entrance of the school. I was on my way around the courtyard to my first-period class when Emily grabbed my arm.

"Hey."

"Hi, Emily," I said.

"Look, I don't know what you've heard, but…" She adjusted her book bag on her shoulder. "You don't know him very well, but my brother is a good person."

I blinked at her.

"He was really upset about what happened to your little brother. You should have seen him. And I don't know what your problem is, but there's no reason to get all your friends after him." She put her hand on her hip. "So I'd just appreciate it if you'd tell them to back off."

I opened my mouth to say something, but she turned and walked away before I could answer. Didn't she know I didn't have any friends? I headed to English class.

Garrett sat at his desk reading a novel with his head so low I couldn't see his face. I put my book bag down and got into my seat just as the bell rang. He continued to read his novel all the way through the announcements. He dog-eared the page he was reading and tucked the book into his bag. He sat up straight and looked over his shoulder at me. His eyes had dark circles under them. It might have been residual black eyes from the fight, but it could easily have been from lack of sleep. There were a couple of small cuts on his face. He looked like I felt. What the hell was Levi thinking?

I took out a piece of paper and wrote the words *Talk at lunch* on it. I folded it in half and waited until Ms. Hughes was writing on the board to hand it to him. Garrett opened the paper and read it. His shoulders slumped. He folded the paper back up and slid it under his arm.

"If anyone is interested in trying out for *Godspell*, I have audition forms," Ms. Hughes said.

"*Godspell*?" Jennifer rolled her eyes. "I thought we were doing *Grease* this year."

"Who told you that?"

"Mrs. Flor."

"She doesn't work here anymore," Ms. Hughes said. "I've looked at the budget, and we're doing *Godspell*. Small cast, easy costuming, cheap set."

"Is it even legal?" Shelly lifted her chin and flipped her hair over her shoulder. "I mean, a play about God in a public school?"

"It's theatre." Ms. Hughes pulled a stack of forms out of her desk drawer. "Auditions are after school tomorrow and Friday. Who wants a form?"

"I studied *Grease* all summer," Jennifer muttered.

Her foot twitched under her desk like a cat's tail, but she raised her hand. I knew she wouldn't be able to resist. Every summer she went to New York to visit family for a week and went to plays. We had all heard plenty about her life up north even though she had lived here since she was seven.

"Come on, guys. The show has two male leads. Help me out here."

"I'll take one," Garrett said.

"Do you sing?" Ms. Hughes asked as she handed him a form.

"A little."

"Anyone else? Josh?"

"No way."

When the bell rang, I gathered my stuff to go to second period. I walked into the hall, and Garrett was leaning against the wall, waiting for me.

"You just want to meet in the lunchroom?" Garrett asked.

"Sure. Where've you been sitting?"

"With my sister and her friends."

"I'll get a table."

"I'll see you then," Garrett said.

He walked down the hallway into a crowd of people. I went back into the classroom. Ms. Hughes sat at her desk, sifting through papers.

"Do you have to sing to be in the play?" I asked.

"It's a musical, so yes. But if you're more comfortable singing with other people you might be more interested in the ensemble. That way, you wouldn't have to sing any solos."

"What about just helping out with the show?"

"That would be great, too."

"Can I have one of those papers?" I asked.

"Absolutely." She handed me a form from the top of her desk and smiled.

❖

I was the first person out of my Spanish class. I raced down the hall and put my book bag on a table in the far corner of the lunchroom to claim it and got into line. I wasn't very hungry, but I got some Tater Tots and a burger anyway.

I sat down at the table and watched people enter. I saw Emily and her senior friends, sitting at a center table. Levi, Manny, Josh, and a bunch of other jocks claimed a table near Emily. Levi kept getting up from his seat to go steal Jennifer's french fries. He was obsessed with her boobs. Last year, I would have been at Levi's table, but I wasn't sure if I was welcome there anymore.

I had already slid my tray with the half-eaten hamburger and most of my Tater Tots away from me by the time Garrett came in. I hated the way my face turned hot every time he stepped into a room. He spotted me but went over to his sister's table. Maybe he'd changed his mind. They talked for a minute, and then Emily looked up at me, smiled, and waved. So I wasn't a jerk anymore. Levi nudged Manny as Garrett walked by them, but they didn't do anything to him.

"Hey," he said. He sat down across from me.

"Hi."

"So are you—"

"How are—"

He smiled. "You first."

"Are you okay? The fight, I mean."

He touched his face. "Oh yeah. It's no big deal. I had these purple marks under my eyes, but you can barely even see it now. My nose still hurts a little." Garrett rubbed it. "You?"

"I was sick. I'm okay now."

"I thought you might stay home just to keep away from this place." Garrett looked across the lunchroom. "I hate it here."

"Most kids don't get beat up the first day," I said.

"Lucky me."

"Are you going to get something to eat?"

He shook his head. "I'm not hungry. I was surprised you wrote me that note. I thought you hated me, too."

"Why would you think I hate you?"

"Uh, not talking to me," he said.

"I talked to you the first day when Shelly—"

"Brushing me off this summer."

Okay, he had me there.

"It's okay. The whole school hates me. I thought maybe when you heard what I said, you got Levi to come after me. It all got twisted around. But I mean," lowering his voice, "I couldn't tell them the truth."

"What did you tell Levi?" I asked.

"Levi?" Garrett said. "I didn't tell Levi anything."

"Then why did he hit you?"

"He didn't tell you what happened?"

"No one's told me anything."

Garrett pressed his lips together. His forehead creased.

"Okay. I guess this is right. I should be the one. It's my fault anyway, right?" He leaned forward, took a deep breath. "People were talking about what happened to Travis. You know, asking questions. So I'm in the hall and everyone is talking—"

"Everyone?"

"People. I don't know their names. And someone asked, you know, when it happened, where was Asher? I said you were taking a crap. And then someone else said, Travis died because Asher had to take a crap? Then people are stopping me in the hall and asking me if it's true, and next thing I know, Levi's fist is in my face."

I was sweating. He couldn't look at me.

"No one thought it was funny. I didn't mean it the way it sounded."

Taking a crap? Immature, stupid people.

"I don't blame you if you hate me. Everyone else does."

"No one hates you," I said.

"You didn't see Levi."

I wanted to tell him that was just how Levi was, but then I remembered how he'd called Garrett a faggot.

"I hate this place," he said. "Everyone knows everyone's business. I didn't even think you and Levi were friends—the way he was at the pool and all. Then he's ready to pound me because I'm making fun of his best friend." Garrett shook his head. "I mean, what else could I say?"

"I don't know. I really don't know."

❖

I sat in the auditorium with what looked like fifty people, mostly girls. There were only three other guys there, and Garrett wasn't one of them. Maybe he had changed his mind about trying out for the play. A few girls stood in a circle and did the warm-up exercises they made us do before class concerts in grade school. Jennifer was stretching in the front row and wearing a leotard. "Eeeeeee-eye-ooooo-yuuuuuu," she sang out. She made me nervous. I decided to move as far away from her as possible before she saw me.

I spotted Kayla's purple hair a few rows back. She was sitting with some younger girls. I shuffled behind them, unnoticed. When Jennifer had first moved here, she and Kayla became instant best friends. I wondered why they didn't hang out anymore.

I checked to make sure I had my audition form even though I knew it was tucked in the front flap of my folder. I stared at the paper while the girls in front of me talked to Kayla.

"What's tech?" asked one girl.

"That's lights, sound, painting scenery," Kayla said.

"That's what you do if you aren't good enough for the show," another person whispered.

"I'm not doing that."

"If you're going to be a thespian, you'll need to put in some backstage hours anyway," Kayla said.

"A what?"

"A thespian, idiot. They run the drama club," Kayla said. I thought about asking her if stage crew had to audition.

"I hear Ms. Hughes won't cast you in a major role unless you're a senior," a girl said.

"She's new. How would anyone know that?" Kayla asked.

"I was in *Little Shop of Horrors* my freshman year," another girl said.

"I said a *major* role. Weren't you a puppet?"

"It's more than you've done," Kayla said.

"Are you a thespian?" another girl said.

"Well, I've changed in front of you in gym," someone answered.

"That's *thes*pian, not lesbian, you idiot."

I got up and moved to the end of the row.

Finally, Ms. Hughes stood in front of the group.

"We'll start with the vocals. Mrs. Barrow is going to lead the warm-up, and then we'll take you in the order in which you signed up. Mrs. Barrow?"

Everyone stood, so I did, too. We went through the scales. When we finished the warm-ups, I picked up my book bag to leave the auditorium and wait to be called, but everyone else sat back down. Ms. Hughes called a name. This older girl handed Ms. Hughes her audition form and hurried to stand next to the piano. I slid back down into the seat. I drummed my fingers against my knees as the girl started singing.

A few of her friends were nodding and waving, but most of the crowd just watched. Her voice shook once, but she recovered by rolling her eyes and wrinkling her nose. She was okay, but you could hardly hear her.

"Thank you." I stared at Ms. Hughes for some sort of reaction, but she gave nothing away. She just made some last notes and then called the next name.

I tried to remember where my name had fallen on the sign-up sheet. It had been close to the top. Did stage crew have to sing, too? I wished I'd asked Kayla before auditions got started. She would know.

I didn't want to sing. What had I been thinking? I didn't belong here.

I grabbed my book bag and hurried down the long aisle of the auditorium to the double doors. The door swung open and I stepped out into the open lobby. A note was posted outside: *Do Not Enter. Auditions in Progress.*

The lobby was quiet. This is where I had imagined I would be—waiting for my turn with all the other people, not sitting in the auditorium being judged by the whole school.

"Hey, did they start?" Garrett jogged up next to me.

"Auditions? Yeah."

"Are you trying out?"

I hesitated and then nodded.

"I went yesterday. Forgot my form."

Garrett started to open the door, but we could hear a voice singing. We peeked into the space. Jennifer stood on the stage, finishing her song.

"She's good," Garrett whispered.

"Yeah."

Jennifer held the last note long after the piano had stopped playing. She raised the note higher. After a moment of silence, a bunch of people in the audience applauded. Ms. Hughes held up her hand to silence everyone. Garrett and I slipped inside.

"Thank you." She didn't even glance at Jennifer, who stood smiling on the stage. "Asher Price, you're next."

Garrett nudged me. I stepped forward.

"Uh, I'm just here for stage crew."

"What?" Ms. Hughes held a hand over her eyes and peered out into the dark auditorium for me.

"Stage crew."

"We need guys," she said.

"I…I can't sing."

Ms. Hughes took her glasses off and rubbed the bridge of her nose.

"Just go," Garrett said to me, then called out to Ms. Hughes, "He's getting his form."

I opened my book bag and took my paper out as Garrett ran up the aisle to give his to Ms. Hughes. I passed him as I made my way up to the stage.

"Break a leg," Garrett said. Then he hurried out the door.

The walk to the stairs that led up to the stage was long. Luckily the other kids started talking among themselves, so it drowned out the sound of my shoes against the wooden steps. But I could hear it. The group grew quiet again as I reached the stage. I looked down at them. I could barely see Kayla and the girls in the back. Jennifer smiled at me and waved from the front row.

"Why don't we just have him match pitch?" Ms. Hughes said. "Asher, Mrs. Barrow is going to play a note and you're going to try to match it with your voice, okay?"

I nodded. Mrs. Barrow hit a key. I started to sing it back, but my breath caught in my throat. Someone was sitting in the last row of the theatre in the shadow. My eyes strained to see, and I got it in my head for a second that it was Travis. My right leg started to tremble.

"It's okay. Just take your time," Mrs. Barrow said. She played the note again. My voice shook, but I sang the note back. She went up the scale and then back down again. That was it.

When it came time to dance, I managed to go in the same direction as everyone else, although I did accidentally trip Iggy's little sister. Then Ms. Hughes had us each read for Jesus. Most of the guys auditioning stumbled over the words. Some read it like a person talking in everyday English. I read it just like I did every Sunday.

Chapter Thirteen

On Sunday, we were late to church because of me. I had ignored Mom's nagging to get up. My left shoe had disappeared, so I had to wear my muddy sneakers. We hurried into the vestibule ten minutes late. John stood outside the sanctuary handing out bulletins. He had buried his wife, and he had managed to make it to church on time.

We tiptoed into the second-to-last row in the sanctuary. I looked at the bulletin. Youth Bible study was cancelled. At least I wouldn't have to worry about how to get through that.

"Hope in God," Pastor Cole read, "who has created you. Open yourself to the one who knows you well."

"God accepts us, even when people do not," the congregation read from the screen. "God affirms us, even when we fail." My lips tried to move along with everyone else's, but I couldn't make myself speak.

I spotted Garrett in the front row during the hymn "God of Love and God of Power." I didn't bother singing along. I felt like I was running a fever again.

Pastor Cole moved on to Children's Time. He talked about how he had once gone to a church like this one and how God had called on him to be a pastor.

"God calls each of us," he said. "You may be teachers, doctors, police officers, parents…any number of things. But God calls each of us. I need a volunteer."

Pastor Cole chose a little girl who looked around Travis's age.

"I was called to be ordained, or approved, to be a pastor. And that meant I got to wear a stole." He helped the little girl into a pastor's robe and draped a piece of fabric over her shoulders.

Mom leaned over to me.

"I always thought you'd make a good pastor," she whispered. I inched away from her.

"This is a stole," Pastor Cole said. "Can you say *stole*?"

She giggled. "Stole?"

"It sounds like when something is stolen, but that isn't what it means at all. I don't know that you'd earn one if you stole one." Everyone laughed. "This is the uniform of a pastor, just like a fireman or nurse or police officer has a special outfit to wear to do their job."

The little girl waved at her mom and dad. She had light brown hair pulled into pigtails. The robe swallowed her up. If Travis had volunteered, he would be grinning devilishly right now. The congregation would still be smiling. I would have slid down in the pew hoping to disappear, praying that Travis would have the good sense to stay quiet.

He always said he wanted to race cars, but there was no telling what he would have been when he grew up. I thought about Hector and the hermit-crab races I'd read about online. Travis would have loved that.

That was when I noticed Mom had raised her hand. Pastor Cole was calling on people in the congregation to share things they were grateful for or worried about. I wanted to yank her arm down. I nudged her.

"What are you doing?" I whispered.

She ignored me. Maybe he wouldn't see her; we were pretty far in the back. She sat with her back straight, reaching her hand as high as she could.

Pastor Cole nodded as an old man talked about his sister's upcoming operation. Then he pointed to Mom. I saw Garrett turn to look.

Mom cleared her throat as she stood up. The other people hadn't stood up. Why was she standing?

"Asher and I just wanted to thank all of you for your thoughts and prayers. It's been really, really hard," her voice started to break, "but it's easier knowing there are people out there who are praying for us. Thank you."

Garrett's eyes shifted to me. It was a good thing for Mom to say, but I wished she hadn't stood up like that. Now people were looking at us.

A bunch of people crowded around Mom and me during the greeting. Some of them were crying. I let them hug me. A tall older guy came over and hugged Mom, too.

"Let's talk after the service, Margaret," he said.

I saw Garrett watching us. He didn't come over. It was a long walk from the front of the church to the back.

After the service, Mom and the tall old guy went to Pastor Cole's office. I headed toward the library. When Travis was little, we used to check the *VeggieTales* movies out from the church library. I loved those movies. The DVDs still lined the bottom shelf along with puzzles of Noah's ark. A kid-sized table and chairs were in the center of the room, and a worn sofa sat under the one window. I sank into the sofa and stared out the window at the people from the traditional service heading to their cars and the ones coming in for the contemporary service.

I watched Dad and Helen park the Land Rover. She put lipstick on before they got out of the car. Mom hardly ever wore makeup. They held hands as they walked across the lot. Dad said something and Helen laughed.

The thud of the band playing for the contemporary service in the sanctuary annoyed me. Dad and his wife were in there. Mom was probably freaking out trying to find me, but I didn't care. Except that she might get hysterical. She hadn't seemed too worried the night she took off.

I hauled myself off the library sofa and peered into the vestibule. Mom wasn't there, so I got some of the juice and doughnuts they had for after the service. I picked an empty table close to the door, so I could see when Mom came out of Pastor Cole's office. I really hoped she wasn't setting up another appointment.

John sat down next to me. In his hands were two doughnuts and a cup of coffee.

"Hey, Asher," he said. "Mind if I join you?"

"Go ahead," I said. I expected him to start talking, but he didn't. He just sat there eating his doughnuts.

I wasn't comfortable with it so quiet, so I tried some of the small talk I'd been getting lately. "So, how *are* you?" I hated that my voice had that same heavy tone people had been using with me.

He smiled. "I don't know, Asher." He brushed some crumbs off his fingers. "How are *you*?"

"I don't know."

"Doughnuts are good," he said.

"Yeah."

"How do you think we're supposed to be doing?" he asked. It seemed weird to hear such a deep voice ask that kind of thing.

I hadn't really thought about that. "I think we're supposed to be sad."

He nodded. "It's quiet at my house."

"Yeah, it's quiet at ours, too. It got real noisy at first with people coming in and out, and then it got too quiet."

John's mouth was full. He spit crumbs when he said, "It's not like it was a surprise with Meredith. We knew she wasn't doing well."

"Is it still hard?" I asked.

"I miss her." He wiped his mouth with his napkin.

John had led a bunch of retreats and bowling nights with the youth group. He spent a lot of time talking about Jesus, but he had never talked much about his wife.

"Was she born that way? Needing a wheelchair?"

"No, no," John said. "No, we met in college. It's only been in the last five years that she needed the wheelchair to get around."

It was quiet again for a minute. Even though John was done eating, he didn't seem in any rush to go anywhere. People started to put the juice and doughnuts away.

"We got a hermit crab," I said.

I was in the middle of telling John about Bobby coming by and Irene making him give us the crab when Mom walked up. She stood smiling next to the table while I finished the story.

"So, I hear you've got yourself a hermit crab," John said to my mom.

"Well, Asher does. He did all the research on how to care for it."

"That's good."

"Come on, Asher. Let's get going," Mom said. "Thanks for hanging out with him, John."

I hated that she made it sound like he was doing her a favor.

"The radio," John said as I got up from the table.

"What?" Mom asked.

"Try the radio. It helps with the quiet."

We walked toward the car. Normally, Mom would ask me questions about what I had talked about with John. She was pretty paranoid about people asking me things about Dad. But she didn't ask me anything. We got in the car, and she sat for a long time without turning on the ignition.

"Are we going home?"

She didn't look at me. "I need to talk to you first."

But she didn't. She just sat there, looking out the window.

"Okay."

I didn't know what to do with myself, so I watched a dog tied up in the yard across the street from the church. It wasn't doing anything either but sleeping in the grass.

"Charles isn't filing the papers."

"Who?"

"Charles."

"What papers?" I asked.

"The custody papers. Your Dad was going to try to get full custody of you."

"What?"

"It's okay. We talked to your Dad. He's dropping it."

"You talked to him?" I asked. "When did you talk to him?"

"Just now. In Pastor Cole's office. Didn't you see me go in there with Charles?"

So that was Charles.

"Yeah, but...You talked to *him*?"

"Your dad? Yes. That's what I need to talk to you about." She took a deep breath. "I know this isn't something you want to do, but he does have a point."

"What are you talking about?"

"He wants to see you Sundays and Tuesday nights. Starting next Tuesday." Mom looked me straight in the eye. "You have to understand, that's what we agreed to in the divorce, Asher. I think you should do it."

She said it like I had had some personal vendetta with Dad. She said it like I was the one who had been crying when he came to pick us up that first time.

"Are you okay?" she asked. "Do you think you can do this?"

"O-kay," I said, not bothering to hide the irritation in my voice. "Whatever makes you happy, Mom. Because that's all that matters."

"What's that supposed to mean?"

"Are you kidding me? You mean *you're* okay with this."

The louder I got, the quieter and calmer she got. "I had a feeling you would react this way. Look, Asher, I know you're angry with him for what he did to you, but the alternative is that he will file papers for custody. Do you understand?"

"You think I'm angry at him? He didn't do anything to me. You think this has all been because of how I felt? Why do you think I haven't talked to Dad the past year?"

"Are you saying you haven't seen your dad because of *me*?"

I hit the dashboard with my fist. "Yes! Yes, that is exactly what I'm saying! What happened to you? Why is this okay now? Just the other day, you said Travis died because of him."

"I never said that."

"Yes, you did. You said Travis never would have died if Dad hadn't left us. You did."

Mom's lip trembled. Then her whole face contorted and she was crying. "I was so mad at him, Asher." I thought she was talking about Dad, but then she said, "I sent him to the pool because he was driving me nuts." She covered her mouth with a trembling hand. "What kind of mother does that?" She took a deep breath and sat up in her seat. "I really wish it was your father's fault. It would be so much easier. But I can't put that on him."

CHAPTER FOURTEEN

It would have been easier to pretend I had forgotten he would be there. All I had to do was head from school to the bus loop instead of going out to the pickup lane. I could have gone home, gotten something to eat, watched some television, and done my homework. I did have a lot of homework.

Dad's Land Rover was parked directly in front of the entrance, so there was no way to miss seeing him. He waved at me when I stepped out of the school. I raised my hand to let him know I had seen him. How many Sundays had I scanned the parking lot at church for that car? And now I was going to get in it. I opened the passenger door and plopped my book bag onto the floor. I had to hoist myself up into it. The car smelled new.

"Hi. Good day at school?"

He said it like he picked me up every day, but he gripped the steering wheel and smiled too tightly to convince anyone this was normal. I thought about telling him I'd been cast in the ensemble, but I still wasn't sure I was going to do it. Okay. I'd play along.

"It was okay."

He shifted into drive, but the other cars cornered us in. "This parking lot's a mess. Is it always like this?"

"Pretty much." That was why Mom always pulled forward when she picked me up, but I couldn't tell him that. He put his turn signal on and inched the vehicle into the line of cars.

"Here's the plan. You and I will have a chance to hang out for a while. We'll pick Helen up from work later and have dinner with her. That sound okay?"

Did I have a choice?

"Sure."

"Do you want to go to the house for a while?"

The house. His house.

"Or is there someplace else you want to hang out? It's up to you."

So I did have a choice. I tried to think of something else I could suggest, but my brain blanked. We waited for a space to open up in the cars.

"I don't care," I said, and that was the truth.

The house Dad had grown up in had two small bedrooms and one bathroom. He had left college and moved back in to take care of my grandfather after my grandmother died. He and Mom had lived there when they first got married. As soon as Mom got pregnant with me, they bought the house I live in now. Even though Dad kept the house as a rental property, I can only remember him renting it out a few times. Mom, Travis, and I went over there with him every now and then, but mostly, he seemed to use it as a place to go to be by himself. He'd tell us that something needed fixing, and he would disappear for hours. Mom had wanted him to sell it. It was one of the things they used to argue about.

"Have you been by the house at all?" Dad asked.

"No." It wasn't a lie. Right after he had first left, Mom used to drive by the property all the time, but you couldn't see the house from the road.

"We've done a lot to it."

The only thing we had done to our house was replace the garbage disposal when it stopped working. Mr. Williams and I had repaired the mower when I ran over Travis's baseball bat. Otherwise, everything was exactly the same at our house as when he'd left. Well, not exactly. Worse, I guess.

When Dad turned onto the S-curve road off of Hancock, the tires didn't complain like ours did on sharp corners, and when we made a left over the bridge leading to the house, we didn't bounce around.

"You fixed the bridge."

"It's brand new. Concrete. And we paved the drive."

Sure enough, the old dirt road winding back to the house was smooth. Tree roots used to reach out into the center of the path. The holes were filled. Travis and I had once played in the puddles along the road after a hard rain. No more puddles or mud. No wonder he was able to keep the Land Rover so clean.

"When did you do this?" I asked.

"A couple of months ago. We were going to wait until next summer, but we talked to Shawn at church. He said he could cut us a deal, so we went ahead and did it."

I wondered if Mom knew he had paved the road. Our driveway was cracked, and bits of grass grew in the grooves. We had priced it out to get the driveway repaved, and there was no way we could afford it. It had to have cost a ton of money to pave the distance between the road and Dad's house, even if he got a good deal.

The bushes and plants Grandpa had planted still lined the road, but most of the oaks were gone.

"What happened?" I said.

"To the trees, you mean?"

"Yeah."

"The hurricane last summer took a bunch of them out. It took forever for FEMA to get out here."

I wished I had thought to bring my camera.

"What about that curved pine tree?"

"It's still there."

We rounded the bend and I caught my first glimpse of the house. It had been freshly painted and stuck out farther along the back. The yard was a brilliant green.

"The house looks bigger.""

"Yeah, we added on. It's a three bedroom now. And we doubled the living-room space. You'll see."

Inside, I didn't recognize any of the furniture. The entryway had always been empty, but now a thick oak table with a flower arrangement stood against the white wall. The kitchen linoleum had been replaced with tan tiles. The old kitchen cabinets had been painted white. New appliances, new countertop, new sink, new carpet.

I couldn't help thinking about the day Mom and I replaced the garbage disposal. She had brought a bunch of tools to me from the garage, and we sat on the linoleum floor with the directions. I did my best, I really did, but it took us the whole weekend to get the job done.

"Did you guys do all of this yourselves?"

"We painted the cabinets, but the rest we hired out."

He led me into the living room. French doors lined the back of the house overlooking a screened-in pool.

"That's really cool," I said.

"You'll have to bring your swimsuit. And you can always bring a friend over if you want. You still hang out with Levi?"

Levi.

"Sometimes." Did his wanting to punch my face count?

"How's his mom doing?"

"Fine, I guess."

"Saw his dad at the funeral."

The flowery sofa had been replaced with a white L-shaped couch.

"What happened to all the old stuff?"

"We donated it. Helen has some friends who work at a women's shelter."

I stared out the french doors and swallowed hard. Travis would have loved this. He would have told Mom he wanted to live with Dad.

"Let me show you your room," he said.

I followed him into the hall that used to lead to the single bedroom. It extended two ways now, with a room on either end, and a bathroom between with chocolate-colored walls.

My new room was painted a boyish blue. The bedspread was denim. A framed poster of a guy skateboarding was on the wall. Helen must have done it.

"Thanks, Dad. This is cool." I wondered when they had decorated the room. Had it been like this for over a year, just waiting for me? Or had they decided to after Travis died? I wondered if the other bedroom was supposed to be for Travis. I wanted to see what it looked like.

"I've got some homework to do. Is it okay if I work on it now? Before we go get Helen?"

He looked surprised. "Yes, of course."

I went out to the car to get my book bag. If I took my time, maybe I could convince him I had too much homework to do to go with him to pick her up. The sun was moving toward the horizon. I looked across the field at the curved pine tree. It was a black silhouette with the light behind it. A long shadow mirrored its curve.

On my way back to the bedroom, I peeked into the other one. A huge bookshelf lined one wall. A wooden desk sat against the other. I recognized the office chair. It was identical to the one Dad had left at our house. They had never intended for Travis to be here.

❖

A little over an hour later, we drove into the city to pick Helen up from work. She was waiting for us in front of one of the tall, new office buildings downtown. Her short blond hair didn't move in the breeze. She wore a long black skirt and a blue short-sleeved sweater. She smiled at us. Her teeth were straight and unnaturally white. I got out of the front seat to move to the back, but she stopped me.

"Don't be silly. You stay put. I'll sit in back."

"How did it go today?" Dad asked her.

"Oh, fine. You?"

"Good. Good." He pulled back onto Route 41.

"What do you do?" I asked.

"Accounting." I wondered if she knew Levi's uncle. "So are we going out to eat tonight?"

"I thought it might be nice to. What do you think, Asher?"

"I don't care."

"How about Italian," Helen suggested.

"You still like pizza, sport?"

"Yeah."

The restaurant had fancy white tablecloths and candles and menus written in Italian.

"Do they have pizza?" I asked.

"Sure, it's over here." Dad pointed to the lower-right-hand side of the menu.

Roasted chicken and goat cheese. Sun-dried tomatoes. Artichokes and red-pepper sauce. I decided to order spaghetti to play it safe. I expected Helen to get a salad. She was really skinny. Instead, she asked for some pasta thing with shrimp that wasn't even on the menu.

"We went by the house," Dad told her.

"Oh? What did you think?"

"You guys have done a lot to it," I said.

"Well, it would have been a lot easier to just move into my place, but my house didn't have any character. Plus, I didn't have any trees. You know how it is in the subdivisions with zero lot lines."

"So you guys have two houses?"

"No, I sold it. Just in time, too. Got a decent price, which is saying something in this economy. Good timing. We put the money into renovating your dad's place."

Before the market fell out. That was before Dad left.

"And the new furniture?" I said.

"Oh, that was my stuff. Steven thought we should use my furniture."

He reached over and put his hand on top of hers. "I wanted to make sure it felt like home to you."

"It does," Helen said.

She wasn't as pretty as my mom. She was too skinny and her face had too many angles. I sort of hated her.

"Did you like your room? We weren't sure about what to do in there. I asked your dad if you were into sports or anything, but…"

"It's nice," I said. "I don't know how much I'll use it, you know, sleeping over."

"Well, it's your room," Dad said. "You can do what you want with it, okay?"

Helen tilted her head and rested her hand on her chin.

"I can't get over how much you look alike. Those gray eyes."

I tapped the side of my glass and looked away. Our waiter brought our food.

While we ate, Helen and Dad asked me questions about school. We didn't talk about Travis or Mom. We didn't talk about Dad filing for custody or the day he came by to pick Travis and me up or why he left in the first place. After dinner, they asked me if I wanted to go back to the house for a while.

"I still have some homework to do for tomorrow," I said.

"Why don't you drop me off at the house first?" Helen said.

It was out of the way, but I figured they were avoiding a fight with Mom.

When we pulled up in their driveway, Helen leaned forward in the seat and stuck her head between Dad and me.

"Asher, it's been really nice getting to know you a little better. Your dad told me you were amazing, and I can see what he was talking about. We'll see you Sunday."

"Sure," I said. I couldn't remember having said or done anything amazing.

Once we were alone in the car, I expected Dad to say something, but he didn't. We drove home in silence.

He pulled into the driveway and put the car in park. For a second I thought he was going to try to hug me or something, but he just said, "Thank you for this."

"Thanks for dinner." I picked my book bag up off the floorboard. "See you."

I got out of the car and walked to the front door. He didn't pull out of the driveway until I had stepped inside the house.

Mom was curled up on the sofa with her legs tucked underneath her. She had the phone up to her ear.

"He just walked in the door. I'll talk to you later."

She hung up and reached for the remote. The television was on but muted. She turned it off. Her eyes were a little swollen from crying, but she smiled as she stood up and came over to me. I dropped my book bag by the door.

"How'd it go?" She crossed her arms in front of her and stood a little stooped over, like she was trying to keep her insides in.

"I really missed you, Mom."

Then I surprised myself by hugging her. I rested my head on her shoulder.

"Did everything go okay? Are you all right?"

I nodded and pulled away. "They were nice. It was fine. I just missed you, is all."

She looked closely at my face to see if I was lying. I laughed. She smiled a little, too.

"I promised myself I wouldn't bug you with questions," she said, but I could tell from the way she hesitated that she really wanted to.

"Good."

I went into the kitchen to pour myself a glass of water.

"Are you hungry?" she asked when I sat beside her on the couch.

"We ate out."

"Really? Where did you go?"

Great. I took a long drink from my water.

"What, I can't ask you where you went for dinner?"

I put the glass down on the table.

"Okay. I won't ask anything," she said. "I didn't realize I couldn't make normal conversation."

There was nothing normal about conversation with Mom any more. Helen seemed pretty normal. I couldn't think of anything she had done that should make me think she wasn't. And Dad seemed pretty normal, too. So they'd made the house nice. So they had a lot of things we didn't. Did that mean I shouldn't like them? And they seemed to like each other. Wasn't that normal?

"Oh, by the way, you got a phone call." Mom smiled. "From a girl."

"Who?"

"Jennifer? She said you had her number. You're supposed to call before nine."

"Thanks."

"Don't forget."

"I won't." I stood up, picked up my book bag, and started for my bedroom. "I've got homework."

"She sounded really nice."

"She is."

"But you don't like her?" Mom asked.

I sighed. "She wrote me this weird note. And anyway, I think Levi likes her."

She stared at me. "So?"

"I've got homework."

Chapter Fifteen

Halloween was going to be different. First, we didn't go pick out pumpkins. I let that slide. Digging out the guts never did much for me, anyway.

My second clue was when Mom got ready to go to work on Halloween.

"Who's going to hand out candy?"

"I didn't buy candy," she said.

"What am I supposed to do when kids come to the door? Hide?"

"Why don't you go to a movie with your friends or something?"

Levi and I hadn't hung out in ages. Who else was there? I missed Travis.

Last year, I had worn the Hawaiian shirt Dad had bought when he and Mom were on vacation, a pair of long socks with sandals, shorts, and Travis's mouse-ear hat from Disney World. I had slung my Minolta around my neck for the final tacky tourist touch. It had been weird without Dad around, but Levi and I had a good time taking Travis door-to-door.

The little kids usually came early, so this Halloween I vacated the front of the house around four. We normally had at least twenty groups come by just in the first few hours. This year, the doorbell rang only three times. Maybe it was because we didn't have the jack-o'-lanterns out front.

When my homework was finished, I sat on my bed for a few minutes, counting the rolls of film I needed to take to Harmon and figuring out how much it was going to cost to get them developed. I wrote the number and amount in my ledger and stacked the film back in the box in my top drawer. I remembered I still had two rolls of film to pick up.

I thought I heard a noise from the hall. It sounded like it came from Travis's room. I sat still, waiting to see if I heard it again. There it was—a rustling sound. I peered out into the hallway and turned on the light. I listened. I didn't hear anything, but the second I moved to go back in my room I heard it. I slammed my bedroom door and locked it. There was no way I was going into Travis's room on Halloween, even if he was my brother. I didn't want to be home. I thought about calling someone. Garrett?

I opened my top drawer and dug around inside for the cast list Ms. Hughes had given us. It had the phone numbers of everyone in the play. I pulled the drawer farther out and shook the contents forward. The contact list slid forward, but when I picked it up the framed Bible passage was underneath.

Save me, God,
for the waters have come up to my neck.
I sink in miry depths, where there is no foothold.

Travis had gone through the same swimming classes I had at the public pool, but he had refused to get into the water until he was four. He hated getting his hair wet even when he took a bath, so it was nearly impossible for the teacher to get him to put his face in the water. I had always done exactly what the teacher said, but Travis flat-out rejected everything she tried. We gave up lessons. Instead, Dad taught him, but the most Travis ever did was dog paddle.

I picked the *Webster's New World Dictionary* off the bookshelf above my computer and flipped to the *M* section. *Minute steak, miracle, mirth…miry.* In my head, I had pronounced it with a long *i* sound, which was right. "*Miry. Full of, or having the nature of, mire; boggy, swampy,*" I read aloud. "Okay. Where's mire, then? "*Mire. An area of wet, soggy ground; bog.*"

It didn't sound like the pool. I closed the dictionary and reached for the telephone sitting next to my computer. Garrett probably wouldn't be home, anyway. I held the phone in my hand as I reached back into my top drawer for the phone list, but I glanced back at the framed passage. Two lines stood out from the rest of the words, set off with spaces and centered in the frame.

God, you know my folly.
My sins aren't hidden from you.

I closed the drawer and sat down on my bed, resting the phone in my lap. I thought about calling Mom and asking her to come home, but I didn't. I heard the air conditioning kick on. The trouble was it was too quiet. I started to stand up and go turn on some music when the doorbell rang three times in a row. I jumped. Three times? It was like some determined kid thought I was inside, hogging a big bowl of candy. Then a pounding sounded at the front door. I sat up on my bed and listened closely. I'd figured whoever it was had gone away when the *bam, bam, bam* on my bedroom window sent me scurrying off my bed. I ducked down in case whoever it was could see through the dark curtains.

"Asher. I know you're in there." I recognized Levi's muffled voice. "It's Halloween. Let's go."

I opened the curtain and looked at him through the window. "I thought we weren't talking."

"Don't be an ass."

"We're too old for this," I told him.

"Candy is candy. Come on."

"Don't you have someone else to hang out with?"

"Yeah. Jennifer and Kayla are waiting out front. Stop wasting my time. Move."

I grabbed my camera and started for the hall, but then I heard the rustling sound again—it was coming from inside my room. I noticed Hector the hermit crab moving around in his tank. So that was all it was. I hurried down to Travis's room. I snatched the Mickey Mouse hat from the top of his closet. Then I slipped into my red Converse, not bothering to tie the laces. I pulled a plastic bag for candy from the drawer in the kitchen and hurried out the front door.

"Is your mom home?" Levi asked.

"No, any minute though." I busied myself with tying my shoelaces so I didn't have to lie to his face.

When I stood up, I barely recognized Jennifer. She had dyed her hair black and wore a spiked collar around her neck and a long black trench coat. Her eyes were lined thickly in grays and purples. But Kayla was definitely still the stranger looking of the two. Her pale legs stuck out from under a short red-and-white cheerleading skirt. Her maroon hair was pulled into a high, slick ponytail. Even with a cigarette dangling from her pink lips, she looked wholesome.

"It was my idea," Jennifer said.

Kayla tugged at the hem of the skirt. "They banned my trench coat from school, but you girls can wear this crap?"

"Come on, Kayla. You look cute. Doesn't she look pretty?" Jennifer asked me.

"She looks nice."

"Positively doable," Levi said.

Kayla exhaled a stream of smoke. "Too bad you're so repulsive. We could have had a great time."

"I hear you didn't find Josh repulsive."

"Is he still talking about that? It was the best five seconds of my freshman year," Kayla said.

"He just called her a few times," Jennifer said. "He's such a liar."

"What are you supposed to be?" I asked Levi.

"Oh, wait," he said, reaching in his pocket and turning away. When he looked back, he grinned, exposing vampire teeth.

"Nice," I said.

We started on the opposite side of the street, avoiding the houses like mine that didn't have lights or decorations, and going to the ones that had maximum candy potential. Levi ran through the yard to the front door of a house with four jack-o'-lanterns on the front step while Jennifer, Kayla, and I walked up the driveway.

Levi rang the doorbell as I stared at the cigarette still dangling from Kayla's fingertips. She took a deep drag and flicked it into the bushes just as the doorknob turned.

"Trick or treat!" Levi, Jennifer, and I called in unison. I watched the woman's bright smile fade as she eyed the trails of smoke curling from Kayla's nostrils.

She mumbled, "Happy Halloween, kids…whatever you are," as she dished out some candy. She wouldn't risk being rude. We probably looked like a group who might pull a trick or two—Jennifer, the cheery goth with the black nail polish, and Kayla, the cheerleader with a nicotine addiction. Levi didn't need a costume to look like trouble.

"Did you see how that lady looked at us?" Kayla said once we were back on the sidewalk.

"That was hilarious. Did you hear her? 'Whatever you are.'" Levi poked Jennifer on the arm.

"Now you know what's it's like to have people judge you," Kayla said.

"You choose to be judged, Kayla. No one forces you to walk around like that," Jennifer said.

Kayla shrugged. "It beats walking around in this happy crap."

"What's wrong with being happy?" Jennifer said.

"I don't think it had anything to do with your costume," I said. "It's because we're too old for this."

"Who cares? They're still giving us candy." Levi reached into his bag and opened a packet of M&M's.

"Yeah, because they think we're going to egg their house," I said.

"*Mmph*," Levi crunched noisily. "Now you're talking."

"We need some little kids to follow around," Jennifer said. "That would do the trick."

Like Travis. I wondered if they were thinking of him, too. Nobody said anything. Even Levi, but only until we reached the next house with its front lights on. He cut through the grass again with Kayla trailing behind him. He turned on her, grabbed her bag of candy and ran.

"Give it back," she screamed.

Great.

She stalked after him, yelling, "Levi, it's my candy." I was glad we were a safe distance from Pearl's house. Jennifer and I stood side by side, watching Kayla and Levi in the neighbors' yards.

"I'm sorry," Jennifer said. "Levi told me how the two of you always took Travis out on Halloween. I can't believe I just said that."

"What?"

"About finding kids to follow around. I'm so stupid."

"No. I think you're right. I feel like we're too old for this, but…"

"It beats staying home. I miss being little sometimes." She pulled at her dog collar. "Are you mad at me?"

"No."

"The Christmas after my grandma died was awful. We used to go there Christmas morning right after we opened presents at our house. My mom kept crying. The holidays are the worst."

"Huh."

"It gets easier."

I was relieved when Levi jumped on my back and started singing the theme song from *The Mickey Mouse Club*.

"Now we know why Levi didn't go out for the musical," Kayla said.

"Asher did. Aren't you doing stage crew or something?" Levi asked.

"Lights," Kayla said. "You don't come until tech week, right?"

"Yeah." I shuffled along the sidewalk.

"You did a pretty good job at auditions. I'm surprised you weren't cast," Jennifer said.

"I'd have paid good money to see Asher sing," Levi said. "Why'd they make you do that for stage crew?"

"Kayla didn't have to audition," Jennifer said.

If I'd known I didn't have to do the audition, I wouldn't have. As it turned out, Ms. Hughes offered me a part in the ensemble, but I'd turned it down. There was no way I could get onstage like that.

"Didn't Garrett talk you into it?" Kayla asked.

"You're stage crew, too, right?" I asked to get the attention away from me.

"Stage manager."

"You should hear Garrett sing," Jennifer said. "He's really good."

"That faggot?" Levi said.

Jennifer stopped. "He's my friend. If you're going to talk like that, I'm leaving. Seriously."

Levi smiled devilishly. "Maybe you know better. Got a crush?"

She ignored him. "Doesn't he live around here?" Jennifer asked.

"Definitely interested," Levi said.

"Shut up, Levi," Jennifer said. "He's nice."

On the corner of our street was one of the few two-story homes in the neighborhood. Levi and I had covered every inch of it when it was under construction. While I walked around looking at the progress each day, Levi screwed around, hiding tools and ditching stuff into the stream behind the house. It was only later, after the family moved in, that I found out the guy who owned it sold insurance with my dad.

Levi inserted his fangs and rang the doorbell. I recognized the woman when she answered the door. Dad and Mom used to do things with them before the divorce.

"Asher, is that you?" she said, holding a big wooden salad bowl halfway filled with candy. "It's so good to see you."

"Hi," I said.

"I think you guys are the last ones making rounds tonight," she said, "although I haven't seen Travis yet."

My mouth opened, but nothing came out. How could she not know? Everyone knew.

"He's a ghost this year," Levi said.

"I'll keep an eye out for him," she said as she filled our plastic bags with Snickers bars. "Have fun, kids."

As we walked away from the door, Jennifer hit Levi hard on the shoulder. "Why did you say that?"

"What?"

ELIZABETH WHEELER

"You're so insensitive."

"Who cares what she thinks?"

"I'm not talking about her, you idiot." Jennifer got into step beside me on the sidewalk. "You okay?"

"Uh, yeah."

Jennifer scowled at Levi. He shrugged. "What did you want me to say? That he's dead?"

She spun toward him, her hands curled into little fists. "Just shut up."

"Lighten up," Kayla said.

"Excuse me?"

"He was trying to help."

Jennifer glared back and forth between Levi and Kayla. "Don't either of you get it? His brother died."

Kayla pulled a pack of cigarettes out of the waistband of her skirt. She lit one, drew a breath off, and said, "I'm not saying I don't feel bad about what happened. But really, the only thing we can count on is that we're all going to die."

"Oh, that's real compassionate," Jennifer muttered.

Kayla looked up into the sky. "I find it comforting."

"Yeah, I can see that," Levi said. "You walk around school looking like you're already halfway there."

It was true. In a place where everyone has a tan, Kayla looked like cold death. It occurred to me for the first time that it was possible that she might prefer death.

"Why *do* you dress like that?" I asked.

She shot me a look. "Why do you dress like *that*?"

"You know what I mean. You used to dress more…I mean, it doesn't make any difference to me, but…"

"Just come out with it, Asher. She looks like a freak," Levi said.

Kayla chuckled. "Yeah, that's me. The freak."

"Some people just like attention," Jennifer said.

"Screw you."

"If it's not that, then what?" she said.

"Do any of you ever think about why you do *anything*? I mean, you dress the way you do because that's what society and magazines say you should do. So you can fit someone else's idea of what is right. Don't you see how pointless that is?"

"So you don't want to fit in," Jennifer said.

"Exactly. Why would I?"

"Because it's normal."

"So is death. So what's the big deal? Do you think anything you *wear* is going to make any difference then?"

"Oh, so you dress like that because you're going to die. Got it," Levi said.

"I'm not in any hurry, but I'm not afraid of it."

"I'm not afraid of it, either," I said.

"That's because he's Jewish," Levi said.

"Levi, I'm Methodist."

He grinned.

"Oh, that's right, Jesus boy," Kayla said. "Because Christians don't really die."

"There's nothing wrong with being Christian," Jennifer said.

"So you're not afraid of anything?" Kayla asked.

I remembered being creeped out by Travis's room. "I didn't say that."

"Except hell." Kayla laughed.

"Well, yeah. But it's not like people have to be perfect all the time. I think the idea is that people make mistakes, and if they ask for forgiveness, it's there."

"So if I went to school with a gun and killed fifty people, God would forgive me?" Kayla asked. "No fire and brimstone?"

"What kind of gun?" Levi said. "If you're talking fifty rounds, then you'd need a couple of clips, because…"

"I'm being hypothetical."

"Of course bad people go to hell, Kayla," Jennifer said. "Don't be an idiot."

"No, she's right," I said. "If you kill fifty people and then realize how terrible it was, you're supposed to be forgiven."

"How about Hitler?" Kayla said. "Heaven or hell?"

"I don't know. Probably hell, with all we know about him, but there's no way I'd know."

Levi snickered. "Asher said hell."

"Osama bin Laden? Heaven or hell?" Kayla pressed.

"I don't know. Hell, probably."

"Your dad?" Levi said.

I didn't say anything.

"And your heaven. It's all harps and angels and shit like that?" Kayla asked.

"I don't know. Maybe it's different for everyone," I said.

I was sort of enjoying the conversation, not that I'm an authority on all things Christian.

"Cool. My heaven has beer kegs and football. And boobs," Levi said.

Levi made me smile, but Jennifer turned on him. "You think you're going to heaven?"

"Why not? If Travis can go to heaven, I sure as hell can."

Jennifer smacked his face. Hard.

He pushed her. "You didn't even know him, you stupid bitch."

Jennifer braced herself and glared at Levi. We all stood on the sidewalk in silence. Kayla watched closely to see what was going to happen next. Levi grimaced and shook his head. I could tell he regretted pushing her; he'd been after Jennifer since middle school. She spun away from him and walked toward me.

"Come on, Asher." Jennifer grabbed my hand and started leading me away.

"Are you still staying at my house tonight?" Kayla called after us.

Jennifer didn't answer her. I glanced back at Levi and Kayla standing under the street lamp, the gnats swarming in circles above their heads. We walked in silence. When we arrived in front of my house, my mom's car was still ticking in the driveway. The blue light of the television screen flickered against the living-room curtains. Jennifer's face was streaked with mascara from crying.

"Do you want to go in?" I asked.

"No."

"We could just sit here for a while if you want," I said.

"It's getting kind of cold."

Mom never locked the car door. She said she hoped someone would steal it. We slid into the backseat of the car. Normally there wouldn't have been room with Travis's booster seat, but Mom had moved it into the garage. I cranked the window open a little.

"I don't know how Kayla wears this stuff," Jennifer said, blotting at her eyes with the sleeve of her black trench coat.

"Can you believe they thought I was making a big deal out of things?" she asked as she took the spiked collar off her neck.

I leaned forward and grabbed a few tissues from the glove box. She smiled when I handed them to her.

"They were the ones making fun of your beliefs. I think it's cool that you're a Christian. I believe in God, too."

"It's no big deal."

"Kayla doesn't believe in anything anymore."

All through elementary and middle school, Jennifer and Kayla wore the same hairstyle and clothes, had the same mannerisms and even pattern of speech.

"You guys used to look like twins," I said.

"You know, she didn't make cheerleading," Jennifer said. "I'm not going to feel bad about it. It's her own fault. They had this camp to prepare you for tryouts, but she mouthed off at home and got in trouble so she couldn't go. I offered to teach her stuff, but she got snotty with me about it. And now she's all goth."

"Just because she didn't make cheerleading?"

"We're still friends. But it's just because we always have been. My other friends don't like her because she's all sarcastic, like she thinks she's better than the rest of us. I'm her only friend. I don't even know why I try." She wiped under her eyes with the tissue. "It's like you and Levi. I mean, what's the point?"

"We're okay."

"He treats you like crap. I remember when I first moved here and you guys hung out. Then he gets on the football team, and it's like...Well, you know." Jennifer balled up the tissue in her hand. "You know, I didn't do that to Kayla. I didn't blow her off when I made cheerleading."

I thought she was going to start crying again.

"So you think maybe she's jealous," I said.

She turned and sat cross-legged on the seat facing me, then reached over and took my hand in hers. She opened it, pressed our palms together, and compared the lengths of our fingers before sliding hers between mine and squeezing gently.

"You're so easy to talk to," she said. I glanced at her face, but she was looking at our entwined hands. When she looked up into my eyes, she smiled. "Is this okay?"

I wanted to tell her she had black lipstick on her front tooth, but I didn't. She kept moving her fingers over my hand, sliding down to encircle my wrist and then touching my open palm. I pulled my hand away and rubbed it against my shirt.

"Sorry," I said. "It tickles."

"Oh, are you ticklish?"

I started to say no, but it was too late. She grabbed my side as I squirmed away from her. Then she moved to the left side of my body, higher up, close to my armpit. I retaliated, getting her knee.

She squealed as she turned her back toward me, stretching her legs out on the seat so I couldn't reach her knees. I moved my hands to tickle her waist instead, and she arched her back against me. Then she turned so our bodies were pressed against one another. We stopped.

"Hi, there," she said, a few inches from my face. She smelled like baby powder and some chemical I couldn't identify. She started kissing me. It wasn't too bad as long as our lips were stuck together, but every time she pulled away or she moved a little her lips would sort of stick to mine like tape. She straddled me on the seat. Her hair kept falling into my face. It made me itch. I tried to tuck it back a little, but then I accidentally pulled her hair and she sort of squeaked.

"Sorry," I mumbled.

"It's okay."

She was staring at me.

"Really," she said pointedly, "it's okay."

Her smile was so eager, so happy. My stomach grumbled.

"Sorry," I said again.

She wrapped her arms around my neck and kissed me again. This time, her tongue flicked against my lips. It made me think of how snakes' tongues dart in and out of their mouths. Her right hand trailed down my arm. She pulled her face away from mine. In the streetlight, she looked like a sleepy raccoon—her eyelids all heavy and black. It was easier when I couldn't see her. She took my hand in hers and pressed her mouth against my open palm. Then she licked the length of my index finger. I closed my eyes and tried to focus on the warm wetness, but then she stopped and pressed her boobs against me, all soft and squishy.

Then I heard something else. Jennifer's eyes got wide, and I put my finger over my lips. She started to sit up to look out the window, but I pulled her back down against me.

There were two voices, and it took me about two seconds to recognize Levi's. Then I heard Kayla.

"What are they…?" Jennifer said.

"Shh."

It came from Pearl's house—the sound of a shell cracked against a hard surface. Again. And again. I counted seven. They must have gone to Levi's house and gotten eggs. Then I heard their footsteps running away. Jennifer's stale breath blew against my chin. I waited until I was sure Pearl hadn't heard them and then moved out from under Jennifer. She sat up and tried to run a hand through her hair.

"They egged your house?" she asked.

"No. Pearl's. You should probably go home."

"I'm supposed to be at Kayla's."

Kayla lived on the other side of town.

"Then we should get my mom." We sat there in the car for another minute. Then I crawled into the front scat and pulled down the visor to check the mirror. My lips were black.

Chapter Sixteen

S leep well?" Mom asked.

She didn't look up from her checkbook and the stack of bills on the dining-room table. My scalp itched. I scratched my head and squinted at the bright light from the sliding glass door.

"You know, a lot of people do that online," I said as I moved past her to the kitchen.

I got some cereal out of the cabinet, but there wasn't enough milk left in the carton to get it wet. I shook my head and closed the fridge. I opened the freezer and took out two frosty waffles. I knocked them on the counter to get them apart.

"Eat fast," she said.

"Why?"

I dropped the waffles into the toaster slots.

"We're going to church."

"It's Saturday."

"They're starting this small group on grieving. We're meeting at noon."

I stared at my reflection in the side of the silver toaster. My lips were gray. I rubbed them.

"I think it would be good for you."

I pictured a bunch of sad people sitting in a circle on cold metal chairs, crying. I couldn't see how that would be good for me.

"You need to talk about what happened." She talked about what happened all the time, and it didn't seem to do her any good. "It helps to know other people have been through these things."

I was pretty sure knowing other people suffered would not make me feel better.

"John's leading it," she said. "I told him we'd be there."

The waffles popped up. I put them on my plate, slopped some syrup on them, and slammed the plate back onto the counter. I heard the squeak of Mom's chair against the floor. She stepped quickly into the kitchen and crossed her arms in front of her.

"After last night, I think it would be good for us," Mom said.

I'd only asked her to drive Jennifer to Kayla's house—no big deal. I dug into the waffle with my knife and fork.

"Your lips are still black."

I fought the urge to wipe my mouth again. Instead, I cut diagonally, not neatly along the perforated lines like I usually did.

"It was part of her costume."

"Were your lips part of her costume?"

"Back off, Mom."

"Back off? You didn't even leave a note. How am I supposed to know if you're okay if—"

"I don't even like her."

"Oh, that makes it so much better."

I ground the knife into the plate. A sound like nails on a chalkboard.

"You can't keep pretending like nothing is wrong."

"I'm not going to this thing."

"What about John? If you don't feel comfortable talking in a group, why don't you talk to him?"

I stuffed a big piece of waffle in my mouth and chewed. The cardboard taste of freezer burn made my stomach turn.

"No."

"Excuse me?"

"I'm not going."

"It's either this or the school guidance counselor. You choose."

She marched out of the kitchen.

Ms. Brimsen, our school guidance counselor, organized drug free campaigns and career day. I knew of a couple of girls who went to talk to her about their problems, but I couldn't picture myself sitting in her office. She had a framed poster on her wall that read *I believe in the possibility of miracles*. An image of my framed Bible passage surfaced in my mind.

"Call Pastor Cole," I said. "I'll talk to him."

I wasn't sure if she heard me, but a minute later, the sound of her phone voice drifted in from the other room. The waffles sat soggy and limp. I shoved them away.

❖

I took the framed passage out of my drawer, undid the clasps on the back, and removed the cardboard cover. I slid the passage out of the frame and tucked it into the Bible Travis had stolen from church.

When we went out to the car, Pearl was pacing back and forth in her driveway.

"What happened?" Mom asked.

"Some hoodlums egged my house," she said. "Look at this."

Mom crossed over to Pearl's yard and looked at her garage door. I could see the egg and shell bits from our driveway. I trotted toward them.

"Do you know anything about this?" Mom asked me.

I kicked at a shell near my foot on the driveway and moved the Bible from my right hand to my left.

"No."

Pearl scowled at me. Mom folded her arms and squinted her eyes. She tapped her sandaled foot on the concrete. She was wearing makeup.

"Well?" Mom asked.

"What? I said no."

"Why don't you go sit in the car and wait for me," she said.

"Fine." I spun toward the car and shuffled across the small strip of grass separating our driveways. I opened the passenger door and something black caught my eye. On the backseat was the spiked collar Jennifer had worn last night. Great. I grabbed it off the seat and looked around for a place to stash it. The glove box. I opened it, hid the collar under the map and papers, and closed it. When I glanced up, Mom was just heading back to the car.

"After we get home from church, you're going to clean that mess. Understood?" she said.

"Why me?"

"Don't start." She backed out of the driveway and didn't speak to me until we were just down the road from the church.

"And I expect you to apologize to Pearl."

"I didn't do anything."

"You're only making it worse."

She pulled into the first open space she found in the church parking lot. I spotted Dad's maroon SUV a few rows over, and I glanced at Mom to see if she had noticed. She hadn't. Let her figure it out herself.

My thumbnails were ringed in white from gripping the Bible. I got out of the car and trailed behind Mom into the church. She watched me knock on Pastor Cole's door before heading off to the conference room.

"Come in," I heard him call from inside.

Pastor Cole sat behind his mahogany desk looking at the computer screen. On the window behind him hung about a dozen makeshift stained-glass windows made from colored tissue paper and construction paper. Pale-pink, blue, yellow, and green shapes and hues played along the white walls in his office.

"Asher," he said as he stood and walked around the massive desk. "Come in."

I stepped into his office. He pulled a chair away from the wall and motioned for me to sit. I waited for the heavy *So, how are you?* to come, but instead Pastor Cole smiled at me.

"It's good to see you," he said.

It was good to see him, too. But then I looked down at the Bible in my hands and remembered why I was there. Pastor Cole saw me eyeing it.

I expected him to ask me about it. *Isn't that one of the pew Bibles from the church?* But he didn't. He just sat there and smiled at me until it started to make me sort of angry.

"I know what you want me to talk about," I said.

Pastor Cole's expression didn't change. For a second, I thought he hadn't heard me. I was about to repeat myself when he said, "You think I want you to talk about Travis." I nodded. "I'm glad you're here, but I didn't ask you to come. I was under the impression you wanted to talk to me."

I couldn't think of anything to say to that. I had told Mom I wanted to meet Pastor Cole because I hadn't wanted to go to my guidance counselor.

"Did you ask your mom to call me?" he asked.

"No."

I felt stupid tears coming, so I lifted my chin and bit my lower lip. Pastor Cole leaned forward.

"It's okay. I wish it had been your idea, but I'm still glad you're here." He leaned back in his chair and looked toward his window. A smile crossed his face again. "Now, there's something to talk about." He motioned toward the colorful display. "Did you see what the preschoolers made?"

"They make them every year," I said.

My fingers traced the cover of the Bible in my lap as I watched the colors move along the wall. It was quiet again. I heard the clock ticking, and I had this feeling that if I didn't do this today I never would. I flipped through the Bible pages until I found the creased piece of paper.

"I want to know what this means."

I handed him the passage.

Pastor Cole took the page in his hand and smoothed it out. "You want to know what this means?" he asked.

"Yeah."

"Why?"

I shook my head. I knew what it meant to me; I wanted to know what it meant to him. Pastor Cole looked over the passage. He stood up and moved back to the other side of his desk, opened another book, and then nodded as if confirming something he had suspected.

"Well, this passage is attributed to David, but almost certainly was written in exile in Babylon," Pastor Cole said.

"From David and Goliath?"

"Yes." He rubbed his eyes with the palm of his hand and then studied me. "What is it about this passage that got your attention?"

I ignored his question. "Exile. He was kicked out?"

"You need to look at it in context. You've only got a portion of the psalm here." Pastor Cole held up the scrap of paper. Then he picked up another Bible and brought it back over to me. He pointed to a verse at the end. "David moved the capital to Jerusalem—Zion—early in his reign, but, see here, 'build the cities of Judah' almost certainly refers to a return from exile some four-hundred-plus years later."

I sat silently as he flipped the page back and moved his chair closer to mine. "Verse nine. 'For the zeal for your house consumes me, and the reproaches of those who reproach you have fallen on me.' This is quoted in relation to Jesus driving the money changers out of the Temple."

"What about the water. Right there, it talks about water."

"In Hebrew culture, moving water means life," he said. He paused and looked at me. "Asher, maybe I could help more if I knew what you were looking for."

I shook my head. "Just tell me about the water. What is it talking about here? Is he really drowning, or…"

Pastor Cole stiffened in the chair next to me. "Water can mean many things. Flowing streams are called living water, shallow water is peace," Pastor Cole said. He closed the book. "Asher, does this have something to do with Travis?"

"What about depths? 'Miry depths?' Does that mean something?" I asked.

"It's important that I know your reason for asking about this passage, Asher. We can look at this from a purely theological standpoint, but…"

"That's all I'm asking for. You said shallow water is peace. Deep water. What does that mean?"

"The deep—or *tehom*—is the mortal enemy, death embodied. Sinking in the miry depths would evoke images of Egyptian—or Babylonian—riverbeds, where crocodiles dwell."

I thought about the Caloosahatchee River and the alligators sunning on the riverbeds. Not the pool, the river, but what difference did it really make when your lungs filled with water?

Pastor Cole's forehead creased. "You have to understand that the promise to praise God after being rescued is a standard form for a psalm, and this part at the beginning is typical."

"But what does it mean?" I asked again.

"It's a prayer, Asher. It's a prayer asking that David be saved and his enemies judged."

I chewed on my bottom lip as the clock on the wall ticked.

"Why are you looking at this?" Pastor Cole pressed.

"What did David do?"

He looked confused. I pointed to the middle of the passage, the first words I had ever noticed.

"Here. In verse five, David's talking about his foolishness. About God knowing his sins. What did he do?"

Pastor Cole lifted the torn page. His fingers traced the edge as he looked at the verse, and then his hand stopped in mid-motion. I watched Pastor Cole's eyes shift from the words to the jagged edge of the page.

"We're all guilty, Asher. Every one of us. What matters is that God knows our guilt and loves us anyway."

A series of short knocks sounded at the door. "Asher?" My mom's voice.

"It's my mom," I said.

She opened the door, her car keys in her hand.

"We have to go," she said.

I stood up.

"We're almost finished here," Pastor Cole said. "If you could give us just another few minutes."

"We have to go now." Mom's voice rose in pitch and volume. She grabbed my arm. I pulled free of her.

"Wait, Margaret," Pastor Cole said. "What's going on?"

She clenched her teeth. "I came here to talk. I came to my church. Did you know *he* was going to be there?"

Pastor Cole stood, watching her. Mom yanked on my arm again. I spotted the pew Bible I had left on the chair and the scrap of paper sitting on top of it.

"Hold on," I said as I wrestled free of her and walked back to the chair to get it.

"Leave it," she said.

My hand froze above the Bible, the passage.

"You said I could have it," I said.

"Leave it."

We walked out of Pastor Cole's office and the Community Methodist Church. Dad's Land Rover was still sitting in the parking lot. Mom settled in behind the steering wheel and slammed the door closed.

"Do you have any idea what it was like walking into that room? Just seeing him sitting there?"

So we were back to *him* again, not *Dad*. I looked at the clock on the dashboard. We'd only been at the church for ten minutes. It felt a lot longer.

"I almost turned around and walked out, but there were all of those people sitting there watching me. No, I wasn't going to let him run me off. I wasn't going to make it easy for him."

I folded the plastic end of the shoelace on my Converse over and over the length of the lace. I was tired of trying to keep up with her mood shifts.

"But then we started talking about why we were there, and it was his turn, and he started talking about Travis."

She choked on his name.

"Travis."

She shook her head from side to side.

"He has no right."

She pulled out of the parking lot. We drove past the swimming pool. People splashed and played. It was an unusually hot November day, even for Florida. I would never go there again without thinking about Travis. I wasn't sure I'd ever go there again at all.

Mom didn't ask about how things had gone with Pastor Cole. I wouldn't have known what to say, anyway.

When we got home, there was a message from Jennifer. I didn't call her back. Instead, I dug the hose out of our garage, hooked it up to our spigot, and washed down Pearl's garage door. Pearl came out and watched me work.

"I don't want eggshells on my driveway, either," she said.

"I'm just trying to loosen it up first."

I went back to my house and grabbed an old towel and a bucket. I filled it with water and wiped her garage down, rinsing the hand towel often to get rid of the shells. I scrubbed hard to get the dried egg off. When I finished, Pearl inspected the job.

"It's a different color than the rest of the door. Did you rub my paint off?"

"No, it's just wet. It should be okay when it dries," I said.

"Humph. Well, if it's not, I'll send your mother the bill."

I picked up the bucket and started back to my house. Then I remembered how Mom said I had to apologize. I took a second to get my thoughts together. It was important that I didn't lie. I walked back to Pearl who was searching her driveway for any shells. She looked surprised to see me standing in front of her.

"I'm sorry about what happened to your garage," I said. I really was.

Pearl stared at me hard. She didn't say anything, but I think she could tell I meant it.

CHAPTER SEVENTEEN

When I woke up and realized that I'd slept through the Sunday service, my first thought was that Mom had offed herself. She always pulled my bedroom curtains open early on church days. But then my stomach rumbled. I smelled something good—bacon? I threw the covers off and headed down the hall to the kitchen. Mom stood in front of the stove, a pile of greasy strips sitting on top of a paper towel on the counter next to her. Her hair was pulled back into a high ponytail. She still wore her pajamas.

"Help yourself," she said as she handed me a plate.

She opened the microwave and pulled out a bowl of scrambled eggs.

"What's going on?" I asked.

"You never had breakfast before?"

I glanced at the clock.

"What about church?"

"I think we need a break."

I put a big pile of eggs and six strips of bacon on my plate.

"Toast will be up in a second. Go sit down."

She lifted the last few pieces of bacon out of the crackling grease. I grabbed a fork out of the drawer and sat down at the kitchen table. The bacon was crunchy—the way I liked it. Mom came in with a plate of toast balanced on top of the bowl of eggs. She went back into the kitchen and came back with two glasses of orange juice and a fork.

"There," she said, setting the juice in front of me and putting a slice of buttered toast on my plate.

We rarely had time for a sit-down breakfast on Sunday mornings. The only Sundays we didn't go to church were when one of us was sick, and even then, she called someone to let them know. I took a bite of the eggs.

"Let's pray," Mom said.

I put my fork down on the edge of my plate and swallowed the food in my mouth. I couldn't remember the last time we'd prayed before a meal. We hadn't had many together since Travis died. I folded my hands, but I kept my eyes open. Mom bowed her head.

"Thank you, God, for this food," she said. "And we ask that you give us strength. Amen."

I picked up my fork again.

❖

At eleven thirty, Mom folded the laundry instead of suggesting we get in the car to go meet Dad at church like we had the last few Sundays. I continued looking through my photographs to see which ones I wanted to take to school for a project in English class, but I kept glancing at the clock. When the phone rang ten minutes later, I ran to get it.

"Are you okay?" Dad said.

"Yeah." I walked down the hall to my bedroom.

"I'm sitting in the church parking lot."

"We didn't go today." I shut my door and sat on my bed.

"Well, I know that. Are you sick? Is your mother okay?"

Mom opened my door and walked in. She put a stack of clothes on my dresser.

"We're fine. We just didn't go."

"Is that your father?" Mom asked.

I nodded.

"Are you still coming over?" he asked.

"I think so. Hold on." I covered the phone with my hand. "Should he come here to pick me up?"

Mom's jaw clenched and released. She walked out of the room. "Yeah. Just come pick me up. I'll meet you in the driveway."

I hung up the phone and rushed to get dressed and brush my teeth. This time, I thought to grab my camera. I shouted, "See you later, Mom," as I hurried out the front door.

Seconds later, Dad pulled up in the driveway. I hopped inside, my camera heavy against my chest. As we backed into the street, I saw Mom watching us from the front window. We drove for several minutes in silence before either of us spoke.

"You might want to give me a call if you're not going to be at church," Dad said.

"Sure."

"How's your mother?"

"Fine."

His fingers tapped the top of the steering wheel.

"It's not like her to miss church." His cell phone rang. He dug into his pocket and looked at the small screen. "Yes?" He glanced at me. "Just picked him up."

I wondered if Garrett had been at church.

"Okay. We'll see you there." Dad closed his phone and tucked it into his shirt pocket. "We're meeting Helen for lunch."

This time was at Belle's restaurant. We used to go there as a family before Dad left. It was one of those places that didn't care if your kids were noisy. The waitress led us to the table where Helen was sipping tea. As we got closer, she stood and kissed Dad on the cheek. Then she wrapped a bony arm around my shoulder. It was like hugging a stick insect. She handed me a menu before I could sit down in my chair. I laid it on the table at the empty space next to me.

Dad and Helen's chairs touched. They were probably holding hands beneath the table or pressing their knees against one another.

"Aren't you going to look at the menu?" Helen asked.

"I already know what I want."

Dad smiled. "Let me guess. The cheeseburger followed by coconut cream pie."

It was exactly what I had intended to get, but for some reason when the waitress came, I said, "I'd like the chicken-fried steak with mashed potatoes."

Mom always ordered chicken-fried steak with mashed potatoes. If Dad remembered, he didn't show it.

"So, what did you do for Halloween?" Helen asked me.

Made out with Jennifer in the backseat of Mom's car. "I went trick-or-treating with some friends."

Dad's forehead scrunched up. "Aren't you a little old for that?"

"No."

Dad turned his head toward Helen and raised his eyebrow. She put her napkin in her lap.

"I used to get so many kids in my old neighborhood. I loved handing out candy and seeing them all dressed up," Helen said. "Of course, no one comes to our house now."

"It's a little out of the way," Dad said.

"That first Halloween I bought all this candy, mostly out of habit, and there it sat. I had to take it to work to get rid of it." She shook her head.

Travis would have happily taken the candy off their hands.

"You should have come to the church," Helen said.

Dad took his napkin off the table and tucked it in his lap. "This year we helped pass out candy to the kids there. A lot of the youth were there. Vince Llowell, you know him, right? Nice kid. He helped with the fishing game. And you should have seen Helen. She had this fishing hat and she put all these lures on it. And then she wore this life jacket over her suit."

"I came straight from work. The bright orange really completed the ensemble."

"I'd gotten this little dinghy set up, and the kids had to get in the boat to fish for prizes," Dad said. "And they had to put on a life jacket. Safety first. It was the best booth there. By far."

I sipped my sweet tea. A few drops of condensation slid down the glass and landed on the table. I blotted them with my paper napkin.

"Do you still get a lot of kids over at the house?" Dad asked.

"Some." I didn't want to tell them Mom worked and we hadn't bought candy or carved pumpkins.

"Remember the year you went as Bob?" Dad started to laugh.

When I was into *VeggieTales*, Mom made me Bob the Tomato by covering a pumpkin costume in red fabric and attaching eyes to it.

"No one could figure out what he was," Dad said to Helen. "He was so mad."

"I wanted to be Larry," I said.

"What did you wear this year?" Helen asked.

"I was a tourist."

"Did you go with anyone I know?" Dad asked.

"Levi. A couple other people."

Dad shook his head. "Levi. That's one tough kid. He used to ram his head into people. Do you remember that? This little kid just running as fast as he could toward you."

"That was Travis."

Dad thought for a minute. "Yeah, Travis did that, too."

"No," I said. "Levi didn't do that. It was just Travis."

"When you guys were little, Levi did that, too," he said.

I wasn't going to argue with him, but I felt myself getting angry.

"So what's Levi up to, anyway?"

"Nothing, really."

"I heard he's playing football now."

"Yeah."

"Good for him."

Helen straightened her silverware. "It's important to get involved in school," she said.

I thought about *Godspell*. I could have told them I was doing stage crew, but I didn't. The waitress came with the food. I didn't really like chicken-fried steak, but I ate every bite.

❖

I spent the afternoon outside Dad's house taking pictures. He had tons of pine trees around, and I was planning to take some pictures of the long brown needles, but I couldn't get the right angles. I only had a few shots left on the roll from the funeral home, and I didn't want to waste it. Dad and Helen seemed content to hang out around the pool. They had told me to bring some swim trunks, but I'd forgotten. When they had offered to swing by the store and buy some for me, I said I didn't want to go swimming.

I wandered to the back of the house. Dad floated in the pool. A pitcher of lemonade sat on the table beside three glasses. Two of the glasses were partially full.

"Do you really think she'll stop going?" I heard Helen ask.

"I wouldn't put it past her."

"Why didn't you just ask him about it?"

"I'm not putting him in the middle of all this. She's done enough of that. He doesn't need it from us."

"Then call her. The problem is you don't talk to each other."

"You don't know her, Helen. The woman is…"

Either Dad trailed off or he lowered his voice so much that I couldn't hear him. I took a couple steps backward and then stomped toward the screen door to let them know I was there. When I glanced at them again, Helen's nose was buried in a book and Dad had plunged underwater.

"Did you get some good pictures?" Helen asked as she adjusted her sunglasses and put the book down on the glass patio table. Her feet were tucked up underneath her, but a couple of her toes peeked out. Her nails were painted pink.

"Maybe. It's hard to know until the film's developed."

She poured lemonade into the empty glass and set it on the edge of the table close to me. Real lemon slices floated in it. We made ours with a mix. I was pretty sure we didn't own a glass pitcher.

"Your dad never mentioned you were interested in photography."

Dad swam over to the pool's edge. His hair was slick. "You know how kids are. It's hard to know what's going to stick. Is that the same camera Aunt Sharon gave you?" He climbed up the steps and grabbed an oversized white towel.

"Yeah."

"I knew he liked taking pictures. Remember when you came over here and took pictures that one weekend?"

That was the day I'd taken the picture of the crooked tree. He had moved out that night while I was at Levi's house.

"Yeah, I remember."

"He's always had an eye for things like that. I knew he'd do something with the arts. Sports weren't really your thing."

Dad pulled a chair around so he could sit right next to Helen. He draped the towel over the chair and sat down. "I coached T-ball. Do you remember that?"

"Yeah."

"You were good. You just didn't like it."

"I liked it when you coached. Then Levi's dad took over."

"Right." Dad and Helen exchanged a glance. He took a sip of lemonade. "At least you've found something you like doing. Taking pictures."

Helen perked up. "I know, take one of us."

"That's a great idea. Yeah, take our picture." He put his glass down on the table.

My camera felt heavy against my chest.

I laughed a little and shifted my feet. "I don't take pictures of people."

"Sure you do. Go ahead." He put his arm around Helen's shoulder. I imagined Mom and me at Harmon Photo, Mom looking over my shoulder at the shot of Dad and Helen leaning into one another.

"No, I'd rather not."

Dad's arm dropped from around Helen's shoulder. "Why?"

"It's okay," Helen said.

"I want to know why."

"You don't have to take a picture," she said. "I was being silly."

Dad's eyes narrowed at me. "Is something wrong?"

"I'm sure he'd tell us if there was something on his mind." She turned back to me. She looked sorry.

I shook my head to clear it. "I just don't take pictures of people. I never have. It's not my thing."

Dad laughed. "Not your thing? What are you, Ansel Adams?"

"Please," Helen said to Dad.

"I just want him to explain it to me."

"I like taking pictures of landscapes and stuff." Dad blinked at me. I remembered what Pearl had said and then added, "When you take a picture of a mountain, it never comes back and complains about how it looked."

"That's true enough," Helen said. "So what should we have for dinner tonight?"

"We're not going to complain. Just take the picture."

"He doesn't want to."

"Sure he does. Go ahead, Asher. Smile, Helen."

Helen wasn't smiling. Dad had that smile on he had rehearsed in the mirror a million times. The kind you see in yearbooks.

"Come on. We can't hold this forever." His teeth were clenched together.

My hand shook as I removed the lens cap and let it dangle from the front of the camera. My father and Helen's heads filled the viewfinder. I didn't bother adjusting anything. Helen went ahead and smiled, and I was surprised that she wasn't as good at faking it as my father. I squeezed my eyes closed as I pressed the button. Whir, click.

"See? That wasn't so bad was it?" Dad asked.

I removed the strap from around my neck.

"Why don't you let us give you some money toward getting the pictures developed? I know I'm going to want a copy," he said.

I stood at the edge of the pool looking down at the shiny black camera. I hadn't even taken a picture of Travis when he was alive. I didn't ever want to see that photo, ever, so I let my camera fall through my fingers to the concrete patio. When it hit the edge of the pool, it made a cracking noise. I should have cared, but I didn't. Instead, I nudged the camera into the water with my foot. It broke the surface and sank to the bottom. I could see the black camera on the pool floor through the clear blue water.

Helen gasped. Dad's eyes widened. His mouth opened slightly, the corners turned downward. It took a second for him to piece together what I had just done. Then he was out of the seat, pushing me out of the way, and staring down into the bottom of the pool. He looked back at me.

I only hesitated a second before I ran out the back screen door and through the yard to the field. My ankle twisted on the uneven ground, but I kept my pace. I looked back to see if anyone was following me, but no one was. As far as I was concerned, they all could sink to the bottom.

I hate you. The words formed a rhythm to my running. *I* right foot, *hate* left foot, *you* right foot. Left, right, left. I cut through the field into the undeveloped brush. Instead of taking the paved drive, I ran through the thicket of palm fronds and pine trees until I reached the main road. Thin red lines cut my skin, like a mad cat had attacked my legs. Sand spurs clung to my socks and shoelaces. My skin was wet with sweat, but I didn't care. I lumbered on in the direction of home even though I'd probably die of heatstroke. The thought of dying made my legs pump faster. I'd kill myself running in the heat. But then I remembered Mom's face at Travis's funeral, and I eased to a jog. My dying would kill her. I could stop at the gas station on the corner and call her on the pay phone or something. She could come and pick me up.

I slowed my pace once I reached the steady traffic of the main road, but my breath still felt tight in my chest, like I couldn't suck enough oxygen out of the air. My shirt clung to my body. I felt the hot breeze of the cars as they raced past. I glanced over my shoulder to see if I spotted Dad's Land Rover, but I didn't see it in the stream of cars coming from down the road.

At the corner, I saw the gas station. I darted across the pavement even though the sign warned not to cross and sped up to get to the ancient pay phone. I wondered how Mom would react to a collect call. This was exactly why I needed my own cell phone.

As I walked up to the gas station, tires squealed behind me and a horn blared. I jumped and turned, expecting to see the Land Rover. Instead, the front bumper of a red Jeep Wrangler was angled about six inches from my knees. Levi grinned at me from behind the window. He honked his horn loudly two more times before he stuck his head out the driver's side. The top was down and he wasn't alone.

"What are you doing here?" he asked.

I eased away from the bumper and walked around to him. Manny stuck his hand up from the backseat. At first, I thought he was going to high-five me or something, but instead he reached for the knob on the stereo. The bass thudded loudly. I couldn't understand any of the words, but Manny was shouting every lyric along with the rapper. Josh sat in the front seat bobbing his head. Iggy was tucked behind Levi's seat.

"Can I use your cell phone?" I shouted at Levi.

He tapped his steering wheel, *rat-a-tat-tat*. Then he pulled out his cell phone and dangled it in front of me.

"Who you callin'?" he yelled back at me.

"My mom."

"What?"

"My mom."

Manny shoved Josh. Levi rolled his eyes and handed the cell phone to me. I dialed the number. I held the phone up to my right ear and plugged my left ear to drown out the noise.

"What are you doing here, anyway?" Levi asked as the phone rang.

"I was at my dad's."

Levi's expression changed to serious.

"You saw your dad?" He reached over and shut the radio off.

"Levi, I like that song. What's wrong with you?" Manny said.

"Shut up," Levi said.

Three rings. Mom usually picked up by the third ring. She usually sat on the couch with the phone right next to her. Come on.

"Does your mom know?" he asked.

The answering machine picked up. I turned my back to Levi and took a few steps away from his Jeep.

"Hey, Mom. It's me. Everything's fine, I just left Dad's and I need a ride. Right now, I'm at—"

"I can give you a ride," Levi said.

"Hold on." I covered the phone and turned back to Levi.

"You serious?" I asked.

He nodded. I spoke back into the phone.

"Levi said he'd give me a ride. I'll see you soon."

I handed the phone back and hurried around to the passenger side. I waited for Josh to open the door, but he didn't.

"Climb," Josh said.

I got a foothold on the wheel and stepped into the backseat. Manny moved over.

"Thanks, Levi. Seriously."

He pulled up to the gas pump, put the Jeep in park, and turned off the ignition. He pulled a credit card out of his wallet and handed it back to me. I sat there holding it for a second before Levi reached in the backseat and shoved my shoulder.

"You gonna pump or what?" he asked.

"Oh, yeah. Okay."

Iggy covered his mouth and laughed. "Oh, man."

I climbed back out of the Jeep. When I'd finished pumping and paying for the gas, Levi pulled out onto the street and made a right.

"Shouldn't we be going the other way?" I asked.

Levi nodded. "If we were going straight to your house."

"He's going with us?" Josh asked.

Manny groaned.

"I told my mom—"

"It won't take twenty minutes."

We drove along in silence past the courthouse in the center of town, the Italian restaurant, and Llowell Chevy. The town gave way to the occasional group of trailers and run-down homes scattered among the open fields along the highway. It wasn't until we were about ten miles out of town that I realized where we were headed.

"That's it," Iggy said. "Up there on the left."

There were half-a-dozen old cars parked around the store at odd angles. One guy bent into the open hood of a rusty car, parked in the weeds in front of the station. Two other men leaned against the same car. The windows of the store were so grimy, I couldn't see inside. I searched for the name of the place, but there wasn't a sign. Just three old-fashioned gas pumps sitting side by side in the direct sunlight.

Levi and Josh sat up a little straighter as the Jeep pulled into the lot. There weren't any lines painted on the asphalt to show where to park, but I had a feeling Levi would have ignored them, anyway. He backed up to the left side of the building, closest to the highway. He pulled the parking brake up but left the motor running. Then Iggy turned to Manny.

"It's no big thing. They never check IDs. Just be cool."

Manny took a deep breath and hopped out of the back of the Jeep. The men in the parking lot didn't make any attempt to hide that they were looking at us.

Manny had black hair and tanned skin. He definitely looked older than the rest of us. He had facial hair.

Levi busied himself with the radio while Josh whistled something that sounded like "Zip-a-Dee-Doo-Dah." One of the men in the parking lot was yelling something in Spanish. I forced myself not to look and see if he was talking to us, but the voice kept getting louder, like he was approaching the Jeep. I heard another voice, closer to us, easy and calm. Manny was standing next to the Jeep, a big brown paper bag in his arms. He was talking to someone in the parking lot—in Spanish.

Manny smiled and hollered something else that made the man laugh, and then he handed Iggy the bag and hopped into the back of the Jeep.

He was still grinning, but Manny whispered, "Let's get out of here."

Levi lifted the brake and put the stick in gear. Then we were off, out of the parking lot and onto the highway again. Levi, Josh, and Manny hooted. Iggy shook his head at them, but he was smiling. Levi honked his horn over and over.

"Hold this," Iggy said and handed the bag to me.

The package in the bag felt cool and heavy against my thighs. It pinned me against the seat, weighted me down while I watched Josh pump his fist in the air and Manny stand up. I caught Levi's look of satisfaction in the mirror.

The radio got louder and I didn't know the song—something about being wet, and all I could think about was Jennifer's mouth and Dad's pool and my camera on the bottom.

Someone hollered that they didn't know Manny knew Spanish, and Manny said something about how we should hear his French, and I knew he lied to Mrs. Morales when he said he didn't know what she was saying.

He leaned forward between the two front seats, squishing me into the far corner so he could hear Josh's and Levi's praise.

"What was that guy yelling at us?"

"So did they give you any shit?"

"I knew it!"

"Next time I'm going in."

"Yeah, whistlin' Dixie."

The bag was heavy, so I lifted it off my lap and set it on the edge of the Jeep, and just then, Levi hit a bump and it slipped over the side. I was the only one who noticed the thud wasn't the booming bass of the radio.

CHAPTER EIGHTEEN

Manny was leaning against the wall waiting for me when I rounded the corner to go to my locker Monday morning. I slowed and kept my eyes straight in front of me. He walked toward me fast and got right up in my face.

"You owe me fifty dollars." He had black stubble on his chin.

"Fifty?"

"Yeah. Twenty-five for our purchase and another twenty-five to keep me from kicking your ass. By Wednesday."

He rammed my shoulder as he strode past me. Fifty dollars? I spotted Jennifer coming from the other end of the corridor. She fell in step beside me.

"What was that all about?"

"Nothing." I stopped at my locker and slung my book bag onto the floor. I carefully rested my poster for the introductory speech we each had to give in English class against the wall. The night before, I had taken several of my photos out of my frames and used double-sided tape to attach them to the poster. I couldn't afford to get new copies made from the negatives, particularly now that I had to come up with fifty dollars. I spun my lock to the right three times and stopped on twenty-two.

"Manny looked mad," Jennifer said.

"It's no big deal." I rotated it to the left.

"You sure?"

I paused. Had I turned once or twice to the left? "Great. You made me mess up."

"Sorry," she said. "I called you yesterday. Did your mom tell you?"

"I was at my Dad's."

"Oh."

I got my books out of my locker. Jennifer twirled her hair with her finger. It was back to blond again and the black sticky lipstick was gone.

"So did you get in trouble?" she asked.

"Why?" I opened my locker.

"For asking your mom to take me home. For coming in so late."

"No."

"Lucky you. Kayla told her mom I'd run off with some guy, like she didn't know your name or something, then her mom told my mom." Jennifer rolled her eyes. I noticed the neck of her brown shirt was cut low.

I pulled a book out of my locker and tucked a pen in it.

"I told my mom what all happened. That it was you. What Kayla and Levi said. She understood that part, but she said I should have called her instead of running off with you and making everyone worry. So I'm grounded for a week."

"That's not too bad."

"Are you kidding? A week. At least it isn't next week, since homecoming's coming up." Jennifer hugged her books against her chest and brushed her arm against mine. "Just so you know, it was worth it."

I closed my locker door and started down the hall toward my first-period class. Jennifer walked so close to me that my elbow kept nudging her upper arm.

"Have you talked to Levi?" she asked.

"Not much."

"I wouldn't have either after Friday."

I shrugged. Our arms bumped again.

"I talked to Kayla that night, you know, just to get my stuff and all. But I'm done with her. I'll be nice to her because that's just how I am, but she's not my friend."

"You left the dog collar in my mom's car."

Jennifer turned red. "Oh my God. I'm never going to your house again. Did your mom see it?"

"No."

We were almost to our English class. Jennifer tugged at my sleeve. I stopped and faced her.

"We need to get to class," I said. The bell was going to ring any second.

"I'm not in a hurry."

I tapped my poster against my leg. Jennifer reached up and tucked a piece of my hair behind my ear just as Garrett rounded the corner. His eyes met mine over Jennifer's head, and he rammed into a girl heading the opposite direction.

"Sorry," he said, bending over to help the girl pick up the papers that had spilled from her folder. As Garrett picked up the papers, he kept glancing at us. The girl grabbed the pages from him and continued down the hall. I stepped back from Jennifer. Her hand trailed from my face to my shoulder and down my arm.

"Get a room," Shelly said as she walked by.

Jennifer twirled away from me to chase Shelly into our English class. Garrett stood in the middle of the hallway with his arms hanging at his sides. He looked like someone had kicked him. I felt like I was going to throw up. I took a step toward him, but then the bell rang and Garrett sprinted down the hall.

❖

At lunch, Jennifer stood up and waved at me from across the cafeteria. She had saved me a spot at the drama table. Garrett was sitting across from her. I thought about pretending that I didn't see her waving, but then Manny pointed at me from the other side of the room and curled his fingers into a fist. I went through the line and sat down in the seat next to Jennifer.

"Asher's doing stage crew," she told the other people at the table as she leaned into me.

"When does that start up?" a girl asked.

"It's Wednesday, right?" Jennifer asked me.

I shrugged. I wasn't sure. I shoved a cold Tater Tot into my mouth.

"You can sit in on rehearsals. You should stay after," she said.

"I don't know. Maybe."

"My mom could give you a ride. You'll get to hear my solo." She looked across the table at Garrett. "Why weren't you in English?"

"Late," Garrett said.

"I thought I saw you this morning," someone else said.

Garrett took a bite of his cheeseburger.

"Did you guys hear the principal's house got TP'd Friday night?" someone said.

"No way. Who did it?" Jennifer asked.

Garrett grinned. "Emily might know something about that."

"Don't tell me she was involved."

He raised his eyebrows.

"I didn't think she ever did anything wrong."

"That's my sister. Full of surprises," he said.

"Well, who do we have here?" Iggy straddled the chair next to me, set his tray down, and slung an arm over my shoulder. "Hey, buddy. What's it been, twelve hours?"

I'd forgotten Iggy was in the play, too. I shrugged his arm off. I met Garrett's stare across the table.

"I really hope it was worth it, man," Iggy said. "Those boys want your ass."

"What're you talking about?" Jennifer asked.

I slid my tray away from me and stood up. Jennifer grabbed my hand, but I yanked it away and walked out of the lunchroom. I made my way down the long hall past the bathrooms and my locker to the side door. Someone had wedged a stick in it to keep it open. I poked my head outside. Kayla was wedged between the wooden benches, smoking a cigarette.

"Hey," I said.

She jumped and flicked her cigarette on the ground before she turned to look at me.

"Damn, Asher." She bent over to pick it back up. "That was my last one." She brushed off some dirt and took a long drag off it.

"What are you doing out here?" I asked.

I sat down on the bench near her.

Kayla held the cigarette between her fingers. She blew smoke out of her nostrils. "They check the bathrooms at lunch. What are you doing out here?"

I shrugged.

"Manny? I don't think he'll jump you during school," she said. "But you're probably safer in there than out here."

"I'm not scared."

"That's right." Kayla smiled. "Jesus boy."

"It's not that. I just don't care."

"That's good. That's honest." She squinted up at the clear sky. "You going to rehearsal?"

"I don't know. Maybe. Jennifer just asked me about it."

"She likes you a lot."

"Yeah, I don't know what that's all about."

Kayla laughed. "You like her?" she asked.

"She's nice."

Kayla grinned. "You don't like her."

"I didn't say that."

"Yes you did. Trust me." Kayla dropped her cigarette and stepped on it. "I don't blame you. She's fake."

"I don't think—"

"She walks around acting one way, and I know better. The worst thing a person can do is lie. I do not lie."

"I can't lie."

Kayla laughed. "Can't?"

"I'm not any good at it."

"Lies come in many shapes and sizes, Asher. A white lie is still a lie."

I didn't say anything. She didn't have a clue.

"That whole group she hangs with now—they think I'm a freak. Why? Because I tell the truth."

"She's hanging with the drama people."

"For now. You wait. When the show's over, it's right back to the preps."

"It's like my photos."

Kayla raised an eyebrow at me. A silver hoop was attached to it.

"I don't take pictures of people. They do that fake-smile thing," I said.

"You've never taken a picture of a person?"

"Not their faces."

Kayla's eyebrow arched. "Just parts?"

"I took one of my neighbor when he was burying their cat. It's from the neck down. And I took one of Travis's hands. At the funeral home." I looked out past the football field. "No one knows that."

"Wow. That's pretty morbid."

"He was always bugging me to take his picture."

"I had an abortion freshman year. No one knows that either." Kayla dug around in her black jacket.

"You serious?"

"You were there the night I got pregnant. Right outside the door."

I remembered knocking on the bedroom door, a joint in my hand, and Josh Llowell telling me to go away. What if I hadn't?

She ran her hand through her hair. "I wish I had another cigarette." She wore a silver ring with a black cross on it on her index finger. "My mom said a baby would ruin the best years of my life." Kayla tilted her head back and laughed. "Sometimes people don't even know when they're lying."

❖

Instead of having Mr. Stevens in biology, a fat man reading a newspaper sat at the desk. He glanced over the top of his newspaper at the clock as the classroom filled up. When the bell rang, the fat man sighed and folded his newspaper. He laid it on top of Mr. Stevens's neat desk, took a sip from a Styrofoam cup, and grunted as he hauled himself out of the chair. He limped over to the television cart, picked up a remote control, squinted at it, and pressed a button. When nothing happened, he pressed the button harder.

"You have to turn the television on," Megan said. A few chuckles circulated through the classroom.

He glanced over his shoulder but didn't say anything. Instead, he took two steps toward the cart and lifted his chin as he peered through the bottom half of his glasses at the television set. His index finger extended slowly toward the button. The sound of static filled the classroom. The man strained to see the buttons on the remote again and then found the volume control. He pressed it once. If he held it down, it would go faster. Or better yet, he could just hit the mute button. It was painful watching him. I waited until the sound grew faint enough for him to hear my voice.

"Sir?" I said.

He adjusted his glasses.

"Sir?" I said again.

He stopped and turned slowly toward the sound of my voice.

"Do you want me to do that?"

"No. No, hold on." He attempted to work the remote again.

I got out of my seat, walked over to him, and pressed the DVD button. Then I turned it to channel 3 and pressed play on the remote control he held in his hand. He held up a VHS tape. Seriously? I found the button to switch from DVD to VCR and slid in the tape. He nodded his head slowly at me and then returned to his coffee and newspaper. On the way back to my seat, I glanced at Garrett. He looked away.

"Are we supposed to takes notes or…?" someone asked.

"Shut up," Megan said.

Mr. Stevens's chair squeaked underneath the weight of our sub. Nothing was written on the board. He hadn't given us any instructions.

I shifted in my seat. The video was titled, *Entomology: Insects and Biology (Part 1)*. It was so faded from age that it looked almost black and white. A few groans rose up in the class. We weren't even studying insects. There was no way Mr. Stevens had assigned us to watch this. This guy had probably pulled the video off some dusty shelf in a storeroom.

"Can we turn the lights off?" Alex asked.

The sub ruffled the newspaper.

"Is that a no?" Alex asked. When he didn't get any response, Alex arranged his books on his desk, laid his head down, and closed his eyes. Two desks over, Shelly was doing math homework.

I only half listened to the old movie. The images on the screen of long-haired scientists reminded me of the old album of Mom and Dad from when they'd first gotten married. In the video, a woman wearing a long yellow skirt wandered through this grid on a field to track the movements of some insect. A guy drew lines on a chart based on where she pointed at the bug. Bubbles floated in the wind to show the direction the pheromones were blown, to determine if the scent attracted the insect. It did. There was no way they did it that way these days. The guy wasn't even plotting on a computer.

I'd never considered making movies. Somehow, all those frames put together in a video made it hard to appreciate any of it. Not that I'd be taking pictures of anything. Not with my Minolta sitting at the bottom of Dad's pool. Not that he cared.

When Levi had dropped me off at my house on Sunday an hour after I'd left the message for Mom, I thought for sure Dad's Land Rover would be in the driveway. I wouldn't have been surprised to see a cop car parked out front. But no one was home.

Mom didn't get home from the extra shift until after six. By that time, I had erased the lame message Dad had left on the answering machine asking me to call him as well as the message I'd left for Mom. She seemed to buy that I had come home early to work on my English presentation. When the phone rang later that night, I thought for sure it would either be Dad calling to tell Mom what had happened or Levi calling to let me know exactly how they were going to torture me. I braced myself for whoever it was, but Mom never came to my room after she got off the phone. She went right back to watching television.

"…pines are grown to make telephone poles."

I glanced back at the insect movie. A forest of perfectly straight pine trees filled the television screen. And then the picture switched to curved pine trees like the one at my dad's house. It was a whole forest of weaving pine trees. The camera focused again on a straight pine tree and then shifted to a twisted tree in the background.

"The culprit is the pine shoot moth." I sat upright in my seat. "The moth lays eggs in the tender, main shoot of trees. The larvae stay inside through the winter. This causes the pine tree to use a subsidiary shoot."

I leaned forward. First the video showed a wriggling wormlike creature. Then a fully grown pine shoot moth appeared. It looked like a plain brown butterfly from the middle down, but the texture was different on the upper half of the wing. I wished the video were in color.

"Farmers combat the problem of curved trees with female moth sex pheromones," the voice said. Scientists in labs mixed the chemicals. "The female pheromones attract and confuse male pine shoot moths and interrupt mating." The film showed a man spraying a foggy mist among the trees. "As a result, the moth population dwindles and the pine trees are unmolested."

So the culprit for the curved tree in Dad's yard was an insect called the pine shoot moth. On the television screen, the scientists celebrated their successful creation of a happy suburban street lined with straight telephone poles.

❖

I counted the telephone poles on my street as I hauled my book bag and poster home from the bus stop. There were nine telephone poles. Instead of forming a straight line from the ground to the sky, they leaned toward the west. They'd been like that since last summer's hurricane.

My head busied itself with the fifty bucks Manny insisted I owed him.

Even though it was late fall, Pearl's grass needed a trim. Ten dollars. A shiny Camry was parked in Pearl's driveway, but I walked up and knocked on her front door anyway. A man I didn't recognize opened it. His hair was gray and wispy. He wore a pair of jeans and a brown blazer with leather patches on the elbows. It was eighty degrees outside.

"May I help you?"

"I'm Asher. I live next door. I wanted to know if"—I had never called Pearl by her first name. I couldn't remember her last name— "if she wanted me to mow her lawn."

"Come on in." He held the door open for me. I'd never been inside Pearl's house.

"I'm Mitford, Pearl's brother," he said.

Mitford motioned for me to sit down on a pink couch. I leaned my poster board against the coffee table next to me.

"I think I met you a couple of years ago when my wife and I came for Christmas."

I didn't remember ever meeting him.

"I don't get to Florida as much as I'd like to." He took out a handkerchief and mopped his forehead. The television was tuned to a game show.

"Is Pearl okay?"

I heard her coming down the hall. "I found it. Who was at the door?" she asked as she rounded the corner. She stopped in the doorway. She was holding some papers.

"Just your neighbor." He took a gulp from a large glass of ice water.

Pearl frowned.

"I stopped by to ask about your lawn," I said.

She handed the papers to her brother. "I don't need my lawn mowed."

"Oh, the boy is just trying to be helpful."

"He charges fifteen dollars."

Mitford stood up, opened his wallet, and held a twenty out to me.

"Don't you give him twenty," Pearl said.

I looked from Pearl back to Mitford.

"You want change?" I asked. "I'll need to wait until my mom gets home."

"No, you keep it."

❖

My shoes were stained green from mowing Pearl's yard. I kicked them off just outside the garage door and went inside to get myself some Gatorade. The answering machine light flashed on the counter. I hit the play button.

"Just checking up on you guys—"

I skipped the message from Aunt Sharon.

"Hi, this is Alice from Harmon. Just another reminder that your pictures are—"

I skipped that message, too.

Fifty bucks for Manny by the day after tomorrow. At least another fifty for Harmon. I only had twenty dollars. I started down the hall to my room and stopped outside Travis's door. He never spent his money. He stashed it away somewhere in his room.

I opened his door and turned on the overhead light. I knelt down beside his bed and lifted his mattress. My eyes strained to see under his bed, so I went back to the kitchen and got a flashlight from the junk drawer. I shone the light under his bed. I checked under and around the box spring. I sat down on the bed for a moment and looked around the room. Where would he have put his money?

The closet door was partially open. I started at the top shelf with the board games and worked my way down. I went through the pockets in his clothes and dug inside his shoes. Once I got to the dresser, I started dumping things out on the floor: socks, underwear, pajamas, shorts, shirts. I took every book off the bookcase and flipped through its pages before tossing it onto the floor. It wasn't like Travis was going to use the money now. He was dead. So what difference did it make if I took it to keep Manny from smashing my face? And Harmon wouldn't be getting much business from me anyway. The photo of Travis's dead hands was gone. My nerves felt too close to the surface, as if my body was too full. When the last book on the shelf didn't contain money, I chucked it as hard as I could across the room at the blank white wall. It landed with a loud, gratifying thud. Granules of drywall sprinkled down to the floor, but the book stayed in the wall itself. It jutted out halfway, the other end buried inside the wall.

"Great."

I flopped down on Travis's bed, rested my head on his pillow, and closed my eyes. I could smell him—a combination of sweat and sweet, like sour cream. Rolling over on my side, the scent changed to something musty. When I opened my eyes, Og was looking back at me. I picked him up. I hadn't held Og since the week Travis died. Mom had talked about burying the dog with Travis. I couldn't remember why she'd decided against it.

I flipped him around. Mom had sewn his cover a bunch of times. She had to stop running him through the wash because the fabric was too thin. I looked at the different colored threads that held him together. Most of the stitches were neat and uniform, but the ones along his crotch were jagged and wide, and the threads had been tied in several places. I sat upright. Og's stuffing felt lumpy. I broke the thread with my fingers and dug around inside. Deep in the middle of Og I found a ten, two fives, and seven one-dollar bills.

❖

I was looking in Hector's cage when Mom got home from work. The bits of hamburger, bread, and corn I'd put in there the day before were untouched. The website I had read said hermit crabs could eat human food as long as it wasn't covered in sauces and didn't contain lots of preservatives.

"Asher?" Mom called from the front room.

If he hadn't wolfed down the leftover chicken last week, I'd think Hector was being picky. He hadn't moved around as much as he used to either. I sniffed the hamburger. It seemed okay, but I reached inside and picked it out of the cage anyway and threw it in the kitchen trash can.

Mom stood at the counter sorting through mail. I opened the refrigerator and got a head of lettuce out of the crisper.

"You left the garage door open," she said.

I ripped a leaf of lettuce off the head and stuck the rest back in the fridge. Maybe I'd post something about Hector on the hermit crab website and see if anyone could tell me what was going on. The phone rang. I went back into my room to put the lettuce in Hector's cage.

"I wouldn't have gone to the session at all if I'd known he was going to be there," she said to whoever was on the phone. She came into my room and tapped my arm to get my attention. She pointed to the phone and mouthed the word, "John." I nodded. Then she drifted out of my room and down the hall.

Hector's shell was in the same position he had been that morning when I'd left for school. I reached in the cage and picked him up. I looked inside the shell, but I couldn't see his legs. I thought about how spiders curled up into themselves when they died.

Great.

"Asher?" Mom called.

No wonder he wasn't eating.

"Asher!" Mom's voice had an edge of panic. I heard quick footsteps in the hall. Her voice broke. "John, I have to go." I heard the beep of the phone being turned off. Mom grabbed my arm. "Asher, what happened to Travis's room?"

I put the shell back in the cage.

She shook my arm and I yanked away.

"Don't," I said.

"His room is torn apart!"

"I know."

"What happened?"

"I was looking for something." I motioned toward the cage. "Hector's dead."

"Oh, Asher."

She started to cry and left my room. I heard a series of gentle thuds. She was putting the books back on the shelf.

"There's a hole in the wall," she called. "Asher, what were you thinking?"

I should bury him, I guess. I picked up the orange- and cream-colored shell, walked out of the bedroom and past Travis's open door. Mom was struggling to get the mattress straight on the box spring.

"A little help?" she asked.

"I'm busy."

"Where are you going?" she demanded. I ignored her.

The cement floor of the garage was cold against my bare feet. I could hear a cricket chirping somewhere near the lawn mower. I'd left the garage door open, but insects could get inside whether I closed it or not. I dug through the wooden handles leaning against Dad's workbench until I found the shovel.

It didn't take long to bury Hector. When I came back inside, Mom was sitting on the couch in the dark. She wasn't crying anymore. She was staring at the television set, but it wasn't on. I washed my hands in the bathroom. The pills the doctor had prescribed for her were sitting out on the counter. Mom said they were supposed to take the edge off. The container was still over half full. I dried my hands and picked up the clear orange bottle. I shook it. The pills rattled. Must be nice to take a pill and forget everything. I tossed it back on the counter before I started down the hall to my bedroom.

I paused at Travis's room. Mom had gotten the mattress straight and picked up all the books. The board games and clothes still covered the floor. I could have picked up the rest, but I didn't feel like it. Instead, I went to my room, closed the door, and took the money out of my pocket. I smoothed the bills out and sniffed one. It smelled like Og. I had the money. I should have felt relieved, but I didn't. I considered letting Manny beat me to a pulp. It wasn't like I didn't deserve it.

Chapter Nineteen

A sher, you're next," Ms. Hughes said.
        "Is it okay if I go tomorrow? I left my poster at home,"
I said.

It was a lie. I didn't know where I'd put my poster. I thought I'd brought it home, but I'd searched everywhere and couldn't find it. I'd checked my locker as soon as I'd gotten to school, and it wasn't there either.

"Two points deducted for not being prepared," she said as she marked in her grade book. "Garrett?"

He got out of his seat and walked to the front of the classroom. Ms. Hughes gathered some forms and headed to the back of the class.

"Whenever you're ready," she said.

"My name is Garrett Adams," he said. "I was born August 10th in Orlando, Florida. Some of you know my sister, Emily. She's a senior. We just moved here for my dad's job. He's a city engineer, and my mom's an artist. She's the one who got me into drawing." He walked back to his desk and picked up a thick leather folder. "This is what I've been working on lately." He held up a cartoon of a guy on a bike flying off this ramp into the sky. It looked like some of those Japanese cartoons with the really big eyes. "I'm into racing, too, but you guys don't have any decent tracks around here. Anyway, I'd like to be an illustrator one day. We'll see. There's a lot of stuff I want to do."

Everyone applauded.

"Garrett," Ms. Hughes said. "You didn't mention anything about singing or acting."

He shrugged. "That's cool, too."

"In case you don't know, Garrett has a lead in *Godspell* which opens next week. Only five dollars for students," Ms. Hughes said. "Any questions for Garrett?"

I heard Josh and Manny whispering, but no one raised their hand.

"Manny, you're next."

The whispering stopped. Garrett went back to his seat.

"Manny?"

"I haven't got it, miss."

"Excuse me?"

"I'll take a zero."

"Go on, man. It's no big deal," Josh said.

Manny shook his head. "I don't do speeches."

❖

"Could I get off at the next stop?" I asked my bus driver.

The Land Rover was parked right there at my corner. I thought for sure Dad would sit in the parking lot of the school long enough for me to get home. If Levi and I were talking, I could have hidden out at his house. Dad must have taken a gamble that I'd be on the bus. If he had pulled up in our driveway, I could have cut through a yard or two and waited for him to leave, but there was no way I could get off the bus without him noticing me. Unless, of course, the bus driver just dropped me off at the next stop.

She squinted at me.

"Why?" she asked.

I tried to think of a good lie, but nothing came to me.

"That's my dad. I don't want to see him."

"What did you do?" she asked.

I ran away because he made me take his picture—it even sounded stupid to me. The brakes screeched at my corner. My bus driver pulled the lever to open the door.

"Good luck," she said as I swung my book bag over my shoulder and walked off the bus.

I pretended I hadn't noticed the giant SUV parked across the road. Maybe he'd just go away.

"Asher?" Dad called.

I acted like I didn't hear him.

"Come on. Stop being like this."

I stopped, but I didn't turn to look at him. I stared down the street toward my house. Stop being like what?

"I had to hunt you down on Sunday, and now you've got me driving all over town today."

Had he gone looking for me?

I walked over to his car and tried to open the passenger door, but it was locked. Dad hit the unlock button on his side, and I climbed into the seat. The air conditioner was on full blast. I angled the vent away from me.

He put the car in drive. "We need to talk."

I waited, but then he didn't say anything else. He just squeezed the steering wheel a lot as he headed into town. So we were going to pick up Helen. Maybe the *we need to talk* included her. I didn't want to talk. I felt stupid for throwing my camera in the water.

I was not going to cry. No.

I saw my reflection in the glass of the window. I was glad I looked angry. I rubbed my eyes with a fist. Dad reached into the glove box and handed me a tissue.

"I'm fine," I said, letting the tissue hang there in his hand.

But then he rubbed it against his own face. Was he crying?

Yes, he was. Great.

I slumped down in the seat.

"Helen thinks I should just tell you," Dad said, "but I don't think you're ready for it, and I'm not sure I'm ready to talk to you about it." He crushed the tissue in his hand. Did he have some sort of disease? "But you have to trust me that there's more to what happened between me and your mother than what you probably hear from her."

Oh. That. I rested my foot on my knee.

"Helen thinks you're upset because of her," he said. "Are you?"

"No." I didn't see what the big deal was. I just didn't take pictures of people.

"She was worried sick the whole night. I told her you just needed some time to cool off." He gripped the steering wheel harder. "You should have called."

I wanted to ask him if he'd gotten my camera out of the pool. Instead, I said, "I didn't mean to worry anyone."

"Your choices affect other people, Asher. It's not all about you."

I noticed the bright yellow line running on the pavement outside the Land Rover. I wondered what it would feel like to open the door and roll out.

❖

When Helen got into the car, the conversation switched to whether I'd rather have chow mein or chop suey and how many egg rolls I could eat. The number for the Chinese restaurant was programmed into her iPhone. Then she told me about how she had gone to Hong Kong with some relative of hers when she was just a little older than I was.

"Helen's traveled all over the world," Dad said.

"No. Not all over. There are still a lot of places I'd like to see. We've been talking about maybe taking a family vacation this summer," Helen said. "Where would you like to go, Asher?"

"I don't know."

"Where have you been?" she asked.

It was hard to think, but I didn't want the conversation to switch to other topics. "Chicago. Disney World. We drove up to North Carolina once."

"I'm surprised you remember that. You were pretty young," Dad said.

"I was eight." I'd missed a field trip at school. We had just finished *Charlotte's Web*, and our teacher was going to take us to a farm that Friday. I couldn't go to the farm because we were going to North Carolina. Mom wanted us to see the seasons. I thought that meant we were going to see snow and bragged to Levi. Dad wanted to drive straight through to North Carolina, but Mom argued with him, and Travis cried, and I kept popping his pacifier back into his mouth and singing "Jingle Bells" to him, even though Christmas was still a month away.

"No, I'm pretty sure you were younger than that," Dad said.

When Travis had started coughing again, Dad finally agreed to stop at a hotel. Mom had packed the nebulizer. Dad watched a game on the television while Mom held the mask up to Travis's face and I made faces to make Travis happy.

"Travis was with us," I said. "I was eight."

"Oh, that's right. I guess you must have been."

Dad had wanted to go back home since Travis was sick, but Mom said we were so close that we had to go the rest of the way. The next morning, we drove over the North Carolina border, pulled off at the first exit, and turned around to go home. Mom had cried, but she didn't say anything. The leaves on the trees in North Carolina had looked a lot like the ones in South Carolina: red, yellow, orange. I liked the red ones best, but I had really hoped we would see snow.

When we pulled up to the Chinese restaurant, Dad went in to pick up our food and left me alone with Helen in the car.

"With your interest in photography, I think you'd love the Grand Canyon," Helen said.

I was glad she was sitting in the back so I didn't have to look at her.

"I'm sorry about the other day," she said.

I should have said I was sorry, too, but I didn't. We sat in awkward silence until Dad returned with the food.

When I walked into their house, the first thing I saw was my Minolta sitting on top of a phone book in the middle of the dining-room table. I wanted more than anything to pick it up, but I felt Dad and Helen watching me as they pulled the food out of the brown paper bags.

"I'll go get some plates," I said. I put my book bag on the kitchen counter and pulled three plates out of the cabinet.

"Would you get some serving spoons, too?" Helen called.

I grabbed a couple of spoons out of the drawer and brought them back to the table. Helen took the spoons and walked back into the kitchen. She reappeared a few moments later with larger spoons, napkins, and three glasses. Apparently only certain spoons could be used to dish out Chinese. Dad got a pitcher of water and filled our glasses as Helen and I sat down.

Dad shoveled his food into his mouth like a caveman. Helen looked like she was conducting an orchestra with her chopsticks. I moved my noodles around my plate and tried not to stare at the centerpiece, but it was hard to ignore my camera poking up between the white cardboard Chinese boxes. The edge of the phone book was facing me. A lined piece of notebook paper poked out of the book. A yellow No. 2 pencil rested next to my camera. The point was sharp.

"Is it ruined?" I finally asked.

They exchanged looks.

"My camera. Is it?"

"You were the one who took it down there," Dad said to Helen. "What did they say?"

Helen put her chopsticks down and wiped her mouth with her napkin.

"I took it to a repair shop. It can't be fixed. I checked into replacing it, too, but they don't make that model anymore. I even looked on eBay."

She pushed her chair back and walked out of the room. Dad stared at me from across the table, a sliver of a smile on his face. When Helen came back into the dining room, she had a shiny blue gift bag in her hand. Multicolored ribbons spilled over the top of it.

Dad said, "We were going to wait until after dinner, but…"

Helen handed me the bag and sat back down in her seat. She wasn't smiling smugly like Dad was. The big bag felt light in my lap.

I reached inside. All I felt was tissue paper. Then at the very bottom I felt a smooth surface and the edge of a small box. I pulled the box out and looked at the picture on the front. They had bought me a digital camera. Top of the line.

"Everything's digital now," Dad said.

He took the box away from me and started telling me about all the cool things it could do. He said they had looked into these digital photography classes for me, too. I should see some of the things photographers are doing these days on the computer. They had looked into some software for me to use. They were so excited. Mostly Dad.

I told them it was a really nice digital camera. None of my friends had anything as nice. It was going to take me a while to figure out all the features. It was really nice of them to get it for me. I told them all of that.

Dad joked about not letting me take his picture, no matter how much I wanted to. I managed to smile.

After dinner, I said I had to get some homework done. Helen washed dishes and Dad watched the news while I put my Minolta into the gift bag alongside the digital camera. I took the bag and my book bag into my bedroom. After I locked the door, I pulled my Minolta out. I slid the mechanism from *lock* to *on*, and for the first time there was no whir of the lens. The small screen on the top of the camera reflected only an empty grayish-green square. I opened the battery compartment at the bottom of the camera. A few droplets of water fell out onto my bedspread. Tiny dots of condensation covered the windows to the film and the viewfinder. My hand was ready to open the back, exposing the film, but then I stopped. It was empty.

I hurried out of my bedroom and into the family room where Helen and Dad sat on the sofa watching the news.

"Where's the film?" I asked.

The anchorman was talking about an alligator that had wandered up into some woman's yard.

"There's this place, Harmon Photo, that develops black-and-white film," Helen said. "They were one of the first places I called after you left. They said to put the camera in fresh water and bring it right in so they could try to salvage the film."

The news droned behind her. The school board was proposing some referendum, and local residents were rallying against a strip mall. My patience wore thin.

"Were they able to save it?" I asked.

"They said there was a fifty-fifty chance the film would be okay," she said. "I didn't want to say anything in case it didn't turn out, Asher. I'll call tomorrow and—"

"I'll call," I said. "I want to pick it up myself."

She glanced at Dad.

I didn't know how I was going to manage to get the money I needed to develop the film, but I'd figure something out. I calculated the number of lawns I could mow as the newscaster reported that Floridians could expect insurance hikes.

"What do they call the increases they've already made to our insurance?" Dad said. Had he even been listening to Helen?

"It's terrible," Helen said. "I don't know how people can afford to live here."

The next news story was about some political debate on gay marriage and civil unions. I got up and went to the bathroom. When I came out, Helen was talking to Dad.

"He worked at my elementary school," she said. "They were a nice couple. They even went to the Lutheran Church. But when he died, they discovered he wasn't a he."

Helen glanced at me when I sat down at the far end of the sofa. "My grandmother did the books at the funeral home," she explained to me. "She told me about this. Anyway, everyone had just assumed they were married all those years. So there they were, getting the body ready, and here's this she instead of a he and they're trying to figure out what to do about it. And you know what? They filled out the paperwork without batting an eye. His, well, *her* wife had stayed at home all those years, and if they had released that he was a she, the wife wouldn't have been entitled to a dime."

"Hmm," Dad said.

"That was over thirty years ago, when people were supposed to be so closed-minded. But you wouldn't see that happen these days. Today, the press would just have a field day. No one would think about what would happen to the woman left behind," she said.

I tried to picture a person like that at my school. Then I remembered Helen had said he had worked at her elementary school. "Was he a teacher?" I asked.

"No," she said. "Why?"

"I don't know," I said. There was a rumor that Ms. Hughes was a lesbian. She never talked about her life outside of school, but some kids said they saw her at the grocery store with her partner. They said they saw them holding hands, but I didn't believe it.

Helen's lips pressed together. "He was a janitor," she said. "He was a nice person."

"But he lied, right? He or she. He lied about who he was. I mean, were they even really married?"

"It's complicated," Helen said. "I think they both knew what the reaction in the community would have been."

"The Bible says it's wrong," I said.

"I'd think your Aunt Sharon—" Helen started, but Dad's hand darted out to her arm and she stopped.

"What about her?" I asked.

"Nothing, Ash," Dad said and stood up. "It's getting late. We really should get going. You have school tomorrow."

Helen sat on the couch staring blankly at the television, but her eyebrows were scrunched together and her fingers drummed her leg.

"I'll go get my stuff."

I stopped after I had rounded the corner to my room and listened. They were whispering.

"I'm so sorry," Helen said. "I thought—"

"It's okay." She started to say something else, but Dad cut her off again. "We'll talk later."

I gathered my book bag and cameras while Dad got the car keys. When I went back to the living room to say good-bye to Helen, she said, "We'll see you Sunday." She tried to act like nothing was wrong, and I realized she was just as bad at lying as I was.

❖

"So they think they can buy you?" Mom asked as she turned the digital camera over in her hands. The blue bag sat on our dining-room table, a pile of white and blue tissue paper next to it.

I shrugged and flipped the pages of my photography magazine.

"That's what they're doing." She held the camera up and squinted through the viewfinder. "Trying to buy you."

"It's easier to use the window."

Mom stared at the back of the camera. I reached over and flipped the side of the camera open.

"Oh. That's interesting." She pressed a few buttons as I picked up my magazine. "It isn't working."

"Try putting the battery in."

"I'm not going to compete with them," Mom said. "That's what's going on here. They think by buying you things that you'll like them more. A lot of fathers do that."

Mom put the camera on the table, took out the instruction booklet, and turned the pages. Then she dug in the box and took out the cord and battery.

I tried to find an article on real photography.

"Your father doesn't know a thing about being a parent," she said as she found the battery compartment. She opened it up and put the battery inside. "You break your camera, so he goes and buys you an even better one." She snapped the chamber closed and the camera buzzed. She panned the room. "Did you know you can make movies with this thing?"

"Huh."

Even though my eyes were on the page of my magazine, I could tell Mom was pointing the camera at me. My leg started bouncing under the table. I stared at a capital T that started the next paragraph in the article, but I wasn't reading. I could see her out of the corner of my eye. She held the camera out in front of her. Her index finger tapped the button on top of the camera.

"Your hair is getting long," she said.

Mom snapped the side panel closed and sighed. She held the camera in her lap for a few moments before putting it back in the box.

"Well, I guess we won't be making any more trips to Harmon," she said.

"I still have film there."

"No you don't."

"Yes, I do."

She poked me in the arm. "No. You. Don't."

I closed my magazine and looked at Mom. She smiled at me. "Go look in your room," she said.

I walked back to my bedroom. A plastic bag sat on my bed. Inside was a stack of unopened envelopes from Harmon Photo.

❖

I was brushing my teeth the next morning when the phone rang. I spit into the sink, wiped my mouth, and hurried to the kitchen.

"Hello."

"You left your poster at my house," Pearl said and hung up.

So that's where it was. I opened the drawer to the left of the sink and took out the double-sided tape. I went back to my bedroom and put it inside my book bag. Then I opened the envelope sitting on my dresser. The front picture was the one of Travis's hands. I tucked it into my Spanish book. The twenty I'd gotten for mowing Pearl's yard was sitting out on my dresser. The twenty-seven dollars I'd found inside Og was stashed in my sock drawer. I shoved the bills into my back pocket before I headed over to Pearl's house. Mitford's Camry wasn't in the driveway.

She opened the door before I could knock.

"Come inside."

I did.

She shut the door behind me and shuffled over to the sofa. My poster was sitting on the coffee table. The rubber band was missing.

"Sit down."

"I have to catch the bus."

"Sit."

I sat down in a wingback chair near the door. Pearl reached out and touched the edge of my poster. She lifted it slightly with her shaking hand.

"I used to know a thing or two about taking pictures," she said.

"You're a photographer?"

"Oh no. It was more of a hobby, but I had my moments."

"Oh."

"I know enough to tell you this is all pretty much crap," she said.

I froze.

"Excuse me?" I choked out.

"These photographs."

I didn't care if she was a pathetic old lady, I didn't have to take this. I stood up. "Okay. I've got to go."

"Oh, don't do that. Ask *why* it's crap. Don't just get yourself all worked up because you aren't a genius."

I started toward the door, but then I turned back. If she could tell the truth, then so could I.

"You know, no one asked what you think," I said.

"No one asked you to mow my yard. Sit your ass down."

I grabbed my poster off her coffee table. "You had no right to look at this."

"I didn't know what the hell it was. If you didn't want anyone looking at it, you shouldn't have left it here."

I headed for the door.

"Asher."

"It doesn't matter if they're crap or why they're crap. I won't be taking any more," I told her. "I broke my camera." I slammed the door behind me and headed toward the bus stop where Levi's Jeep Wrangler was parked, waiting for me.

CHAPTER TWENTY

{Photograph of folded hands}

Levi's window was cranked down. I could hear the rap music thudding. Yesterday I might have run home and hid out, but not today. I adjusted my rolled-up poster board under my arm and kept walking. Levi turned down the volume and leaned out the window as I got closer.

"Asher. Get in."

I circled around the Jeep. I ignored him, walked past the passenger door, and threw my book bag on the ground beside the street sign. I sat down in the dirt with my back to him. I didn't think Levi would try to run me over, but if he did, he'd at least dent his bumper against the metal pole. He turned off the ignition. All I heard was the *tick, tick, tick* of the engine cooling. Then the door opened and closed. I watched for the bus. Levi's brown leather boot stopped on top of an empty anthill a few feet in front of me.

"You like taking the bus?" he asked.

"It's a ride I can count on."

"Is that why you ditched the beer? Because you were pissed I didn't take you straight home?"

I ran my hand down the length of my poster. I'd lost the rubber band that kept it rolled up.

"I wanted to give you a chance to hang out with Josh and Manny. Why did you have to be such a prick about everything?"

I flicked a sand spur off my jeans.

"Did you get the money?" Levi asked.

I had the forty-seven dollars in my back pocket. Ransacking Travis's room left me feeling hollow. I considered giving the money to Levi.

"No." Technically, I was three dollars short.

"Shit." He stomped his foot. He rested his hands on top of his head and looked skyward. "What the hell's wrong with you? Manny wants to beat the shit out of you. I'm tempted to, myself."

"Go ahead."

"You're an asshole," he said, sauntering over to my left.

"Levi, I think we both know who the asshole is here."

I watched him lift his boot. It hovered above my poster.

"My photos are in there."

"So?"

"So don't touch it." I pushed his foot away.

He crushed my poster underneath his heel. I grabbed his leg and shoved him backward. He stumbled and landed on the ground. I jumped on him.

"Jesus, Asher."

My fists pounded, but he covered his face with one hand and grabbed at my arm with the other. His bottom lip puckered out and his eyes bugged. He caught my wrist and flung me off him. I scrambled up and landed with my elbow in his gut. I didn't see Levi pull his fist back. He grazed my chin hard enough to snap my neck to the side. He shoved me out of the way and darted toward my poster. I lunged forward and grabbed both his legs.

"Get off me," he said.

He twisted until he got one leg free. His boot caught me in the shoulder and knocked me on my side. My face pressed against the ground, but I still clutched his other leg.

"Let go," Levi said.

I bent his leg backward. I wanted to snap it. He twisted under me and I heard a crack.

"Shit!" he hollered.

The heel of Levi's other boot came up. He mashed it into my left cheek. I pressed back hard, but the edge of his heel was sharp and the boot cut into my skin. He eased up suddenly, then popped his boot back into my face.

I rolled over and looked up at the open sky. I touched my face and squinted to see if I was bleeding. I wasn't. I propped myself up.

Levi sat across from me holding my poster loosely in one hand. He stared at me with his head cocked to the side. Then he picked a sand spur off his jeans and flicked it. I saw the yellow flash of the school bus turn the corner. Levi glanced over his shoulder and stood up awkwardly. He tossed my poster onto the ground beside me.

"You sure you don't want a ride?" he offered.

I rubbed my shoulder and shook my head. Levi's boots clicked unevenly against the asphalt of the street. He limped over to his Jeep. I wiped at my face and tried to make my legs work.

He peeled off down the road just as the school bus pulled up beside me. I picked up my poster. A crease ran the length of it. The door of the bus squeaked open, and I walked up the steps.

"Is everything okay?" My bus driver stared after Levi's Jeep.

"Yeah."

"If Levi's giving you a hard time…"

"No, we're good."

She examined my face. "You've got dirt on your cheek."

I wiped it with my arm. "Thanks."

In the empty seat up front, I unrolled my poster. The photograph of the pine tree was slightly bent. The others were okay.

"Hey, Ash." Vince's chubby face peeked from around the seat behind me. "You okay?"

"Yeah. I'm fine."

I smoothed the surface of the tree photo with the bottom edge of my T-shirt and dug inside my book bag for the double-sided tape.

"What're you doing?"

"I've got a presentation in English."

I took my Spanish book out and flipped through the pages until I found the black-and-white photo of Travis's hands.

"What's that?"

"It's a picture."

"Whose hands are—"

"Why do you even take the bus? Can't you get a ride with Josh or something?"

I felt Vince looking at me as I carefully attached the tape to the back of the picture and pressed it against the poster. By the time I'd rolled the poster up again, Vince was debating with Taylor, another freshman, about why buses should have seat belts.

When we pulled up to school, I scanned the student lot for Levi's Jeep. It wasn't there. I waited until everyone else was out of the bus before I stepped into the aisle. I didn't follow the crowd to the courtyard entrance but went around to the side of the building where the door was usually propped open and walked to the bathroom at the end of the hall.

I laid my poster against the brick wall and looked closely in the mirror. My cheek was red and a little swollen. I rinsed my face and patted it dry with a paper towel. I lifted my sleeve to check out my arm. It wasn't that bad. A little bruised, but nothing compared to what Levi could have done with his work boots if he'd wanted to. The bathroom door opened. I yanked my sleeve down as George, the ancient custodian, wheeled his cart into the space. The bell rang. I heard the Pledge of Allegiance start over the school intercom.

"That's the late bell. Better hurry." He unscrewed a soap dispenser.

"Yeah, I'm going."

I grabbed my poster and walked down the hall to English class. Everyone was just sitting down as I opened the door.

"Do you have a late pass?" Ms. Hughes said.

"No."

She marked me up in her grade book as I got into my seat, then gathered some forms to take with her to the back of the classroom.

"I want to finish your speeches today. Any volunteers to get us started?" she asked.

I pressed my fingertips against my cheek while I waited to see if Josh would volunteer. He hadn't gone yet, either. I glanced around to see if he had raised his hand, and there was Ms. Hughes, looking right at me.

"Thank you, Asher," she said.

Great. I lifted my book bag to get my poster, and as I walked down the narrow row to the front of the class, I knocked a folder off Garrett's desk.

"Sorry," I said.

We both reached to pick it up and bumped heads. His hair smelled like coconut. Garrett put his folder back on his desk.

"It's okay," he said, but he looked away.

I tried to shrug it off and smile, but the edges of my mouth felt funny, like I'd just gotten injected with Novocain.

I held my poster against my body and maneuvered to the front of the class. I rocked back and forth while I waited for Ms. Hughes to tell me to start. Manny whispered something to Josh. Josh leaned forward in his desk.

"Hey, what happened to your face?"

"Josh," Ms. Hughes warned.

At first I thought he was calling me ugly, but then I remembered my cheek.

"Sleepwalking," I said. A lie.

"Again?" Josh said.

Everyone in the class laughed except Garrett and Ms. Hughes, and that was because they were new. I wondered if someone found out about me digging in Mr. Williams's planter, but the class reaction was more likely from the time my parents had freaked out and called the police when they woke up one morning and couldn't find me. I had been sleepwalking and ended up in our shed. By the time I woke up, it was ten o'clock in the morning. The whole town had gathered in my yard to search for me. I climbed out of the shed wearing only my underwear.

"You sure you didn't run into somebody's fist?" Josh said, nodding at Manny.

News spread fast at our school. I wondered who else Levi had told.

Ms. Hughes's eyes narrowed at Josh. Then she checked to see my reaction. I was pretty sure she was trying to decide if she should give him a detention. She didn't know yet that Josh didn't get detentions.

"Two points deducted, Josh."

He spun around to glare at Ms. Hughes, but she wasn't paying attention to him. Instead he turned to Manny and mouthed *bitch*.

Even though I hadn't said anything yet, Ms. Hughes was writing something down on the score sheet. She'd given us a copy last week when she introduced the assignment so we would know in advance what she wanted us to do. I started a mental checklist—name, date of birth—but then Ms. Hughes looked up at me and nodded.

"My name is Asher."

I unrolled my poster a little and wrapped it around me like a shield, the blank side facing the classroom.

"Last name?"

Even though she sat at the end of the room, Ms. Hughes's head poked out above my slouched classmates'. Her short hair looked wet, like a black helmet. I couldn't see her eyes because of the fluorescent glare on her glasses. I cleared my throat.

"Price," I said. My left leg started to shake. I put my full weight on it so it would stop trembling, but then my other leg started up. I wondered if everyone could see it. Ms. Hughes nodded again and smiled, her pen poised over the paper on the desk in front of her.

Okay. Birth date and place. "I was born February 12th. I'm from here. Florida." Family. "My mom is Margaret. She's in sales." That's what she told people when she didn't want them to know she was a telemarketer. Before Dad left, she was just a mom. "My dad's Steve. He sells insurance." I swallowed. "They're divorced. And I had a brother. Travis."

I could hear the clock ticking on the wall. A chair squeaked from somewhere in the room.

Now I was supposed to talk about my interests. I held my poster up to the chalkboard and moved the magnetic clips onto the four corners to hold it flat. I took a deep breath.

"I like taking pictures, so…"

I pointed to the first photo—a black-and-white picture of a Spanish-style stucco tower with a tall white cross reaching up into a gray sky.

"This is my church. Community Methodist. I took this last summer right after Bible study. It was getting ready to rain." I waited for somebody to crack a joke about going to church, but no one did. Last year, they would have.

I motioned toward the next picture—a black box with the white numbers *6440* peeling off the side.

"That's my neighbor's mailbox."

Josh slid down in his chair, yawned and closed his eyes.

"Uh…" A trickle of sweat ran down my armpit to my waistband. "These are some other pictures." I'd planned to tell them about the half-eaten pinecone and the cloud that looked exactly like my Aunt Sharon's profile—she had a big nose. Instead, I went to the one in the lower left-hand corner.

"That's a sign Levi found on the side of the road."

A couple people leaned forward at the mention of Levi since he had been the first freshman to bypass JV and make the varsity football team.

Josh squinted at this picture since he played football, too. "Is that a beer sign?"

"Josh," Ms. Hughes warned.

"Yeah," I said.

"Hey, that was my brother's."

It wasn't his brother's house anymore, but it had been when I took the picture.

Josh squinted at me. "What were you doing, going through my brother's stuff?"

"Josh."

I felt heat on my face and started to answer, "Actually, Levi—"

"I'm just saying." Josh leaned back in his seat.

I pointed to the photo I'd attached to the center of the poster.

"This one's my favorite. It was the first picture I took with my camera. See here, the trunk shoots up from the ground like most pine trees, and then here, it makes a hard left, then a right back toward the sky. I've never seen any tree like it. It's in the yard of the house my dad grew up in."

From the corner of my eye, I saw Garrett lean forward and raise his hand.

"Questions at the end," Ms. Hughes said.

He lowered his arm slowly, his eyes jumping from me to the poster and back again. Aside from the teacher, he was the only person in the room who seemed to take any of the speeches seriously. Ms. Hughes had said they would give us a chance to get to know each other. What she really meant was that *she* wanted to get to know us because most of us had known each other since before kindergarten and could easily have introduced every person in the class. That might have been a better assignment since only Garrett and Ms. Hughes were new. It was hard to take the speeches seriously; taking yourself too seriously could be a death sentence here. Like when Samantha said she liked sports, the class laughed because in middle school she had ripped Nate's shorts clean off during a flag-football game.

"Continue, Asher," Ms. Hughes said.

I had one picture left—two hands folded over each other. The image was grainy. The hands weren't even centered in the photograph.

"That's a picture of my brother's hands."

Jennifer's arms crossed in front of her tight like she was trying to keep herself from exploding. Garrett shook his head slowly from side to side. There was a sniff from somewhere. I hadn't been sure about bringing that one in, but I owed it to Travis. There. It was done. I cleared my throat.

That covered my interests, but I couldn't remember what was next. That was going to cost me a point.

"Future," Ms. Hughes said.

I had planned to tell the class that I was going into business. It seemed like a safe thing to say. Jennifer wanted to be an actress or cheerleader, Garrett wanted to be an illustrator, and one girl said she wanted to be a teacher, but I think she was just kissing up.

"Uh. I like photography. Maybe something like that." I hesitated a second. "And somebody told me I'd make a good pastor."

"Yeah, that's cool," Josh said.

"Josh, for once, why don't you shut up," I said.

A couple of people started to whisper. Garrett wasn't one of them. Jennifer turned around to glare at Josh. Ms. Hughes scribbled notes on the score sheet. I tugged on the bottom of my T-shirt. Finally, Ms. Hughes looked up and said, "Thank you, Asher."

Weak applause. No worse than anyone else. I took my poster off the board and started toward my seat.

"Oh, I'm sorry, Garrett," Ms. Hughes said. "You had a question?"

I stopped and took a few steps backward. I held my poster diagonally across my chest. Garrett pointed to it.

"What made the tree like that?" he asked.

It wasn't the first time he had seen the picture. He had asked the question before, standing in my bedroom, but I hadn't answered him then. This time I did.

"My dad said it's always been that way, but we saw this video in biology that said these bugs make it grow like that. I don't know."

I held the picture up so he could see it better. Garrett stared at the photo for what felt like a long time.

"It's a cool picture," he said. Then he ran his hand through his hair and looked down at his desk.

"Josh," Ms. Hughes said. "You're next."

He sauntered up to the front of the class.

"I am Josh Llowell. Born August 22nd at Davis Memorial Hospital like, let's see, just about everyone else here. My folks are Jim and Chrissy Llowell. You all know my older brother, Evan. Got an annoying little brother, Vince. I like muddin', fishin', huntin'… gettin' into this and that when the opportunity presents itself. When I grow up, I'm gonna be mayor. Or maybe just run Pop's dealership. Maybe both."

A couple people high-five'd Josh on his way back to his seat. His parents owned the Chevy place. Everyone in town had watched Evan, Josh, and Vince grow up in the TV commercials for Llowell Chevy.

"No visual?" Ms. Hughes asked.

"What?" Josh asked.

"A visual. You're supposed to have a visual."

"I brought me. Do I count?" he asked.

"Uh, no. You don't. Let's see. Rayanne isn't here, so we'll have to finish tomorrow," Ms. Hughes said. "If you look on the board, you'll see your journal topic for today. Let's take fifteen minutes to work on that." People started pulling out their journals. "Oh, and *Godspell* people, don't forget we've got our first tech rehearsal tonight."

I took my journal out of my book bag and placed it on my desk. I read the statement on the board: If the school board decided to make uniforms mandatory based on evidence that implementation at other schools resulted in a decrease in misbehavior and violence, would you support or oppose their decision? Why or why not?

I tapped my pencil. Uniforms would never fly here. I turned to check the time. Five minutes until the bell.

I slowly walked up to Ms. Hughes's desk.

"Ma'am?" I said.

She stopped sifting through the papers on her desk.

"I can't go tonight." I kept my voice low.

"What?"

I cleared my throat. "Tonight's practice. I can't be there."

"You've known about this for over a month."

"Yeah. I know."

She shook her head. "Well, I suppose we can fill in tonight, but—"

"Actually, I'm not going to do it at all."

She blinked at me. "Why not?"

I didn't say anything. The idea of staying in this place one minute more than necessary was too much to handle.

"Is there something else going on?" she asked. She glanced at my cheek.

It was a valid question, and I didn't have an answer. I stood in front of her desk and didn't look at her.

"Fine. Okay, Asher. We'll find someone else." Ms. Hughes took her glasses off and rubbed the bridge of her nose. "But I'm very disappointed."

I turned away and started for my desk.

"Oh, and you might as well take this."

Ms. Hughes held a piece of paper out to me. I stepped back to her desk and took it from her. It was the evaluation sheet with her written comments. At the upper right hand corner of the paper was a bright red A- and the words *Interesting presentation—well done! You might want to consider making a PowerPoint in the future, so the photos are easier to see.*

At the bottom of the page, in smaller letters, Ms. Hughes had written *I'm so sorry about your brother.*

Chapter Twenty-one

After English class, I stuffed my poster into my locker. I started to reach in for a book, but my locker slammed closed. Kayla grabbed my shoulder and spun me toward her.

"Is it true?"

"What?"

"Ms. Hughes told me you dropped out of tech."

I reached to open the door again, but Kayla stepped in between me and my locker. Give me a break.

"I was counting on you for lights."

"Move, Kayla," I said. "I need to get my stuff."

She leaned against my locker and got in my face. "You need to find a replacement, then."

"I'm not in the mood for this."

"Too damn bad."

I brushed past her and started down the hall. She jogged up to me and moved in close to peer at my cheek. I jerked my head to the side.

"Rumor has it you ran into Levi's fist."

"Since when did you start listening to rumors?" I asked.

"I talked to Vince on your bus. He told me he saw Levi at your stop."

"So what?"

"I thought you didn't lie."

"It's not like anyone really thinks I was sleepwalking anyway."

Kayla got up in front of me. "I don't care about them," she said. "Don't lie to *me*."

I stopped. "Okay. Just between us. Levi and I got in a fight. I started it. He finished it."

"His dad came and picked him up," Kayla said. "People are saying he busted his knee when he was kicking your ass."

I remembered the crack when I twisted his leg.

"I wanted to hurt him," I said.

Kayla shrugged. "Looks like you might have."

"He didn't want to hurt me."

"Of course he didn't. You're his best friend," she said. "So are you going to run the lights or not?"

❖

A saw screeched. When it stopped, I could hear the steady thud of a hammer. People were all over the auditorium—I caught a glimpse of Kayla's maroon hair poking out from behind a black platform. The antenna from her headset stuck straight into the air, and she reminded me of a cockroach scurrying around in the dark. Ms. Hughes held something black in her hands.

"Has anyone seen Jesus?" she called.

"He's getting makeup," someone said.

"Tell him he needs to get his microphone."

I slung my book bag into one of the back rows of the auditorium and walked down the aisle toward Ms. Hughes. She spun toward the stage.

"Who is going to paint the rest of those letters?"

Kayla stepped out from behind a curtain with a paint tray and a thin brush. "I'm on it."

"Get someone else to do it," Ms. Hughes said. "I need you on mics."

Kayla headed back behind the curtain. Ms. Hughes turned around and bumped right into me. I thought she would be happy to see me, but instead she rushed past me.

"Uh, Ms. Hughes," I said as I followed her up the steps of the stage.

"Five minutes," she yelled as she handed Kayla the small black box. "Actors, five minutes."

"Ms. Hughes."

She finally noticed me.

"I'm here for lights," I said.

"I thought you weren't coming," she said.

"I worked things out so I could be here."

"I got someone else for the light board," she said. "Kayla?"

"Yes?" I noticed Kayla standing to the left, attaching the small black box to Garrett's jeans. She fed the wire through his shirt to this tiny microphone that wrapped around his ear.

"Who's doing spotlights?"

"I got Manny. I was going to put Sarah on the other one."

"Put her with makeup," Ms. Hughes said. "Asher's going to do it."

Garrett glanced over at me. Kayla pressed a button on her headset.

"Mic one is ready for sound check. Okay." She turned to Garrett. "Go down center. They want to test the mic. Speak naturally."

I turned to ask Ms. Hughes how to run a spotlight, but she was gone. Kayla walked toward me.

"Follow me," she said as she rushed by me.

Kayla led me down the steps of the stage to the back of the theatre. She reached inside a cardboard box and handed me a script and a headset that looked like hers.

"Put this on. Don't talk on it unless something's on fire."

She headed up the stairs that led to the balcony. I had to jog to keep up with her.

"Wait, Manny is on the other spotlight?"

"Yeah." She didn't break stride. "The script has the light cues in it. Just read along. You're going to follow Garrett mostly, but when there's a scene with two actors close together on the stage, just make the beam bigger so it covers both of them. It looks better. Test it out a bit and you'll see what I mean. You know stage directions, don't you?"

"Uh…"

"It's all written like you're standing on the stage. So left is the actor's left, not your left. Downstage is the front of the stage, upstage is the back of the stage, center is center."

She stopped in front of a big metal spotlight.

"Got it?" she asked.

"Can I write on this?" I asked, holding up the script.

Kayla handed me a pencil that was tucked behind her ear.

"I'd recommend it," she said. "Good luck."

She turned and started walking away.

"Wait," I said. "How do I operate this thing?"

"Ask Manny."

I looked across the balcony. Manny sat in the last row on the other end beside another spotlight. I put the script and pencil down and tried to attach the headset to my jeans. Just then, Garrett's voice filled the auditorium.

"Testing one, two, three."

I walked over to the edge of the balcony. Garrett stood in the center of the stage wearing a red muscle shirt with the Superman emblem on the front. I had been ready to be nervous for him, but I didn't need to be. Sweat didn't shine on his face. His legs didn't shake and his voice didn't tremble when he spoke.

"Is that okay?" he asked. He shielded his eyes from the overhead lights and looked out into the audience.

I heard someone say, "It's good. Go ahead and sing something."

Garrett sang about saving all the people. His voice was like the choirboy CD my mom listened to at Christmastime. It was prettier than anyone I'd ever heard.

"He sounds like a girl," Manny said. I hadn't noticed him come up beside me.

The fall from the balcony could probably kill me, but I didn't care much, other than the fact that it would likely hurt a lot first. We stood there side by side until Garrett trailed off behind the curtain. I backed away from the edge of the balcony and attached the clip of the headset to my pocket.

"You know how to work this thing?" I asked Manny.

He walked toward me, snapping his fingers.

"It'll cost you, man."

"Never mind. I'll figure it out."

"You still owe me." He snapped again, pointed at me, and poked my chest.

I sighed and dug in my back pocket for a single bill. I managed to pull one out without dropping the wad of cash on the floor. The twenty from mowing the grass. I held it up to Manny.

"It's all I've got."

Manny took it from me. "What about the rest?"

I pointed to the bruise on my face.

"And the other five?" he said as he tucked the twenty in his front pocket.

"Come on, Manny, give me a break."

I put on the headset and moved over to the spotlight. There was a switch on the bottom and another two levers on each side. I moved the metal cylinder from side to side. It swiveled pretty easily. I pointed the light up high on a far wall and flipped the bottom switch. A large beam of light shone brightly. I tried the other levers, and the light changed from yellow to blue to red. Another knob changed the size of the beam. I turned the spotlight off and sat down in one of the seats close by and flipped through the script. Manny walked over to me.

"You done this spotlight thing before?" he asked.

"No," I said. "You?"

"No way. Extra credit for Ms. Hughes's class," he said. "She made me come in yesterday and spot the whole show. And that new kid, Garrett. Watch how he moves around on the stage. I swear that kid's a faggot."

CHAPTER TWENTY-TWO

{Photograph of man and woman smiling}

"It's a good show, isn't it?" Jennifer said.

"Yeah."

I was trying to get the image of Garrett crucified out of my mind as I dropped my headset into the cardboard box.

"Was that number seven?" Kayla asked, looking at the clipboard in her hand.

"I don't know."

She rolled her eyes and dug inside the box.

"Seven," Kayla said and marked down that I had returned it. "So you'll be here tomorrow, right?" She didn't seem to notice Jennifer standing right beside me.

"Sure," I said.

"See you then," Kayla said.

Jennifer grabbed my hand and pulled me out of the auditorium.

"She's being such a bitch. I said hi to her in the hall today, too, and she wouldn't even look at me." She was squeezing my hand, so I squirmed free and pretended like I needed both hands to pull my jeans up. "And, no offense," she said, "but why is she talking to you? I mean, you were the whole reason everyone got mad."

I shrugged. I could still hear Garrett singing in my head about dying, calling on God, hanging there on the lifeguard stand.

"My mom should be out front. We'll give you a ride."

As we stepped out of the school, I saw Garrett's Mongoose chained to the bike rack.

"I think I'm going to walk home," I said.

"What? Why?"

"Just feel like it."

Jennifer stared hard at me. "Okay, whatever." She flipped her hair. "Call me later. I mean, if you feel like it."

She turned and headed over to where her mom was parked, waiting for her. I walked down the sidewalk toward the road. I looked up as they drove past me, but Jennifer was staring straight ahead. Her mom was watching me, though. She wasn't smiling. Once they had disappeared from view, I slowed my pace and glanced back over my shoulder. A few cars still lined the pickup. Some upperclassmen trailed out to the student parking lot. When Garrett stepped out of the double doors, I started walking normally again. It didn't take him long to catch up to me on his bike.

"Hey," I said.

"Hey."

I thought he might pedal on, but he swung his leg over and glided to a stop a few yards ahead of me. He waited for me to catch up and guided his bike along beside him.

"How's it going up there with Manny?" he asked.

"We're straight," I said.

Straight. Good. Cool.

"So I've heard," Garrett said.

I checked his face to read his expression—he was smiling. The air felt warm against my face. Some kids played tag in the yard across the street. An older girl ran slowly, so a boy about seven could catch her. When she pretended to be upset that she got caught, the boy laughed.

"You've had some week," Garrett said.

"Yeah."

"Why did you get rid of the beer?" he asked.

So he'd heard.

"I didn't." I paused. "I didn't mean to. I had it up on the edge of the Jeep, and they hit a bump."

"So it was an accident?" Garrett laughed. "Why didn't you tell them?"

"You think they'd care?"

We turned off the main road to a shortcut through a neighborhood lined with oak trees. There was no sidewalk, so we walked along the right side of the street. Most of the homes were ranch-style stuccos in beiges and dark browns.

"Did you hear about Levi's leg?" Garrett said. "He's got a cast."

I thought about the games remaining in the football season.

"Great."

"Iggy told me you and Levi got in a fight this morning."

"Levi was waiting for me at my bus stop."

"That guy needs anger-management classes."

"I started it," I said.

"Seriously?"

I nodded. "I know. Hard to believe."

"You didn't strike me as the violent type."

"Like you said, it's been a rough week."

I heard a car approaching and moved farther to the right. We walked in silence until we turned down a side street.

"You can really sing," I said.

"Thanks."

"No, I mean *really*. I've never heard anyone sing like that before, except on CDs."

"We used to take lessons," Garrett said. "My mom's kind of into the arts and all, so Emily and I were always in classes. You should hear her sing."

I stared down at the asphalt as we walked. I cleared my throat.

"Manny said something at rehearsal. It may get around, so I'm telling you. He said you were, you know. Gay."

Garrett shrugged.

"If he said something to me about it, he's probably going to say stuff to other people," I said.

"It's no secret," Garrett said.

"I just thought you'd want to know. So you could be ready for it."

"And what? Find a girlfriend like Jennifer?"

I could feel him looking at me.

"Look, about Jennifer…"

"You don't have to explain. I shouldn't have said that," he said. "I mean, you like her. Trust me, I get it. It's my problem."

I sighed. "Garrett, I don't know how I feel about anything anymore."

Evan Llowell's old house was up ahead. Garrett's family had added plants and mulch to the yard.

"Come in for a minute," he said.

We crossed through his green yard. Thick curtains covered the front glass window. Garrett punched in a code on the outside of the garage door and it opened. Hammers, wrenches, and saws hung neatly above a clean workbench. A red riding lawn mower was parked to the right. Emily's blue Civic was to the left. Garrett lifted his bike onto a hook on the wall next to three other bicycles. He opened a door that led into the kitchen, dumped his backpack on the counter, and nodded for me to do the same. He reached into the fridge to pull out a bottle of Gatorade.

"How was practice?" I heard Emily call.

"Okay," Garrett said as he handed the drink to me. "Asher's here."

Emily poked her head into the kitchen. Her hair was tied in a low ponytail. She wore gray shorts and a red shirt that looked like it probably belonged to Garrett.

"Hey." She looked at me and then smiled at her brother.

Something about the exchange made me realize Emily knew her brother was gay. I gulped down some Gatorade. Garrett yanked it from my hand and took a swig. He gave it back to me. I stared down at the opening.

"How's it going?" she asked.

"Good," I said.

"Where's Mom?" Garrett asked.

"Office."

"Come on," he said.

I started to walk out of the kitchen with the Gatorade in my hand. Garrett took the bottle from me and put it on the counter.

"Mom freaks if we spill stuff."

In the dining room, a rectangular oak table took up most of the space. It was hard to believe a bunch of guys had once played drinking games in the same room. On the opposite wall, a painting hung of two kids building a sand castle, the waves reaching up to the moat. I stopped to look at it.

"She painted that when we were little," Garrett said.

Their backs were toward the artist. An Emily close to Travis's age knelt down beside a pudgy Garrett.

"Your mom is really talented," I said.

"Yeah."

I wanted to look at it longer, but I followed Garrett into the living room. They hadn't put their television on the wall across from the window. Instead, they'd hung a flat-screen TV on the far wall, above a low bookshelf. Images from MTV flashed silently across the screen. Emily stretched out on the pale-yellow leather sofa under the large window but didn't turn up the volume. The room had been painted a rich red. Two black wingback chairs stood in the far corner of the room. A small antique-looking table was wedged in between them. Any evidence of Evan Llowell was gone.

Garrett walked past the sofa and down the hall. I thought he was leading me to his bedroom, but instead, he knocked on the door. The same door I'd knocked on the night of the party.

"Yes?" a voice called from inside the room.

The door squeaked as he opened it. The light from the room spilled out into the hallway. I'd seen Garrett's mom at church, but never this close. She sat at a purple desk with a large pad of paper spread out in front of her. Round dark lines marked the page. I couldn't tell what she was drawing. Her hair was twisted and clipped awkwardly on top of her head. Her face was dotted with freckles. Her thick glasses magnified her pale blue eyes, which crinkled at the corners when she saw me.

"Asher, isn't it?"

She didn't stand up or extend a hand. She didn't even put her pencil down. The room was stark white aside from the colorful canvases and supplies. No curtains covered the wide windows. The sunlight was fading. I realized I hadn't told my mom I was going to rehearsal.

"Are you staying for dinner?" she asked.

"I can't. Thanks though."

"Some other time, then," she said. "Garrett's told us a lot about you."

"We'll let you get back to work," he said.

"So good of you to stop by."

Garrett closed the door and headed toward the living room.

"Call your mom," he said. "See if you can stay."

"I can't."

"Emily, what are we having?" he asked.

"I didn't get anything out."

"It's your turn."

She groaned, turned off the television, and rolled off the sofa. We followed her into the kitchen. She opened the freezer door.

"How about chicken?"

"You like chicken?" he asked me.

"I've got to go home." I got my book bag off the counter.

"Call her."

I shook my head. "I'm sort of in huge trouble at home."

"At least come see my room."

His walls were covered with colorful illustrations of wide-eyed kids with spiky hair on skateboards and bikes. The drawings were attached by pushpins to a strip of corkboard that went all the way around the room.

"This is cool," I said.

"Thanks. I've only been really into it the last two years or so."

"Did you do all of these?"

He nodded.

I walked around his room taking in the images. I noticed one character that seemed to emerge over and over again—a happy guy with big brown eyes and wild hair. I grinned in recognition and pointed to Garrett.

"That's you," I said. "Self-portrait."

"Yeah. Kind of obvious, huh?"

Then I noticed one that looked like two guys about to kiss, their eyes wide open.

"Don't you worry about hanging these up?" I asked.

"What do you mean?" He sat down on his bed.

I motioned toward the kissing one. He shrugged.

"They know I'm gay," he said.

"Who? Your parents?"

"They knew before I did."

"Your dad?" I asked.

"Yeah."

I stared at the drawing of the two guys. The one character looked like Garrett. The other one had gray eyes. Like mine. Bare chests, a tiled background. I felt Garrett watching me.

"Garrett," I whispered.

"Yeah, that's you," he said. "I hope it's okay."

The illustration had managed to capture an...innocence. I had tried to bury that moment, but there it was. And Garrett had gotten it right. It wasn't—

"Seriously, don't worry. I was actually going to take it down since I'm sort of seeing someone," he said.

Seeing someone? My stomach clenched.

"What? Who?"

Garrett did this impish grin. "It's still pretty new, so I'm keeping it sort of quiet until I see how things work out, but you know Iggy, right?"

Iggy? Scrawny, druggy, rock-band Iggy? No.

"You do know he does drugs, right?" I said.

"Actually, he's been clean for two months."

Of course they'd been hanging out at drama club—I'd seen them—but not in a relationship. Not like that.

"I don't think I've ever met anyone who plays the guitar better. Did you know he writes his own stuff? Anyway, we've been hanging out a lot. I like him. We'll see how it goes."

I thought about Iggy's long, stringy hair. Imagining Iggy and Garrett kissing just about made me sick.

"You can't date him, Garrett," I said.

"Why not?"

Because I couldn't stand the idea of Garrett with him.

But I didn't have the right to say that.

It had never even occurred to me that Garrett would date someone. "Look, you can do what you want behind closed doors and all, but people will annihilate you if you go public."

"Wow," Garrett said. "Well, I guess that would be our problem, not yours."

"Wait. That came out wrong."

"I was out at my old high school," he said. "My problem with this school isn't homophobia. Being gay isn't a big deal. Being inauthentic is."

I stared at the illustration on the wall. He was going to take it down and put it away.

"Do you want it?" Garrett asked me.

It killed me that he didn't want it for himself, but I tried to figure out where I could possibly put it. I'd have to hide it in my drawer or something. Something else to hide.

"No."

My eyes stung, so I blinked and said, "I've got to go."

Garrett stood up and led me down the hall, through the living room, to the front door. I heard something sizzling in the kitchen. I thought about saying 'bye to Emily, but I just wanted to leave. I opened the door and glanced up and down the sidewalk.

"I'm glad we got a chance to talk," he said as he stood in the doorway.

"Right." I stepped out into the empty street.

❖

I walked past Levi's house and cut through his neighbor's backyard to my street. I saw Mom's car parked in our driveway.

Pearl looked out the front window at me, so I picked up the pace. I pretended like I hadn't seen her, but she opened her front door.

"Asher!" Pearl called.

I jogged up my driveway.

"Get over here."

She hobbled down the steps.

"Don't you make me chase you."

I stopped. The idea of Pearl chasing me just made me sad.

"Get over here. I want to show you something."

"I'm late," I said. The front door of my house opened.

Mom stepped out, her hand on her hip. "Asher," Mom said. "Where've you been?"

"School. I forgot to tell you I had rehearsal."

"Rehearsal? For what?"

"*Godspell*. I'm doing lights."

"Until seven at night?" she asked.

Pearl harrumphed. Mom noticed her hobbling over to our driveway.

"I need to talk to that boy of yours," she said, pointing her bony finger at me. "I've been watching for him since three thirty this afternoon."

Mom crossed her arms and glared at me. Great.

"What did you do?" she asked.

"Nothing," I said. I turned to Pearl. "Will you tell her? I haven't done anything."

The expression on Pearl's face brought me absolutely zero comfort. She huffed. "Well, he didn't egg my house again."

Like it would kill her to show a little kindness.

"Go," Mom said. "But I want you home in ten minutes."

I took a deep breath and followed Pearl inside her house. A big box sat in the middle of her living room. I wondered how she'd managed to drag it from wherever she'd kept it. It looked heavy. A big black file folder sat in the center of her coffee table. She nudged it toward me.

"It's a portfolio."

"So?"

"A portfolio. My work." She picked it up and tossed it at me. "Look at it."

My jaw tightened. I didn't want to look at her portfolio. I didn't even care if Pearl once worked for *National Geographic*, but I picked it up off my lap and flipped it open. Black-and-white photographs of people. On the first page, there was a picture of a woman trying to comfort a crying baby. The woman looked like she was about to cry herself, and she was oblivious to the photographer. Her face said, *I'm so embarrassed.* I could practically hear her saying it.

"I started out with landscapes," Pearl said. "You know, when you take a picture of a mountain…"

"I know…it never comes back complaining about what it looked like."

She stared at me for a long moment. "You making fun of me?"

"You said it to me once before, is all," I said. "I just remember."

"Don't play games with me, you hear?"

"You're the one playing games," I said. "My mom's going to be ticked at me. I didn't even do anything."

"You've got some nerve."

"Me?" I stood up and tossed her portfolio onto the coffee table. "You looked at my photos. No one asked you to, but you did, and then you tell me I suck?"

She stood up, too. "I know what I'm talking about."

I flung my hands up at her. "You don't know anything about me."

"Do you think I'd waste my time on a little shit like you if I didn't think you had some potential?" I stopped. "Now sit your ass down."

I sank back down into the chair.

"Pick up my portfolio."

I bent over and scooped it off the table. Pearl grimaced as she lowered herself back onto the sofa. I considered helping her, but she'd probably hit me.

"Now where were we?"

"Mountains," I said.

"Landscapes." She took a deep breath. "Right, landscapes. That's all I did for a long time, but then I took a couple of psychology classes." She tapped her temple. "I started doing things like this." She pointed to the one of the woman with the baby. "You see this kind of thing everywhere, now. I did it first."

"Well, every time I pull a camera out, people start acting like idiots," I said.

"That's because you're a teenager. Everyone around you is an idiot. You're the biggest idiot of all. The key is to take pictures when they don't realize you're doing it. When people are most real." Pearl leaned over and turned a few pages. "Here's one that might interest you."

It was a picture of Levi and me racing so fast we're blurred. I'm wearing a baseball cap. A bat sits in the yard. We must have been about six or seven. Across the yard from us, in the background, my mom is standing next to Levi's dad. One of Mom's hands is covering her mouth. The other one is resting on Levi's dad's upper arm. He's grinning. They don't even notice Pearl is taking the picture.

"I remember this."

"It's a crappy photo. The composition is off. See here, how you aren't centered? And the lighting...terrible."

"I remember Levi's dad coming over."

"He used to. That summer."

I looked at the photograph for a long time. Levi's dad coached us when my dad gave it up. I remembered now.

"If it's not any good, why did you keep the photograph?"

"Look at you, Asher. The way your body is moving. And see here. Your mom's expression. She's so proud of you." She smiled at me and turned the page. "Now this is an interesting one. Look here. The composition is good." Pearl rubbed her hands together and struggled to stand up. "I'll be right back."

I turned the page back to the one of Levi and me and leaned in closer. Mom is happy. She's leaning into Levi's dad. I slid the photograph out. I heard a crash from the other room. I started to stand, but then I heard Pearl say, "I'm okay." I tucked the picture into my book bag and closed the book. A few moments later, Pearl rounded the corner from the hallway carrying a camera.

"It's a Canon A-1. It's both an automatic and a manual, so you can learn on it."

She put it down on the coffee table in front of me.

"Uh…"

"If you break this one, I'll hunt you down and kill you."

Even though I'd just stolen her photo, I said, "I can't take your camera."

"I'm not asking you to take it. I'm not giving it to you. You're using it to learn."

She reached into her robe pocket and pulled out a yellowed booklet.

"I expect you to know the parts of this by the next time I see you." Pearl tossed the pamphlet down next to the camera.

"I can't borrow your camera," I said.

"It's not my nice one. I wouldn't give you my *nice* one." Pearl sighed. "If you don't take it, I'm not going to let you come over anymore. And then all your pictures will stay crap."

❖

The phone was ringing when I opened the front door.

"Hello?" Mom said. She marched into the front room to stand directly in front of me. "No, Jennifer, I'm sorry but Asher's not allowed to talk right now. He's grounded."

I walked around her and headed to my bedroom. She followed me down the hall.

"I'll tell him you called."

I put my book bag down on the floor next to my computer and faced her. Mom held the phone in her right hand. She turned it off and dangled it in front of me.

"No more calls for a week."

I blinked at her.

"No more computer either." She stared hard at my face and then leaned in close. She lifted her hand. I took a step back. "What happened to your face?"

I'd forgotten about the fight with Levi.

"Nothing."

"How did you get that bruise?"

I put the camera Pearl had given me on the center of my bed and took out the instruction manual.

"And where did you get that camera?" Mom asked.

"It's Pearl's."

She snatched it up off my bed with her left hand. My instinct was to yank it away from her, but I didn't want to risk breaking it.

"You already have a camera," she said.

"That one's digital."

"Does Pearl know you have this?"

Now she was accusing me of stealing. Unbelievable. I ignored her and flipped through the manual. Mom tucked the phone under her arm and grabbed the pamphlet away from me.

"Does she know you have this camera?" Mom pronounced every consonant, like I was slow.

My lip curled. "You think I stole it?"

"I don't know what to think anymore."

I leaned back on my bed and looked up at the ceiling. I noticed a thin crack from the edge of the wall to just above my head. It looked like a lightning strike.

"Fine," she said. "Then I'll take the camera, too."

I bolted upright. "Why?" I demanded.

"You come home after dark all bruised up, no phone call or anything, and you don't know why you're grounded?" she said.

"I told you I was helping out at school!"

"And I'm supposed to believe you? You tore your brother's room apart. You egged Pearl's house." She held the telephone up. "And God only knows what you're doing with that girl. I found a dog collar in the glove box."

"It was part of her costume."

"Nice. Is she in this play, too?"

"Give me the camera."

"Not until you start telling me the truth."

"Give me the camera."

"Is she in the play?"

"Yeah. So what?"

"I called. Play rehearsal ended at five thirty," she said. "Where've you been? Were you with her?"

I wanted to sling my book bag at her. I wanted to smash the monitor. I wanted to rip my secondhand bedspread to shreds.

"You're out of the play. I want you home right after school tomorrow."

"Give me the camera." I kept my voice even and low.

"You can have it back after you put Travis's room back together," she said. "We'll start with that."

My hands shook. I tried to steady my breathing. Finally I stood up.

"It's just the closet, really," she said. "We need to get some stuff to fix the wall."

She moved out of the pathway to Travis's room to let me pass, but instead I walked over to my dresser and dug out my empty picture frame, the one that used to hold the Bible passage. I pulled the grainy pictures from the Harmon photo envelope. I flipped through them until I came across the one of Dad and Helen by the pool. I removed the back of the picture frame, slid the smiling photo of my dad and stepmom in, and set it on top of my dresser in front of Hector's cage, facing Mom.

I picked up my photography magazine and stretched out on the bed. When I looked up again a few minutes later, Mom had left the room, but the Canon A-1 and its instruction booklet were sitting on the edge of my bed.

CHAPTER TWENTY-THREE

{Old photograph of boys playing}

I watched the football coach jog across the field to the storage shed as my bus pulled up to the school. I wondered how much grief the coach would give the team with Levi injured and Manny ineligible.

Coaches. I thought about that year Levi's dad coached us. I'd wanted to quit after the first practice, but Mom refused to let me. I cringed every time the ball came toward me, but Mom made up for it by organizing pizza parties after the games. She got the team together to go to the movies and out for ice cream. She sat with Levi's dad and asked him about the orange grove business. I thought she was thinking of me.

My bag felt heavy with Pearl's camera inside, but there was no way I was going to leave it at home where Mom could get it. I walked past the courtyard of the school. Then I saw the *Godspell* poster. They had been hung all over the school earlier in the week. Each letter in *Godspell* was a different color of the rainbow, starting with red. The word God was crossed out and GAY was written above it.

"Jerks." Jennifer reached up and ripped the poster off the wall. She studied it for a moment before tearing it in two pieces and tossing them in the trash.

"I really hoped people would be more mature about this."

"About what?"

"Garrett. I mean, so what if he's gay?"

I stared at the top button of her shirt. A loose thread dangled from the murky white button.

"People in this school are racist," she said.

Racist? We continued down the hall.

"Did your mom tell you I called?" she said.

"She found the dog collar," I said.

Jennifer covered her mouth.

"Are you serious?"

"Yeah."

"I need it back. Kayla wants it."

"It was in the car."

"Is that why you're grounded?" When I didn't answer, she closed her eyes and tilted her head back. "Ugh!"

"She's making me quit the play, too," I said.

Her head snapped forward. "Because of me?"

I got my books out of my locker.

"She knows that we were in her car," I said. I closed the metal door and spun the lock.

"That's the stupidest thing I ever heard," Jennifer said. "We didn't do anything. Not really."

I focused on the brick wall across the hall.

"Speaking of that night," I said. "You know, I've been thinking about it and I just think it might be better if we, you know, just…"

"Just what?" Jennifer asked.

"Well, that night. You know, I really liked spending time…with you…but…"

Jennifer's eyes narrowed. "Asher, you're an idiot."

"What?"

"We're friends. I don't think either one of us was really feeling it that night," she said. "No offense, but it was kind of like kissing my brother."

"Oh. Right."

The bell rang.

"Anyway, I've sort of been talking to Levi, lately," she said.

Levi?

She scrunched up her nose at me. "I know, right? I actually called him about you, and we just started talking. He comes off as such a jerk, but when you talk to him one-on-one, he's kind of sweet."

Sweet. Not a description I'd have used for Levi. I imagined his fist pump if I told him Jennifer described him as kind of sweet. She was delusional.

❖

At the end of the day, I spotted another poster outside the library. A Jesus wearing clown makeup grinned in the center. Someone had drawn a penis in Jesus's mouth. The words *I like dick* were written above the clown's head in black marker. A couple of freshmen were pointing at it and laughing. Without slowing my step, I ripped the poster off the wall and kept walking. I was just rounding the corner to the bus loop when I passed Kayla carrying a heavy box.

"Hey, Ash," she said. "Help me with this."

"Can't right now." I continued past her, the crumpled poster still in my hand.

Her forehead creased. "Aren't you coming to rehearsal?"

I spun toward her but kept walking backward. "Got to go home. My mom." I put on a worried face, like something had happened, no time to waste talking. "Talk to Jennifer. She knows."

Kayla ditched the box and came running up to me. I took a deep breath and kept moving.

"What's going on?"

The last thing I needed right now was the wrath of Kayla. I glanced toward the buses to avoid meeting her eyes. She touched my shoulder gently, and it was so unexpectedly nice I could barely stand it.

"Hey." She said it so soft and worried that I wanted to curl up and cover my ears. "Are you okay?"

I switched directions on her, paced back and forth. People moved around me to get to their buses and cars. My hands tightened around the poster.

"What's this?" She tried to take it out of my hands, but I jerked away. "Okay. All right, Asher. Come on, let's get somewhere private."

I didn't want to go, but I let Kayla pull me by the arm off the sidewalk to the back of the school where I'd caught her smoking. She leaned me against the wall.

"I need to catch my bus," I said.

She took the poster out of my hands and smoothed it out. I stared off into the distance while she looked at it.

"Not bad," she said.

"What?"

"Someone has a future as an artist," she said. "Well, just look at the detail on the balls there."

I didn't crack a smile.

"What if Garrett saw that," I said, flicking the poster.

She shrugged. "He's a big boy. He can handle it."

Kayla was right. Garrett could handle it. Oh God, I didn't want to cry. Kayla just stood there.

I managed to choke out, "You've got rehearsal."

"I've got time."

I opened my mouth to say something about being grounded and missing rehearsal, but nothing came out. Those were reasons people could understand. The rest, the truth, proved too confusing for me to begin to discuss. I blinked, pressed my lips together, blinked again. Kayla got right in front of me—too close to lie to. My chest filled up with something heavy and I covered my face.

"Jesus, Asher," she said.

She dropped the poster, hooked an arm around me, cupped my head in her other hand and guided me to her shoulder where I tried to steady my breathing. I closed my eyes tight.

"Okay," she said, stroking my hair. "It's okay."

I took deep breaths to try and pull myself together. She smelled like Ivory soap. She patted the back of my head like you might a dog you liked a lot. I pulled back and looked down at her. Kayla wiped at her eyes with her sleeve.

"Damn. We're both a mess," she said.

I sucked in a deep breath and exhaled slowly. She wiped my face with her sleeve, too.

"There. You're all better."

I was pretty sure it was the first time anyone ever comforted me without asking me to explain what was wrong.

"Shut up," she said even though I hadn't said anything. "You're going to miss your bus."

❖

Our back screen door poked out of the back of the car. Mom was stretching bungee cords in a crisscross to keep the trunk from popping open as I walked up the driveway.

"Get in. We're going to the hardware store."

I opened the car door, slid into the passenger seat, and set my book bag on the floor in front of me. Mom latched her seat belt. I leaned forward and opened the glove box. I shoved the maps out of the way.

"Where's the collar?" I asked.

"I have it."

"It's Kayla's."

"Have her mom come pick it up."

I glared out the window.

"Put your seat belt on," she said.

I pulled the belt across me and latched it. Mom eased out of the driveway. I stared at our neighbor's yards. Kristen and Michelle rode past on bicycles. They waved. Mom waved back.

"That camera Pearl gave you," Mom said. "If you break it, you'll have to replace it."

I stared out the window at the cars lined up at the bank. The digital clock read 3:45. They would be into the first act by now. I wondered who was working the spotlight.

"You're the only person I know who could break a camera and get two new ones," she said. "You need to tell Aunt Sharon you broke the one she gave you."

At least Kayla and Jennifer would be talking. I was pretty sure Kayla would ask her about what happened.

"And make sure you tell her you already got two new ones, otherwise you'll end up with three."

"Why isn't Aunt Sharon married?" I asked.

"You know Aunt Sharon. Married to her job."

"Has she ever dated anyone?"

"Sure."

"Isn't she lonely?"

"I don't know, Asher. Who isn't?" she said

Liar. Mom must have thought I was an idiot. I glanced at the speedometer. She was driving twenty miles an hour.

"You know, you can change digital pictures to black and white on the computer," she said. "Then you can print them out yourself. A guy at work was telling me—"

"I don't like digital."

"How do you know if you've never tried it?"

I ignored her.

"Your dad spent a lot of money on that camera, and it's just sitting there, collecting dust."

"Then you use it."

"I would think you'd need to know about all different kinds of photography. If you're serious about this and want to go to school, then you'll have to."

I thought about how frustrating it was to get the Minolta to focus on the clouds at Travis's funeral. The Canon A-1 would let me. All I had to do was select a manual setting.

She eased into an empty parking space and opened the car door. I expected her to ask me to help her get the screen door out, but she didn't. I didn't feel like offering.

"I'll be back in a minute."

I watched her struggle with the bungee cords in the rearview mirror. The trunk popped open, and she maneuvered the screen door awkwardly up to the door of the hardware store. An older guy with a lined face and blue jeans hustled up to help her. He took the screen from her with one hand and opened the door with the other. Mom smiled, and they both went inside.

I reached in my book bag and took out the old instruction manual and the Canon A-1. I rolled down the window. The air blowing in was hot, but at least it was moving. I turned the camera over in my hands and looked through the viewfinder. Next door, Wild Bill strolled through the grocery parking lot gathering carts. I wondered if they paid him to do it.

I rolled up the window, got out, and closed the car door. I took the camera inside the grocery store with me. I walked past the greeting cards to the photo department. I wanted to see Iggy, but he must have had the day off. A man who looked around my dad's age stood behind the counter.

"May I help you?"

"I'm just looking at film."

"What kind?"

"The 35 millimeter. I usually use black and white."

He scratched his chin. "I don't know if we have that," he said. "Sorry, I don't usually work over here."

"You don't carry it anymore. I go out to Harmon Photo on Six Mile Cypress. In another few months, I'll be able to drive myself out there. If I can afford the gas."

"That's quite a hike."

"Yeah. My mom thinks so." I looked over the color film.

"Your last name Price?" he asked.

I nodded. "Asher."

"I thought so. You've got those gray eyes. You know, we're looking for someone for the photo lab." I glanced at his nametag: *Doug McKinney, Store Manager.* "You interested?"

"I might be." I picked up a roll of color film. "I'll get this instead. Thanks, Mr. McKinney."

"You tell your dad I said hello."

I headed for the checkout and tossed the film on the conveyor belt. I dug into the back pocket of my jeans and pulled out $47. The cashier started to put the film in a bag, but I said, "No, thanks."

I tore the film canister out of the package as the automatic doors opened. I tossed the cardboard box and my receipt in the trash. I stood in the shadow of the building, loading the color film into the Canon A-1. Wild Bill sat on the curb, singing to himself. I looked at him through the viewfinder. His hair was greasy and his shirt was missing two buttons. His cheekbones stuck out and his mouth looked like the opening to a cave, but his thin lips curved up at the edges. He tapped his foot on the ground in time to a beat I didn't hear. I adjusted the zoom, focused, and centered him in the frame, but I didn't take his picture.

❖

My hands were covered in white clay when the doorbell rang. I'd just finished filling in the hole in Travis's bedroom wall. I walked down the hallway and saw that Mom was outside installing the screen, so I went to the front door and looked through the peephole. John from church stood on our front step.

"It's unlocked. You have to open the door," I called through the closed door. "I've got stuff on my hands."

The doorknob turned. John opened the door and smiled.

"Hey, sorry to stop by unannounced," he said.

"That's okay." I held my pasty hands up like the surgeons did on television.

"Is your mom around?"

"She's working out back."

"Oh." He looked down at a small book in his hand. "I wanted to give this to her."

"You can go out back if you want."

"I don't want to bother her." He eyed my hands. "You look like you've been busy."

"Yeah."

He paused in the doorway. He didn't seem to know what to do with himself.

"Why don't you go on back?" I said.

"Yeah. Okay. I'll just…" He pointed to his right, backed off the step, and walked around the side of the house.

I closed the door with my shoulder and went back to Travis's room. The drywall mud was thick and gray against the white wall. I took the supplies into the garage, rinsed the mud off the trowel, and set it on the edge of the scrub sink. I rubbed my hands under the warm water and dried them with an old towel. According to the directions on the side of the bucket, in twenty-four hours I'd be able to sand down the patch on Travis's wall.

I started to head out back to help Mom, but the phone rang. I checked the caller ID. It was Aunt Sharon.

"Hello."

"Asher. I'm glad I got you. How's everything going?"

I headed back to my bedroom.

"Okay, I guess."

I straightened one of the picture frames on my wall. I stared at the photograph of Dad and Helen on my dresser.

"Your mom left this message saying you wanted to talk to me. What's going on?"

Nice one, Mom. I sat down on my bed next to the envelopes Mom had gotten me from Harmon Photo. I opened one and pulled out the two pictures on top. I studied the two grainy photos side by side as Aunt Sharon waited.

"Asher," she said.

Both were taken at the pool right before Travis had died, and I hadn't taken either one of them. The first one, Travis had taken of Levi while I was swimming with Garrett. Levi must have taken the other one of Travis when I wasn't around. I took in their dark hair and bulging eyes, the jutting chins and the puffed-out cheeks. All the pictures from the submerged roll had survived, but there wasn't much contrast between the dark and the light. The images were washed out. It made the photos eerie, but none of them compared to these two photos next to each other. Even though the one of Travis was sort of blurred, anyone could see his face mirrored Levi's.

"You know that camera you gave me?" I said.

"Yeah."

"I broke it. It was a stupid thing to do, and I've got a new one, but Mom told me I had to tell you."

"So are they going to have to name a hurricane after you?"

I rubbed my eyes. "I don't know, Aunt Sharon. I really don't want to talk about it."

"Hold on." I heard a muffled female voice, then Aunt Sharon said, "I'm not saving it. You can have it if you want."

"Who was that?" I asked.

"My roommate."

I heard a woman call, "I have a name. It's Carol."

"Yes, that would be Carol. And she's eating the last piece of tiramisu," Aunt Sharon said. "But seriously, what's going on?"

"I don't know."

I tucked the two photographs along with the one I took from Pearl into my book bag.

"Your mom told me you're out of control—egging houses, tearing rooms apart. She's worried about you."

"I know."

I stood in front of my dresser where Hector's cage still sat. It had been three days since I'd buried Hector, and I still hadn't gotten around to cleaning the cage and putting it away somewhere. There was something morbid about keeping an empty cage.

"She thinks you need counseling. It wouldn't hurt, you know."

I heard a rustling sound in the silence that followed. I put my face up to the cage. There on the far side a big shell scooted over the pebbles.

"He isn't dead," I said.

"What?"

"My hermit crab. Hector. He isn't dead." A smile spread across my face. "I read about this—hermit crabs molt. He just outgrew his shell."

"Hermit crab?"

"Aunt Sharon, can I call you back later?"

I got off the phone and hurried into the dining room. The sliding glass door opened. Mom poked her head in and smiled at me.

"Check this out," she said.

She slid the screen door closed and open.

"John, come on in," she said.

He stepped inside and Mom shut the door.

"When it cools off again, we're actually going to get some fresh air in here. Thanks so much for your help, John."

He wiped his hands on his jeans.

"Sure."

"You want something?" I asked. I opened the fridge.

"I'd love some water," Mom said.

"Maybe I should get going," John said.

"Just stay for a minute. I want you to show me that book."

"Oh!" he said, like he'd forgotten why he came over in the first place. He pulled it out of his back pocket.

Mom motioned for me to get something for John, too. I took two glasses out of the cabinet and got out the plastic water pitcher. They sat down at the kitchen table.

"It's the book we're using in that group at church."

He handed it to her. I set the two glasses on the table and stood next to the table and lingered.

"Hey, Mom?"

She looked up at me.

"Yes?"

"I was wondering if I could go to Levi's for a few minutes."

Mom took a deep breath.

"I know I'm grounded. It's just, he hurt his leg and I want to check on him."

She glanced from me to John and back again.

"Okay. But you need to be back here in an hour."

❖

If I hadn't known it was November, I would have sworn it was August by the way the air hung heavy as I crossed through the yard behind my house. I could feel the heat of the pavement through my shoes as I walked along the road to Levi's house. His Jeep was in the driveway, so I knew he was home.

I rang the doorbell once and then knocked three times. A shadow passed over the sun, and I glanced up at the sky. It was going to rain.

Levi opened the door.

"Hey." He left the door open and limped back into the house. I followed him inside.

"It's Asher," he called.

Levi's mom came out of the office to hug me. She wore a pair of jean cutoffs and smelled like orange blossoms.

"We haven't seen you in a while. You doing okay?"

"Fine."

"Levi said you've been seeing your dad. How's he doing?"

"Okay."

"C'mon, Ash." Levi headed toward his bedroom.

"It's good to see you," I told Levi's mom. She headed back into the office.

As I walked down the hall to Levi's room, I noticed the Keep Out sign was now posted outside his door. His mom must have let him move it. I wondered if the Budweiser sign was up.

Levi opened the door. The extreme sports posters were gone. He had replaced them with a corkboard, a full-length mirror, and a bookshelf. A football schedule was tacked to the corkboard, along with a bunch of pictures of people I knew from school and phone numbers. The bookshelf didn't have any books on it. Three trophies sat on the top shelf. His football jersey was folded on another shelf with his helmet and assorted pads. A weight bench sat at the foot of his bed with a bunch of handheld barbells underneath it. He still had the denim bedspread.

"Your room is different." I sat down on the edge of his bed and put my book bag down on the floor.

He looked around absentmindedly. "Yeah. I took the posters down."

"I think my dad found them." Levi gave me a strange look. "He did my bedroom for me at their house. Extreme sports. And a denim bedspread."

"Are you shitting me?"

I shook my head, and he laughed.

"You still have the Budweiser sign?"

Levi smiled. He grimaced as he knelt down next to his bed and slid it out from underneath. A layer of dust covered the mirrored sign. "I've been working on Mom. Did you see the Keep Out sign? I'll have this up before the summer. You watch."

I nodded. Levi moved over to his computer desk and sat down. He swiveled the chair to face me and then leaned back, stretching his legs to the bed.

"How's your knee?"

"I've got to wear this brace thing for a few weeks." He grinned at me. "Thanks for asking, asshole."

He tucked his hands behind his head. He looked like a football player. I thought about mentioning the conversation with Jennifer, but Levi's face was smug enough already.

"I broke my camera."

"That sucks."

"I knocked it into the pool at my dad's house."

"Your dad's got a pool now?"

"Maybe you can come over sometime," I said.

"Maybe." Levi turned toward the computer and moved the mouse. The screen lit up.

"I went by Pearl's the other day."

"That must have been fun." He was checking to see who all was online. "How's the old bat?"

"Turns out, she used to do photography. She gave me her camera to use. She was showing me these old pictures she took, and there was this one of you and me."

He turned back toward me.

"No shit."

I reached into my book bag and dug around for the photograph. I handed it to him.

"Check it out. We're racing to get the ball."

Levi laughed. "That sounds about right. What are we, seven?"

"Six, I think. Travis wasn't born. My mom doesn't look pregnant. See there?" I pointed to our parents in the background of the photo. "I'd forgotten how your dad used to hang out at the house," I said.

Levi took his feet off the bed and placed them solid on the floor. He rested his elbow on his good knee and stared at the photograph. He sucked in air and puffed his cheeks out as he exhaled. Just like Travis used to.

"My dad." Levi flicked the edge of the picture.

"Remember how our families used to do stuff?"

"Yeah."

"Before Travis."

He continued to stare at the photograph. I saw the muscle in his jaw tighten and loosen. He sniffed and wiped his nose on the back of his hand. I'd known Levi most of my life, and I didn't recognize any of the things flashing across his face. He shook his head and tossed the photo onto the bed next to me.

"Are you thinking what I'm thinking?" I said.

"I don't know. What're you thinking?"

"That maybe...you know...that they..." I reached back inside my book bag for the other two photos from the pool and handed them to him.

He made a *humph* noise.

"I took this one," Levi said, holding up the photo of Travis.

"I know. Levi, really look at them," I said.

He held one in each hand. His eyes darted back and forth between the two photographs—the one of him and the one of my dead brother. Dark hair and eyes, puffed-out cheeks. Anyone could see they could have been brothers. Levi took a deep breath and handed the pictures back to me.

"Levi, remember T-ball? My mom was always hanging around your dad. And then that summer, he was always at the house."

"I know," he said.

"And then afterward, when Travis—"

"I know, Ash."

"What do you mean, you know?"

"My dad told me," he said.

"Told you what?"

"About Travis. About your mom."

"How long have you known?"

"Just since Travis died."

Months then. For months my best friend had walked around knowing this crap about my family, and he hadn't said a word to me.

"Why didn't you tell me?"

"It seemed like you had a hell of a lot of other stuff to deal with. Did you really need that?" he asked. "I didn't want to know it myself. My dad was a prick. No wonder Mom's on his ass all the time."

I thought about Dad's long hours at work, the arguing, the fact that everything changed after Travis was born. I'd wanted to blame Travis for the change in their relationship, but it wasn't his fault.

"I hate her," I said. "She acted like it was all Dad's fault, and the whole time she was the one."

Levi tilted his head. "You know, Ash, come to think of it, everyone in the whole damn town probably knows except us. Seems to me, your folks worked it out, at least for a while. I know mine did."

"Then why lie about it?"

"Us?" Levi's eyes fixed on his bookshelf. "People do all sorts of crazy shit when they're scared."

He stood slowly and hobbled across the bedroom. He lifted a trophy off the shelf and slid something out from underneath it. He sat down next to me on the bed.

"Travis," he said. "That day at the pool. He was screwing with me. You know how he was. And then he got up in my face and took that picture." Levi shook his head. "So when I saw him standing in line, I got your camera from him and took the picture of him. He tried to get the camera from me, but I wouldn't give it back." Levi opened his hand and showed me a five-dollar bill. He held the bill between his thumb and index finger. "I took this from him, too. And then he ran off and died."

The money for ice cream.

Levi stared at the five-dollar bill.

He turned it over and over in his hands.

"Why did you take it?"

"I don't know. He pissed me off. I'm an ass."

If Levi hadn't taken Travis's money, then he would have been right where I'd left him. If Mom hadn't been annoyed by him, he wouldn't have been at the pool with me. If Dad hadn't left us, if the pool had been less crowded, if I hadn't followed Garrett. If Mom and Levi's dad…

"I'm the one who should have been watching him," I said. "He's my brother."

"Just yours?" Levi laughed and tossed the bill into my lap. "You were taking a shit. How can you blame yourself for having to take a shit?"

I let the five-dollar bill rest in my lap. I didn't say anything.

"You thought he was standing in line. He would have been fine." Levi's voice trailed off.

Levi was right. I wanted to latch on to that. It would be easier to blame someone else. He glanced at the pictures on the bed. I picked them up. This wasn't Levi's fault, and I couldn't let him think it was. I unzipped my book bag and slid the photographs back inside. I picked up the five-dollar bill.

"I was in the bathroom. But it wasn't because I had to go."

Levi stared at me, his eyes almost black. I couldn't look at him. Instead, I squeezed the bill tightly. My face felt hot.

"Garrett," I said. "We were...I mean...he lied. I wasn't—"

"So you were hanging out in the bathroom. So what. You still thought Travis was safe."

I could have left it there. Levi shifted his weight. He fidgeted next to me. I leaned forward.

"But we weren't, Levi. You punched Garrett, but he was trying to protect—"

He held up his hand to cut me off.

Levi lowered his voice and spoke slowly. "You don't need to say anything." He rubbed his hands on his jeans and leaned back in the chair. "It doesn't make a damn bit of difference one way or another."

❖

Halfway home from Levi's house, the wind picked up. I heard the *rat-tat-tat* of heavy raindrops grow louder against the pavement. The sky divided in two: the sun shining from behind me, the inky black of the storm rolling toward me. My tall, lanky shadow got hit with drops first, and then it was on me, a downpour. My hair matted to my forehead, and my clothes clung to my shoulders and thighs as

I walked steadily toward home. Steam rose off the street. The sky rumbled, but I wasn't in any hurry.

I cut through the yards separating Levi's street from mine just like I had my whole life. I squinted through the rain at Mr. Williams's red and yellow crotons and the dirt bed where he'd buried Sam and where I'd tried, in my dreams, to dig up Travis. As I got to the back screen door, the rain let up as quickly as it had started. The sky was still dark. There'd be more.

I slid the new screen and the sliding glass door open. They moved smooth and quiet on the track. I stepped inside and hopped over the carpet onto the linoleum kitchen floor, where I put my wet book bag on the counter and peeled off all my clothes, except my boxers. I started to close the door, and a lizard darted across the concrete patio, through the open doors, and into the house. Out of habit I opened my mouth to call for Travis to catch it. It didn't make it past my throat. I swallowed.

I spotted the lizard moving under the dining-room table. It stopped by a chair leg, its body stiff with adrenaline. I pictured Travis crouched down to trap a lizard, attaching it to his ear lobe, its mouth clinging and its body arched. Travis swinging his head from side to side, with a lizard dangling, like an earring.

I knelt down next to the table to cut off the path to the living room. The lizard scurried back toward the sliding glass door. I had it cornered against the glass, its legs shoving against the metal grooves in the track. If it just moved to the right a little, it would be outside. I inched the door open, and the lizard sprang against the screen, then turned the opposite direction away from the opening to the yard. I edged the gap wider, but the lizard was already down at the other end where the doors lined up. Its tail got wedged in the screen door.

"Great."

I slid the glass door open just as the little reptile wiggled loose of its own tail. The lizard ran blindly into my cupped hands. It squirmed, kicked its legs, tried to leap free. I set it down outside the screen door and watched it run off into the grass before I closed the doors and went to my room. As I pulled on a T-shirt and jeans, I watched Hector eat the chicken I'd put in his cage earlier.

I found Mom asleep on Travis's bed with the nightstand lamp on. The book John had brought had fallen onto her chest, her place lost. Her right hand rested on top of the book. The other was on the pillow beside her head, fingers curled loosely. She had a smudge of something on her cheek—probably from handling the old screen door. I studied the lines on her face, the sides of her nose to the corners of her mouth, across her forehead, and around her eyes. Her skin was discolored without makeup, purplish half circles under her eyes, sort of like a bruise, but not quite, and blotchy with darker brown patches around her temple and hairline. Her eyebrows crept together with worry.

I tiptoed out of the room to get the Canon A-1. I looped the strap of the camera around my neck and returned to Travis's room.

I took off the lens cap and knelt down beside the bed. I centered her face in the viewfinder, angled away in profile. The lamplight caught her cheek. Her loose hand on the book appeared in the lower right corner. Faded Og sat on top of Travis's pillow in the upper right corner of the shot. I watched her and waited. Her body moved up and down with each breath. Her forehead creased, her eyes searched beneath those lids, and her mouth twitched open.

Her guilt wasn't hidden from anyone. It was plain on her face; she didn't even rest peacefully. People do all sorts of crazy shit when they're scared, Levi said. But everyone knew. And Dad left her—I'd been right, *her* not me—and Travis was dead. It should have made me feel better, being right, but it didn't. The only thing left was me. She was afraid if I knew the truth, I'd leave her, too. She had reason to be scared—I meant it when I said I hated her. But sometimes people didn't even know when they were lying. It was hard to hate when I knew why she lied.

I took the picture.

Author's Note

Asher Price is a fictional character, but while writing his story, I spent time in Florida, taking his photos. You can see them on my website: www.elizabethwheeler1.com.

About the Author

Elizabeth Wheeler's passion for writing, directing, and teaching is driven by a quest to unleash the authentic human experience in literature, on the stage, and in life. As a teacher, she is touched and inspired by the real-world examples of how students, facing adversity, assimilate the lessons learned from those experiences to persevere and transform into triumphant adults. A former Chicago model and actor, Elizabeth now teaches English in rural Illinois. She is a graduate of the University of Florida and the inaugural novel writing program at the University of Chicago's Graham School. As an advocate for student storytelling in the print and digital world, she has spoken internationally as well as at educational conferences in Illinois. Elizabeth is co-founder of a professional theater company, Heart and Soul Productions, and director of her school's drama program. A fifth generation Floridian, Elizabeth now lives in Illinois with her husband, two sons, and nephew. *Asher's Fault* is her first novel.

Soliloquy Titles From Bold Strokes Books

Asher's Fault by Elizabeth Wheeler. Fourteen-year-old Asher Price sees the world in black and white, much like the photos he takes, but when his little brother drowns at the same moment Asher experiences his first same-sex kiss, he can no longer hide behind the lens of his camera and eventually discovers he isn't the only one with a secret. (978-1-60282-982-4)

Lake Thirteen by Greg Herren. A visit to an old cemetery seems like fun to a group of five teenagers, who soon learn that sometimes it's best to leave old ghosts alone. (978-1-60282-894-0)

The Road to Her by KE Payne. Sparks fly when actress Holly Croft, star of UK soap Portobello Road, meets her new on-screen love interest, the enigmatic and sexy Elise Manford. (978-1-60282-887-2)

Kings of Ruin by Sam Cameron. High school student Danny Kelly and loner Kevin Clark must team up to defeat a top-secret alien intelligence that likes to wreak havoc with fiery car, truck, and train accidents. (978-1-60282-864-3)

Swans & Klons by Nora Olsen. In a future world where there are no males, sixteen-year-old Rubric and her girlfriend Salmon Jo must fight to survive when everything they believed in turns out to be a lie. (978-1-60282-874-2)

The You Know Who Girls by Annameekee Hesik. As they begin freshman year, Abbey Brooks and her best friend, Kate, pinky swear they'll keep away from the lesbians in Gila High, but Abbey already suspects she's one of those you-know-who girls herself and slowly learns who her true friends really are. (978-1-60282-754-7)

In Stone by Jeremy Jordan King. A young New Yorker is rescued from a hate crime by a mysterious someone who turns out to be more of a something. (978-1-60282-761-5)

Wonderland by David-Matthew Barnes. After her mother's sudden death, Destiny Moore is sent to live with her two gay uncles on Avalon Cove, a mysterious island on which she uncovers a secret place called Wonderland, where love and magic prove to be real. (978-1-60282-788-2)

Another 365 Days by KE Payne. Clemmie Atkins is back, and her life is more complicated than ever! Still madly in love with her girlfriend, Clemmie suddenly finds her life turned upside down with distractions, confessions, and the return of a familiar face... (978-1-60282-775-2)

The Secret of Othello by Sam Cameron. Florida teen detectives Steven and Denny risk their lives to search for a sunken NASA satellite—but under the waves, no one can hear you scream... (978-1-60282-742-4)

Andy Squared by Jennifer Lavoie. Andrew never thought anyone could come between him and his twin sister, Andrea...until Ryder rode into town. (978-1-60282-743-1)

Sara by Greg Herren. A mysterious and beautiful new student at Southern Heights High School stirs things up when students start dying. (978-1-60282-674-8)

Boys of Summer, edited by Steve Berman. Stories of young love and adventure, when the sky's ceiling is a bright blue marvel, when another boy's laughter at the beach can distract from dull summer jobs. (978-1-60282-663-2)

Street Dreams by Tama Wise. Tyson Rua has more than his fair share of problems growing up in New Zealand—he's gay, he's falling in love, and he's run afoul of the local hip-hop crew leader just as he's trying to make it as a graffiti artist. (978-1-60282-650-2)

me@you.com by KE Payne. Is it possible to fall in love with someone you've never met? Imogen Summers thinks so because it's happened to her. (978-1-60282-592-5)

Swimming to Chicago by David-Matthew Barnes. As the lives of the adults around them unravel, high school students Alex and Robby form an unbreakable bond, vowing to do anything to stay together—even if it means leaving everything behind. (978-1-60282-572-7)

365 Days by KE Payne. Life sucks when you're seventeen years old and confused about your sexuality, and the girl of your dreams doesn't even know you exist. Then in walks sexy new emo girl, Hannah Harrison. Clemmie Atkins has exactly 365 days to discover herself, and she's going to have a blast doing it! (978-1-60282-540-6)

Cursebusters! by Julie Smith. Budding psychic Reeno is the most accomplished teenage burglar in California, but one tiny screw-up and poof!—she's sentenced to Bad Girl School. And that isn't even her worst problem. Her sister Haley's dying of an illness no one can diagnose, and now she can't even help. (978-1-60282-559-8)

Who I Am by M.L. Rice. Devin Kelly's senior year is a disaster. She's in a new school in a new town, and the school bully is making her life miserable—but then she meets his sister Melanie and realizes her feelings for her are more than platonic. (978-1-60282-231-3)

Sleeping Angel by Greg Herren. Eric Matthews survives a terrible car accident only to find out everyone in town thinks he's a murderer—and he has to clear his name even though he has no memories of what happened. (978-1-60282-214-6)

Mesmerized by David-Matthew Barnes. Through her close friendship with Brodie and Lance, Serena Albright learns about the many forms of love and finds comfort for the grief and guilt she feels over the brutal death of her older brother, the victim of a hate crime. (978-1-60282-191-0)